Red Hot Reunion

ALSO BY BELLA ANDRE

Take Me
Tempt Me, Taste Me, Touch Me

Red Hot Reunion

BELLA ANDRE

POCKET BOOKS

New York   London   Toronto   Sydney

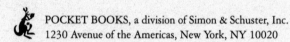 POCKET BOOKS, a division of Simon & Schuster, Inc.
1230 Avenue of the Americas, New York, NY 10020

ISBN-13: 978-1-4165-2418-2
ISBN-10: 1-4165-2418-5

This Pocket Books trade paperback edition March 2007

10 9 8 7 6 5 4 3 2 1

POCKET and colophon are registered trademarks of Simon & Schuster, Inc.

Manufactured in the United States of America

For information regarding special discounts for bulk purchases, please contact Simon & Schuster Special Sales at 1-800-465-6798 or business@simonandschuster.com

For Paul. My real-life hero.

acknowledgments

As always, I want to thank my family for getting behind me and my writing in the biggest way possible. The Fog City Divas and the San Francisco RWA have helped to make this career more fun than I could have ever possibly imagined. You're the best, ladies! Selena, I'm thrilled that I got the chance to work with you on my past three books. Jessica, thanks again for helping my books find their way to the bookshelves. For all of the booksellers who have recommended my books, big kisses. And to everyone who has read my books and taken the time to write and say hello, I want you to know how much I appreciate your emails and letters. They are an absolute joy to read.

one

J ason pulled off his silk tie, letting it dangle from his fingers as he stood in the doorway to the bedroom. "Hi,
honey, I'm home."

Emma paused with one hand on her pearl earring, no longer able to breathe normally when the most gorgeous man
in creation was drinking her in, devouring her with his eyes.
Her hands trembling with anticipation, she placed the pearls
in her jewelry box, and waited for him to come to her.

Waited for Jason to take her to that naughty place she
secretly loved to go.

His long stride ate up the hardwood between them. Jason
threw his tie onto the duvet cover and then he was standing
behind her in the mirror, his front to her back, running large

tanned hands over her arms. Her nipples peaked beneath her thin silk blouse and she bit her lip at the erotic picture of her aroused pink areolas pressing against the thin white fabric.

"Bad girls don't wear bras," he said in a low tone that heated Emma's blood another ten degrees.

As soon as she'd come home from the office, she'd removed her bra and panties, knowing how much it would turn Jason on.

"Or panties," she whispered. Jason pulled her ass into his hips and the full, hot length of his erection throbbing against her sent a flood of wetness straight to her pussy.

"Bad girls need to be spanked," he said as he brushed her blond hair away from her neck and bent his mouth to her exposed flesh. She shivered as he nipped at her skin, kissing her between love bites. His hands moved across her rib cage, making the slow trip up her torso, to the sensitive swell of her breasts. At last he covered her tits with his hands and squeezed them, rubbing his thumbs over her nipples. His touch was light at first and then when she thought she couldn't stand it anymore, he squeezed them between his thumbs and forefinger. Emma cried out her pleasure, nearly coming where she stood.

"Take off your skirt," he commanded in a quiet voice and she immediately obeyed, her shaky fingers fumbling at the clasp and zipper on the left side of her gray wool pencil skirt.

The thick fabric dropped with a whoosh to the floor and cool air blew across her exposed mound. Oh God, all she wanted was for Jason to slide his big hand over her pussy lips. She'd been dreaming all day of the moment he touched her clit, the perfect instant that his thick fingers penetrated her again and again, harder and harder as she exploded.

He lifted her up into his arms and carried her over to the bed. "I'm ready Jason," she breathed. "Fuck me. Now."

But he was not to be deterred from his plan. "All in good time," he said as he pulled her arms up over her head and secured her wrists to the iron bed frame with his blue-and-yellow-striped silk tie.

"You're tying me up?" she said, her words sounding far more like a request than a question.

Jason didn't bother answering as he moved over to her dresser, pulled out two scarves, then returned to the bed and spread open her legs. Her cunt throbbed with heat and need as he exposed her wet flesh by tying first one ankle and then the next to the iron posts.

He stopped and stared at her and Emma was overwhelmed with the need to please him. Her silk shirt was in disarray, her breasts were thrusting up at him, her pussy slick and plump with arousal.

"You don't know how long I've dreamed of doing this, Emma. Tying you up. Making you scream with pleasure." He slid one finger into her with no more pretense, no more fore-play, and she arched into his hand. "You were such a good girl in college. Now look at you. Waiting for me naked beneath your silk and wool. Letting me tie you to your bed, spreading your long legs open for me. Begging me with your eyes to do anything I want to you."

He fell silent then and she knew he was waiting for her to reach the next level of desire, the one that would have her pleading with him to take her all the way to heaven.

"Are you ready for more?" he asked, his control seeming to slip as his voice shook. "Do you want me to slide another finger into your sweet pussy?"

"Please," she moaned, her eyes closing as he complied with her desperate request. "More. Give me more Jason."

"I would do anything for you," he said a millisecond before his hot breath covered her pussy. Holding her breath, she waited for his tongue to press down on her clit. But as the seconds ticked by, and the first pulse of an orgasm sounded within her, Emma couldn't wait any longer. Bucking her hips as far up as she could, she pressed her cunt into his lips.

She could feel him silently urging her to let go, to make herself come against his lips, his teeth. As if she could do anything else, when her body was already straining to reach the peak. She was so close, and as she pushed against his wet tongue again and again, as he thrust his fingers relentlessly, Emma spiraled into an earth-shattering orgasm, the likes of which she'd never known.

Her entire body shuddered beneath his delicious onslaught and then he was poised above her, his hazel eyes burning with desire. He ripped open her blouse, taking one taut nipple into his mouth. The thick head of his penis pressed against her open pussy lips and she arched to take him in.

"Not so fast," he murmured, taking her lips in a savage kiss, pulling the breath from her lungs as if it were his right. As if he owned her, body and soul.

Which they both knew that he did.

All she wanted was for him to plunge his nine rock-hard inches into her. To screw her hard and long, to make her come again from the inside out.

And this time she was so close, so close . . .

Emma Cartwright woke up from her wet dream, the sheets soaked and twisted beneath her, her arms above her head, her legs spread. Exactly the way she'd been tied up in her dream.

Disappointment flooded her. She should have known it was just another X-rated version of the ongoing fantasy she'd been powerless to control for the past decade.

Jason Roberts. With her. In bed. Making wild, passionate love to her. Doing all the dirty things she could never admit to wanting in real life, but that she knew would be astonishing and beautiful in his arms.

After so many years of frustration, she only wished for one thing: Why couldn't they get to the part where he actually slid into her before she woke up? Where he took her and made her his. Completely.

Because then, at least, she would know what it felt like to be a part of Jason. To have him be a part of her.

But Emma knew with utter certainty that suffering without Jason, even in her dreams, was her price to pay. For what she had done to him ten years ago in college. For teasing him with her virginity, never giving in, telling him she loved him, and then choosing to date and marry another man.

Like a zombie, she got out of bed and turned on the shower. Hopefully the ice-cold water would help her erase her unmanageable arousal. A need that she knew damn well could never, ever be assuaged. Because no matter how much she wished her life had turned out differently, Emma had made her choices.

Too bad they'd all been bad ones.

Tonight's fantasy had been her most potent, most realistic one yet. And she knew why. At six P.M. she would be coming face-to-face with the two most important men in her life at her ten-year college reunion.

The man she'd loved and left.

And the man she hadn't loved who had left her.

⁓

"Judy, how are you? I can't believe it's been so long since we've all gotten together."

"Hello, Eileen. How's your son? Thank so much for coming tonight."

The crush of bodies entering the Stanford University Faculty Club momentarily dwindled away and Emma let out a breath of relief. She had spent all day decorating the large event room with tasteful flowered centerpieces, cardinal red tablecloths, and dozens of "then and now" photo collages. She had been smiling so hard, for so long, that her lips were numb and her cheeks felt like they were going to crack. Trying to focus on what Eileen had been saying about her three-year-old had been nearly impossible with Steven, her ex-husband, groping his new, extremely young, very beautiful girlfriend not twenty feet away. The ink was barely dry on their divorce paperwork from the county clerk's office, but Steven had already moved on.

Worse than that, so much worse, was the knowledge that at any minute, Jason Roberts would be walking through the door.

And she'd be expected to greet him with an impersonal smile. A smile that said no more than, "Hello, it has been a long time, hasn't it?"

The sad truth was that Emma didn't know if she had it in her to act like a composed, mature thirty-two-year-old woman. Not when all she really wanted to do was wrap her legs around Jason and beg him to do her.

Just then a good-looking young waiter sauntered her way. "Would you like a drink, ma'am?"

Ma'am? When had she graduated from Miss? Was that what Jason would think when he saw her? That she was a shriveled excuse for a woman? Oh God. She couldn't stay at the reunion another second longer. She'd done her duties as organizer and now she'd have to flee. Wimping out was the only option.

The waiter's voice cut through her frantic planning. "Margaritas and martinis are all I've got left right now." She could barely focus on him as he looked her up and down and decided, "You look like a fruity-drink gal to me."

Something in his voice snapped her out of her panic, something flirty and young that made her feel like maybe calling her ma'am had been a mistake. Maybe she wasn't old and shriveled after all. Besides, she knew that taking the coward's way out wasn't really an option tonight.

Everything she'd feared for so long, everything she regretted was coming back to slap her in the face tonight. Maybe this time if she faced her mistakes, she prayed silently, she could finally recover.

"I really shouldn't," she said as she looked down at the drink in her hand, but she was so desperate to escape from the awful reality of her life that before she knew it the glass was at her lips.

The strawberry liquid eased its way down her throat into her belly. Had she been a fruity-drink girl all these years and not known it? And if that were true, what else had she not permitted herself to be? Fun? Happy? Satisfied?

One sip was enough, however, to make her think about how many calories were in the glass she was holding. And the workout she'd have to do tomorrow to burn this drink off. Normally, she would never allow herself to drink anything but bottled water—empty calories were not something she allowed herself to ingest, no matter the occasion—but if ever there was a night to bend the rules, it was tonight.

Surveying the crowd, Emma turned her thoughts forcefully back to the successful party well under way. She knew she should be pleased by how well the evening had turned out, especially considering she'd been organizing the ten-year reunion for more than a year. On any other night, she would have been right in the middle of it all, talking about jobs and kids and vacations.

Tonight, it was all she could do just to keep the smile on her face.

The waiter passed by again and said, "Need a refill?" but she had already grabbed a full glass. "Bad day, huh?" He gave her a sympathetic smile before walking away.

You have no idea, she thought, giving in to the stupid impulse that made her say, "Keep 'em coming," even though she could practically feel the fat molecules attaching themselves to her hips.

"Downing margaritas while checking out that waiter's ass looks like fun. Can I join you?"

Guilty as charged, Emma jumped at her best friend Kate's sudden arrival at her elbow. "That's not what I'm doing," she said, but the empty glass in her hand was evidence to the contrary, as was the wink the waiter gave her from across the room.

"Bull," Kate said, dragging Emma over to a dimly lit table in the corner behind the DJ. "I know you're freaking out about being at the same party as Steven, aka 'the man you never should have married,'" Kate added with a contemptuous twist of her blood-red mouth, "but trust me, dating the head cheerleader when you're in your thirties is desperate and pathetic. You're the kind of classy babe his Playboy bunny wishes she could be."

The words were out of her mouth before Emma realized they were coming. "Thanks, Kate, but I seriously doubt that most supermodels wished they were a huge failure in their parents' eyes for getting divorced *before* providing them with grandchildren." The alcohol made Emma feel bold enough to admit, "What if I *want* to be a Playboy bunny like her? What if I *want* to drive men wild with my huge, perky breasts and wicked ways? What if I *want* to weigh fifteen pounds too much but somehow make it look good anyway?"

She grabbed another drink from a passing waiter, thinking that the only man she'd ever wanted to drive wild—Jason—would likely cut her in two with nothing but a jagged glance when he finally arrived.

Kate grabbed Emma's hand. "You're wonderful and sexy and Steven never deserved you."

"So then why did I marry him? I'm the one who made the decision. Who chose *him*."

Kate cut right to it in her typically straightforward way. "You were so young. Way too young. Your parents were in love with him and you thought getting married was the right thing to do. You were so certain that you would grow to love him."

Emma blinked away the tears that were about to fall. It was true, her parents had adored Steven from the minute they laid eyes on him at a Stanford faculty function ten years ago. As the reigning football star on the West Coast, he was perfect son-in-law material. So she'd paid the bills and gotten his suits dry-cleaned, but there had never been passion between them. Glimmers of friendship, but never desire.

"You pulled me aside before the wedding, Kate, and told me I didn't have to go through with it. Why didn't I listen to you? Even when you pointed out that I still loved—"

No, she couldn't say his name out loud. Not now, when all of her perfect choices had turned out to be anything but. Not when the memory of her latest middle-of-the-night fantasy was still burning between her legs.

Kate, of course, had no such qualms. "You have wanted to be with Jason Roberts since the day you met him. You still do."

Emma looked at Kate with surprise.

"What? You think just because you don't ever talk about him that I don't know how you feel?"

Emma hated how transparent she was. How even though she'd tried to deny her feelings for Jason for years they were still written all over her face.

"I need more to drink," Emma said, craning her neck, looking over Kate's shoulder for the cute waiter. Emma knew that she was going to feel bloated and sick tomorrow, that she was going to have spend the entire day at the gym with nothing but lettuce and rice cakes for dinner, but she didn't care. Booze was taking the edge off. And Lord knew she needed the edges of her life hacked off with a machete tonight.

Pathetic loser that she was, she had TiVo'd every single one of Jason's Food Network shows, all of his book signings, anything where his name was listed as a guest.

And even though she'd fantasized about seeing him again a million times, a part of her still hoped that he wouldn't come tonight. That he'd be too busy with his top-rated cooking show. Or his world-famous restaurant. Or one of his supermodel girlfriends.

Because then she wouldn't have to face him. Wouldn't have to figure out what she could possibly say, if he would even talk to her.

I always loved you. No, too pathetic.

I'm sorry. Definitely not good enough to make up for what she'd done. For how she'd done it.

Make love to me. He'd laugh in her face. Jason could have any woman in the world. Why would he possibly want her? Even her own husband, make that ex-husband, hadn't wanted her.

Emma was reaching for another truth-blotting drink when Kate's red-tipped hand gripped her forearm. "He's here."

Emma's blood grew cold. She craned her neck in desperation, praying for a back door to appear out of thin air. "He can't see me looking like this," she hissed, desperate for a hiding place.

She had always dreamed of looking like a goddess the next time they met. Of blowing him away with her allure and sophistication and irresistibility. Instead, she was drunk and nervous and only now realized how boring and dried up she was in her silk-lined cream Ann Taylor linen dress.

Kate turned to face her. "You know what you have to do tonight, don't you?"

Emma blinked hard and tried to swallow, tried to speak, but her mouth was the Sahara. Finally finding her voice, she whispered, "I can't."

Kate's eyes hardened. "Yes, you can. You're single. You're gorgeous, no matter what you seem to think. Just once, if only for tonight, take this chance for you. Stop trying to please everyone else, honey. It's time to please yourself."

two

Eighteen-year-old Jason Roberts looked around at his new home for the next four years and wondered if his acceptance to Stanford University had been a big mistake. Everyone was white-collar. Wonder bread. Perfect. He'd only been on campus for an hour and already he'd met a cute brunette who was an Olympic gymnast. She hadn't made a big deal out of it, but he was star-struck anyway.

Not that he'd ever show it, of course. Leaning against the bottom of the stairs in a Rolling Stones T-shirt and faded jeans, he watched one fellow student after another drag heavy suitcases into the dormitory lounge. He memorized every detail—the oversized diamonds on the mothers' hands, the well-groomed fingernails on the fathers', the confident, excited expressions on their kids' faces—and yet to the *casual observer he looked almost disinterested in the comings and goings around him. It was something he'd perfected over the years, a casual, effortless presence: cool enough to fit in with anyone in any situation, but not too cool that people thought he was a snob.*

And then she walked in and his cover was blown.

The girl was blonde and thin, nearly too thin, but what really stood out to Jason was how nervous she was. Painfully so. He wanted to reach out and pull her away from her parents, who were obviously more concerned with assessing the wealth of the fellow students than they were with their own daughter's welfare. He kept his face averted, but his eyes remained on her.

Something about her pulled at him, made him want to hold her, kiss away her uncertainty. He wasn't a virgin by any means, but he'd never felt this way about a girl within the first minute of setting eyes on her.

He waited until her parents had disappeared, then moved to stand beside the girl.

"I'm Jason. Need some help with your things?"

The grateful smile she gave him lit her up from the inside out. All the beauty he suspected beneath her overly pale skin, her prominent cheekbones, bloomed to life before him.

"That would be great," she replied, staring into his eyes, seeming to get lost for a second.

His groin jumped with awareness and his gaze moved to her lips instinctively. He couldn't wait to taste her. A taste that he was certain would be sweeter than anything he'd ever had on his tongue.

And then, polite little girl that he knew she'd been raised to be by the stiff-as-a-board couple who had dropped her off, she held her hand out. "I didn't mean to be rude. My name's Emma. Emma Holden."

He curled his large fingers around the fine bones of her soft hand.

And in that moment Jason Roberts wanted Emma Holden more than he'd ever wanted anything in his life. He might have been only eighteen, but already he knew he'd have her. And it would be exactly right. The best thing they'd ever done. For the both of them.

⌒

Jason Roberts firmly believed that charging in on his white horse to save Emma Holden that first day of college was the stupidest thing he'd ever done. And somehow, he couldn't escape the foreboding that attending his ten-year reunion might also end up at the top of his list of worst decisions.

He hadn't been planning to come back to Palo Alto tonight, but his old drinking buddies had been hassling him for months to show up at the reunion. "The three of us are the reigning heroes of our graduation class," was what they kept telling him. "It's up to us to do a victory round, to show all those chicks with their noses in the air what they could have had."

Jason had never thought about it exactly like that, but yeah, he supposed they had a point. None of them had hung out with the jocks, the sorority girls. They hadn't been the big brains or future Olympic champions. Just a crew of good guys, tough guys who knew that they weren't going back to where they came from. Each and every one of them had made a name for themselves in atypical ways, not by any means your average Stanford graduate who becomes an investment banker.

Rick Stodler had created an international construction empire. Ace McKinty had turned his flying lessons into one of the hottest low-cost airlines in the country. And Jason, well, he was proud of everything he'd accomplished. Damn proud.

He'd left Stanford as a poor kid who'd earned a fancy Economics degree on scholarship and had returned a multi-millionaire. A world-famous chef. A *New York Times* bestselling cookbook author. And the recipient of *People* magazine's Sexiest Bachelor of the Year Award. Two years running.

The moment he walked into the Stanford Faculty Club, he saw that Rick and Ace were right about the hero thing. Women surrounded him, phone numbers were pressed into his palms, slid into the pockets of his slacks.

His buddies waved him over and as he made his way across the room, Jason fought the urge to scan the room for Emma. He planned on looking laid-back, completely at ease when she saw him. Only half there, he'd settled into a conversation on great Thai restaurants in the city when a stacked redhead rubbed her tits against his arm and handed him a beer.

"Jason," she said, her tongue coming out to lick the corner of her lips like a viper, "I can't believe it's been this long."

"Did we have a class together?"

She pouted and it wasn't a pretty look for a woman in her thirties, especially when she'd had a boatload of collagen injected into her lips. She reminded him of the trout he had on special at the restaurant last week.

She walked her fingers up his arm. "How could you forget our science labs in Chem 101?" She raised her voice in the gathering crowd to stake her claim. "Just you and me in a deserted lab, late at night. Up to all sorts of naughty things."

Despite his act, Jason knew exactly who she was. Alicia Haynes, head of the Pi Phi sorority. One of the girls who had been too busy running after the frat boys and the jocks and the heirs to notice a boy on scholarship. She had made his freshman year chemistry class a living hell, all because he'd been unfortunate enough to land her as a lab partner.

Taking a long swig of his beer, Jason nodded. Her eyes perked up as she waited for him to fall into her ready arms. "Sorry," he said, "don't remember," pausing just long enough to see her deflate like a punctured blow-up doll.

After the way Rick and Ace had built things up, Jason had expected to feel some sort of triumph about returning to Stanford as the poor-boy-who-made-real-good. But frankly, after his run-in with Alicia, he realized he didn't really feel anything either way.

Then again, hadn't he known that none of this was about some girl in his chemistry lab who hadn't given him the time of day?

This was about Emma.

And after ten long years of keeping his distance, of making sure he wouldn't run into her under any circumstances, he knew the time had come to face his past.

To face the one woman he'd truly loved. And could never have.

He could feel her in the room. A decade might have passed, but her power over him was stronger than ever.

He couldn't put it off any longer. He knew that. But this time, he decided, he wasn't going to let her get the best of him. He'd had too many women, been in and out of too many beds to let one little slip of a girl wreck his life again.

Tonight, he would finally show her that even though she'd yanked his heart out of his chest in college, he'd had no trouble forgetting all about her. And moving on with his life.

Just like she had.

After issuing his buddies a blanket invitation to drop by his restaurant soon, regardless of the fact that the reservation book was full four months out, he headed for the bar. The room was crowded, but every nerve in his body was alive.

Slowly scanning the room for his quarry, he saw her. Sitting in the corner with Kate, her loud, opinionated best friend. As strange a pair today as they were in college.

Kate stepped away from the table, and when Emma's ice blue eyes connected with his, Jason unexpectedly lost his breath. She was even more beautiful now than she had been in college. Thin, far too thin, and as prim and proper as a nun, but the raw need in her eyes drew him to her like a moth to a flame.

Ten years had passed since that day in the quad when he'd caught her swapping spit with Steven Cartwright. Jason had fooled himself into believing she saw past his poor boy, country roots. He'd loved her so much he'd ignored all the signs. Not being invited to lunch with her parents after that first, disastrous meal where he used the dessert fork instead of the salad fork. Not knowing anything about polo horses or real estate or yachts. He'd invited Emma into his world—his family had easily welcomed her into their fray—but she hadn't wanted him in hers.

Still, wanting to be with her was instinctual. Like jumping out of a tenth-story window of a building on fire. And just as dangerous. For ten years he'd steered clear of her, turned down every alumni event invitation on the off chance that she might be there. He hadn't wanted to see if he still needed her more than he needed to breathe.

He was sick of hiding from her. Sick of letting her think that she'd won. He hadn't come here with a big plan. Frankly, he still didn't have one. For all he knew the best thing to do was get the hell out of here, head back to Napa, try and forget all about her again. All he had to do was get in his car, get on the freeway, and head north.

19

And then what? He would slide into his plush king bed knowing that he was too much of a wimp to face her, that's what. A self-made, multimillionaire, world-famous chef wimp.

Forget that.

It was time to take care of unfinished business. Namely, proving to himself that Emma didn't have a hold over him anymore. And then he'd head back to his fields of Chardonnay and give 100 percent focus to the only thing that really mattered: Good food.

So he wasn't going to turn and run. He wasn't going to hide in his gleaming stainless-steel kitchen, hacking at animal bones with knives sharp enough to do serious damage to anything they came in contact with.

Rolling the tight muscles of his neck through his strong fingers, Jason fingered his Stanford University Ten-Year Reunion badge. Then he got ready to show Emma how badly she'd messed up in college by flaunting his fame, his money, and his fully intact hairline in her face.

three

Emma saw the man she loved for the first time in a decade and forgot how to breathe as the final piece of her perfectly ordered world broke and fell to the floor. He looked the same as he had the first day she'd met him in their freshman dormitory, only wiser, stronger.

And even more gorgeous.

Jason Roberts was no longer a boy. He was a man. The most delectable man she'd ever seen.

Jason stood several inches over six feet, and his muscled limbs held the promise of incredible strength. Emma's memories told her what was beneath his shirt and slacks and she shivered at the decadent thought of seeing him naked. Even if getting naked with Jason was the world's most unlikely scenario.

His arms and legs would be corded with muscles, the natural, powerful physique of an athlete. He still pulled his slight, dark waves into a short ponytail at the back of his neck. It was a hairstyle that would have looked ridiculous on any other man in the room, but on Jason, the too-long hair just accentuated his masculinity.

Emma knew for a fact that every woman in the room had the same what-would-it-be-like-to-get-naked-with-him daydream running through their minds. He was the kind of man that women noticed on the street, or in a restaurant, and couldn't take their eyes off of, even if they were with a lover or husband already.

His sensuality was raw and impossible to ignore.

Seeing him, here, tonight, was the final blow. Emma started to slide off the chair as everything went black. But before she hit the floor, strong arms caught her. She inhaled a wonderfully familiar smell of freshly cut wood.

Jason's aftershave.

"Emma," he said and all it took was the sound of her name on his lips for every cell in Emma's body to rev up with a combination of desire, hope, and fear. But the tingling in her breasts—plumper, fuller than they had been just five minutes ago—told her which of the three was winning out.

Desire.

Licking her dry lips, she croaked, "Welcome to the reunion."

Jason's face was hard. And so beautiful she thought she was dreaming. "Thanks," he said, the sound of his voice sending shivers through her, from her toes to the tips of her breasts.

Her eyes locked on to his and she realized that if she couldn't feel his tanned skin under her fingertips, if she couldn't taste his lips on her tongue, if she couldn't wrap her thighs around his hips, she'd go insane.

More than ten years after their first kiss, Emma's world came down to Jason. Just as she must have always known it would, his first kiss as vividly imprinted in her brain as if it had just happened.

⌐◠⌐

It was freshman orientation day at the beach and Emma couldn't believe she'd forgotten to bring a dry T-shirt to change into at the end of the day. Cold and feeling incredibly foolish, she decided to wait in the backseat of the dorm's van for everyone to finish up and pile in. A few minutes later Jason poked his head in the door.

"Hey, loner. Wanna be loners together?"

She grinned as he scooted onto the long, fake leather bench seat to keep her company. Too shy to sit around in nothing but a towel and bikini top, and sure that she looked fat in her revealing clothes, she shivered in her wet T-shirt, partly from the dampness that was seeping into her skin, but mostly from being alone with Jason in such close quarters. There wasn't enough air in the van for the both of them.

She was certain she was probably just imagining things, but even though they'd only known each other for a week, she already felt a special connection with Jason.

Particularly in the sexual sense.

Which explained why she couldn't quite meet Jason's eyes as he started stripping off his T-shirt.

"Here," he said, startling a gasp from between her sun-reddened lips.

She looked at the bundle of fabric in his hands, uncomprehending for a moment. Dazedly, she realized he was offering her a chance to change into something dry.

"Thanks," she said, as she took the shirt from him and slipped it over her head. His T-shirt, which said NICE GUYS COOK on it, was huge on her slim frame. She scooted her butt off of the seat and slid the hem of the T-shirt past her hips, pulling the wet towel away from her legs as well, semi-decent again and blissfully dry.

Jason's T-shirt was warm from the heat of his body. Emma was branded with his scent—an elementally male essence of clean soap and sunshine that set the tips of her small breasts into tight buds. She sent up a silent prayer of thanks that she had his shirt on to cover up the telltale signs of her body's sensual betrayal.

All throughout high school Emma had barely felt more than the slightest twinge of attraction for a guy. But now, the slight scent of Jason on his T-shirt was making her feel warm and moist between her legs.

How embarrassing was it that she was falling for the first guy who was nice to her in college? Especially when a gorgeous guy like Jason could have any girl he wanted, and every girl in their dorm had been flirting like crazy with him.

Her hands were still tingling from the quick exchange, as if they were anticipating more touches. Peering at him from underneath her lashes, Emma admired Jason's body in his bathing suit, sans shirt. His chest was rock-hard, his abs a well-defined six-pack, and the vee of his chest between his well-muscled pecs sported a light dusting of gold-tipped brown hair. Just enough chest hair to be sexy, she thought, as she ran her eyes over his toned, tanned legs as well.

Emma forcefully cut herself off. What was she doing ogling him so obviously? Her mother would be having a coronary if she could see her oversexed daughter now. Forcing a bright smile, she said, "Everyone at Stanford seems really nice, don't they?"

He grinned at her, saying, "They sure do," and the force of his smile just about blew his T-shirt right off of her. For the first time in her life, Emma knew what it was like to yearn for someone. She felt as if she were in heat under the full wattage of his smile.

Just then, the hired driver slid into the front seat and called back to them, "Looks like it's just the two of you heading back right now." The driver shot off and as they rounded a sharp corner in an effort to keep from falling on top of him, she placed her hands up against his bare chest. But Jason's arms were already around her, just barely keeping her from sliding off the seat.

Pressed against each other, their lips just a breath apart, she looked up into his eyes. Unable to resist the pull he had over her, she leaned in the final inch. Jason pulled her into him and bent his head, lowering his full lips to hers.

She felt his breath and then the soft, alluring pressure of his warm skin against her mouth, already swollen in anticipation of his kiss.

The kiss was sweet and sensual and the most powerful sexual experience Emma had ever had in her life. She slid her tongue into his mouth, wanting to know his taste, wanting to devour him.

Jason groaned as her tongue slipped into his mouth, and he deepened the kiss, pulling her even closer to him. Her hands danced over the hot skin of his chest, and began, of their own volition, to move lower, toward the waistband of his swim shorts. Emma was unaware of the driver, oblivious to anything but how glorious it felt to be held in Jason's arms, to be kissed into delirium by him.

The way Jason was looking at her was scary yet exciting, like he wanted to devour her, just as he had so many years ago. He was so close that Emma could feel his elemental warmth envelop her, pumping life into her cold blood.

The only time she'd ever let herself really live was with Jason. And she wanted to live again.

"Come outside with me," he said and those four simple words excited her more than anything ever had, even though somewhere in the back of her brain a warning bell was sounding, alerting her that Jason wanting to be with her out of the blue like this made no sense at all.

But Emma had the rest of her life to examine her mistakes, to see where she'd gone wrong in betraying him and choosing a plastic existence over the real, flesh and blood life that she and Jason might have created together. Tonight was her one chance to be with him, to finally give herself to him fully and completely. And she was going to take it.

A whispered, "Yes," was all Emma could manage as she walked to the door, knowing that Jason was behind her with every step, his heat, the potency of his gaze burning through her.

Sudden, powerful lust coursed through her veins. She felt wild and far more wicked than she ever had before, except in her secret erotic dreams. From this moment on, tonight was for her, damn the consequences.

With Jason dangerously close behind her, so close that she could hear his even breathing in her ears, Emma pushed through the heavy double doors and inhaled the cool night air. It did little to quell her fever. Her desire. She welcomed the chill after the heat of too many bodies, all trying to outdo each other with bragging about how far they'd come in the ten years since college. Amazingly, the headache that had been building up all day behind her eyes, threatening to break her skull apart, disappeared.

The thought was fleeting—*Jason is the best medicine, just as he always was*—floating around inside of her, waiting for a quiet time when she could dissect it.

She'd always loved the Stanford campus with its mature oaks and palm trees, large expanses of lawn, and the mix of old stone buildings with modern glass and steel structures. But tonight, as Emma moved away from the faculty club into the night, buoyed by Jason's silent urging from behind her to go farther, beyond the clinking of wineglasses, away from the overly bright laughter, she was oblivious to her surroundings.

Under the fronds of a palm tree, she turned to face him, praying for boldness, hoping for the strength to see this through.

Jason's smile was feral, intense. "The usual place?"

Emma shivered at his words, knowing that she didn't deserve his invitation to revisit their past. His offer was a gift, the most valuable gift she had ever been offered. Far more precious than a BMW or a diamond bracelet or anything her ex-husband had ever given her.

Another fleeting thought passed through her—*I would give up everything for this man*—and again she let it sink deep into her. Something else to add to her list, to deal with later.

"Yes," she whispered again, her eyes bright with unforgotten memories. "The lake."

Eighteen again, they ran through the night, traversing familiar, well-worn dirt paths through campus, past the dorms, past the faculty offices, out into the University wild lands. The leather rims of Emma's shoes bit into her heels, her lungs whooshed and pumped for air, her hair fell from its tight ponytail to dance at her shoulder blades. She felt free. Like anything was possible. Like dreams came true. And even though she knew from experience that real life wasn't ever going to be a fairy tale, tonight she was going to pretend that it could be.

Through their clasped hands, Jason's lifeblood infused her with renewal. Like a vampire, Emma sucked at his power and let it fill her until the dried-up stick of a woman from just minutes ago was nearly erased.

And then the lake on the edge of campus stood before them, a full moon revealed on its clear, still surface.

Fear hit her like a jackhammer, right at the place in her skull that had been on the verge of detonation in the ballroom. Who was she kidding? She wasn't a woman who ran with the wolves, for God's sake. Soft visions of fairy-tale endings fled and she felt more vulnerable than ever before.

As if he could sense her sudden panic, Jason said, "It's now or never, Emma."

His words were neither an invitation nor a condemnation, and a picture of the rest of her life assaulted her. It wasn't pretty. It wasn't interesting.

If she didn't take this "now" there would only be "never" for the rest of her life.

Turning to face him, holding his hazel gaze with her own she spoke the word that would seal her fate.

"Now."

What the hell am I doing?

Jason knew he should leave. Right now. Five minutes ago, even. He was supposed to make a little small talk, put the past firmly in the past, then forget Emma and get on with his life.

But with Emma's lips mere inches from his, with her breasts close enough for him to lean into, Jason was hard-pressed to think of anything but touching her. Kissing her.

Making love to her.

A ruthless voice inside him—a voice that Emma had unleashed with her betrayal in college, a voice that had never been silenced since—quickly reminded Jason that love had nothing to do with it.

And so he admitted to himself that from the moment he'd seen her across the crowded room, he'd wanted to own her, to possess her with everything he had. His hands. His mouth. His teeth. His cock.

Especially his cock.

But just as he had known that coming to the reunion was not one of his better ideas, he knew that taking Emma to the lake, taking everything she had kept from him in college was a bad idea. He'd heard that she was newly divorced and, therefore, vulnerable. And yet, all the wisdom in the world didn't matter tonight.

Because the look in her eyes from the moment he'd entered the room told him she was going to serve herself up to him on a platter tonight. She wanted him and he was desperate to see if fireworks shot off when he touched her.

If dynamite exploded.

If the inferno still raged.

Which meant the last thing he needed to do was come on too strong. He knew Emma better than anyone else, knew it wouldn't take much for her to run from him back to the safety of her boring, perfect little life. And then he would have lost his chance.

To take all that she'd withheld from him in college.

And then, hopefully, to forget all about her. Something he should have done ten years ago.

Standing on the edge of the lake where they'd shared so much, Emma had made her choice. "Now," she'd said, but still he waited. He waited for her to make the first move that would seal her fate.

And he would keep waiting, even if it killed him. Because when all was said and done, he didn't want to give Emma any cause to blame him for ripping apart her perfect little world.

He wanted her to know that *she* had destroyed her life all by herself.

four

Emma stood as still as a statue, waiting for Jason to do something. Anything. Why wasn't he kissing her? Touching her?

A small tick at the corner of his jaw—the same one that she used to kiss away before a big test—was the only indication that he was the least bit on edge. The seconds ticked away and Emma held her breath. Waiting, still waiting. And then Jason began to move away from her—it couldn't have been more than a millimeter—but loss hammered her across the chest

She suddenly understood. *Now* wasn't good enough unless she made it happen. She reached for him and then she was in his arms, held so tightly that she finally knew what safety felt like.

She was sick of waiting. Now or never was what he had said and he was right. It was time to leap into the unknown.

"Now," she breathed again as she pressed her mouth to his. A shudder ran through her as his heart beat against her lips. And then he was slipping his tongue inside her mouth and Emma felt as if she were being devoured whole.

As Jason's tongue found the sensitive corner where her lips came together, Emma threaded her hands through his thick hair and boldly pulled him down onto the damp sand. His weight settled hard over her and she arched her pelvis into the thick bulge between his legs.

He tasted like summer and wine and joy.

His hands worked up the front of her dress. Finally, God it wasn't soon enough, he cupped her breast in his hand. Her nipple, already painfully aroused from their kiss, arched up into his palm. Jason's thumb ran over the tight bud and pleasure overtook her. She rocked her pelvis against his thighs and knowing what she needed, Jason joined her rhythm, bucking against her.

And then his hands found the zipper on the back of her dress, and her shoulders and breasts were bared.

"Touch me," she begged, possessed by an inner wild woman who would stop at nothing in her quest for sexual satisfaction, but it was as if he couldn't hear her, so intent was Jason's focus on her nearly naked skin.

"You're so beautiful," he whispered. "So damn beautiful." Emma had never felt so cherished before. Never felt so lovely. Even though she didn't believe him. She knew she wasn't beautiful. But she still loved hearing her lover say it. Who wouldn't?

But when the heat of his mouth covered one breast, his hand stroking the other, Emma stopped thinking. Stopped second-guessing. She simply felt.

Felt his moist tongue through the sheer lace of her bra as he teased her beyond sanity.

Felt his large, magical hands—one cupping her breast, the other against her bottom—pulling her closer to him.

Instinctively, Emma wrapped her legs around his waist, unable to get close enough. Something was building up inside of her, something much more powerful than an orgasm.

Something more like an explosion that had the power to change her life forever.

～⦵～

Silently, Jason pledged allegiance to taking what Emma so freely offered with no strings attached. To sticking to his plan to show her what she'd missed out on and then getting the hell out of Dodge before the paint had a chance to dry.

But right now all he could concentrate on was the incredible woman who was coming apart in his arms. The woman who made him feel things he had sworn to never let himself feel again.

After having spent the past decade steering clear of women like Emma, he now knew that it hadn't mattered that he'd searched out plump, full women who were generous with not just their flesh, but their appetites as well. It hadn't mattered that these women came from nothing like he had. It didn't matter that they had said they loved him. Two called-off engagements said a heck of a lot more than words.

The truth was that Emma was the blueprint. And no one had ever come close to comparing to her memory.

And now, Emma in the flesh.

Because during all the years that he had imagined what being with Emma again would feel like, the reality was above and beyond anything he could have ever dreamed up.

His hands curved over her small, perfect breasts, and as he rubbed the taut peaks of her nipples against his palms Jason couldn't believe how good her curves felt in his hands. Her legs wrapped around him and he was lost, drowning in a violent need that he had never been able to transcend.

Her sweet tongue did crazy things to his insides, things he had never felt with anyone else, no matter how talented they were with their mouths and their bodies.

Erotic memories returned along with renewed desire.

"Remember how it used to be?"

His fingers began their slow descent from the center of her breasts, past the small clasp at the front of her bra, and Emma's eyes changed color as heightened awareness infused her.

"Remember how slow we went?" he said, letting his finger play down the center of her rib cage, around her neatly indented belly button. In college she'd never let him get very far, but he'd finally worn her down enough to let him pleasure her with his fingers. He'd promised her that she was still a virgin even if he fondled her, stroked her, made her cry out in his mouth. Jason had always prided himself on being a convincing guy.

Especially when he'd known just how bad Emma wanted it back then, how badly she'd craved those stolen, secret orgasms.

Just like she craved one right now.

But he wanted to hear her say it. Admit how hot she was. For him.

"Do you want me, Emma?"

Her "yes" was little more than a groan of desire.

That wasn't good enough. He wanted her to beg a little, to wonder if he would walk if she didn't say the right thing.

"How much?"

Her whispered response brushed against his neck. "More than anything."

The only way he could stop himself from plunging into her wet heat in that moment was to keep talking, spewing useless words when all he wanted to do was slide his fingers, his cock, into her slick, wet pussy.

"Remember how wet you'd get?"

Emma didn't respond with words. Instead she arched into him. With his free hand Jason quickly unclasped her bra and then her rosy, heated flesh was in his mouth.

She was so aroused that he knew she'd come the minute he touched her clit. How could he ever forget the feeling of slowly running his fingers down the soft skin of Emma's stomach, under the waistband of her jeans, inch by inch until he found the edge of her panties? Waiting until the final moment to travel those final inches, into her wetness, exploring and rubbing her swollen clit until she cried out in his mouth.

Her legs opened for him and Jason could hold back no longer. But just as his fingers slid beneath the fine lace of her panties into her pubic hair, slick and wet, the bright high beams of a car broke through the bushes.

Nothing was going to stop him now, not when he had her on the brink of giving into him completely. Still, he couldn't take her like this, out on the beach, in full view of anyone who might walk or drive by.

Grabbing a condom from his pants, he stood up, quickly dropping his pants to the sand. Emma pulled herself up onto her elbows, blinking uncertainly at him.

"What are you doing?" she asked in a tentative voice.

"I think you mean, what are *we* doing?"

He reached under her shoulders and knees and picked her up, cradling her tightly in his arms as he headed into the water.

"We're not about to do what I think we're about to do, are we?"

He lowered his voice to a husky growl. "Everything you can imagine and more."

In the moonlight, he could just make out the flush that spread across her high cheekbones. Which was why he was so damn surprised when Emma wrapped her arms around his neck and said, "Thank God."

~~~

Every one of her fantasies was about to come true.

Only once in college had Emma been brave enough to touch Jason's penis. And she'd never been able to forget the feel of his smooth, huge erection in her hands. She had spent so many years wondering what it would have felt like if she had let him stretch her wide. If she hadn't been so afraid of her own shadow, maybe she could have risked giving her virginity up to Jason and he would have plunged into her again and again until they both cried out.

She whimpered with pleasure at the X-rated images as he slowly lowered them into the lake, finding a spot deep enough to completely sumberge their bodies. "Are you cold?" he said into the curve of her neck, gently punctuating each word by nipping at the sensitive spot behind her ear.

Emma shivered, but not because she was chilled. She had never felt so inflamed. "I'm perfect," she said. Although the water was cool, to Emma it felt heavenly rushing across her heated skin. As she floated in Jason's arms, he wrapped her legs around his waist, his enormous erection thrusting into the lace of her panties. His fingers skimmed her stomach and she held her breath. Any second now and he was going to . . .

"Tell me what you want, Emma."

His words sent fear hammering across her chest. Fear that he would be disappointed with her complete lack of sexual prowess.

Fear that he would see what a dried-up excuse for a woman she was.

Fear that he would laugh at her for thinking she could be anyone but Emma Holden Cartwright, Palo Alto mortgage broker, daughter of two pillars of the community, ex-wife of a hotshot lawyer.

"Tell me what you want," he whispered again against her neck, causing the tiny hairs to stand up as a shiver coursed through her, and she felt that he was trying to help her over the massive hump of her trepidation.

Biting her lower lip, she shook her head. "I . . . I can't," she whispered, knowing what a hypocrite she was, with her legs wrapped around his waist and her breasts pressed up against his incredible chest and his erection jutting into her.

He tipped one finger under her chin, forcing her to look at him. "You can."

She swallowed, but her tongue felt like sawdust. In college they had explored each other in silence, with the occasional moan as a soundtrack. Never dirty words. The only dirty words had been in her secret fantasies.

But Emma knew that tonight was about firsts. If she could think words like pussy and cunt in her dreams, she could say them out loud, couldn't she?

"Tell me," he said yet again, so wonderfully patient with her as she fumbled toward ecstasy, straight toward some wild place she'd never been before. What could she have possibly done right to deserve this amazing moment of intimacy with Jason?

She took a deep breath and her nipples rubbed against his pecs in the most delicious way.

"Touch me."

Jason grinned that gorgeous half-grin of his and she knew she wasn't going to get away with being so obtuse.

"Where?" he murmured into the hollow of her collarbone.

Before she knew it, "Everywhere," was out of her mouth.

Jason groaned and his mouth was on hers again and he was sucking all of the remaining breath from her lungs. Oh God, maybe now he would get back down to the business of making her come, something that she needed more desperately than she had ever needed anything in her life. But he pulled his lips away, his hand flat on the concave lines of her stomach.

"Where should I start?"

"Between my legs," she said so softly that her words were nearly carried away by the breeze.

"Tell me where," he insisted, his words a low growl. "Where do you want me to touch you between your legs."

She blurted out, "My pussy," and all of the humor left his eyes. In an instant his large, warm hand was in her panties and his thumb covered her clitoris so lightly that if she hadn't been in a state of hypersensitivity, she might not have felt it.

His soft words brushed by her ear. "You've certainly learned some dirty words, haven't you?"

She blushed, hating herself for giving in to the urge to act like a bad girl. Of course he saw right through her. He knew her better than anyone, even now.

He drew her back under his spell, saying "What do you want me to do to your . . . pussy, Emma?"

Emma gasped at hearing the sexy words fall from his lips, just as they had leapt from her own. She was so close now, if only she could be brave enough to keep playing this game maybe he would take her to that heavenly place that even her dreams wouldn't allow her to go.

Forcing herself to be bold, to risk everything yet again, she said, "Rub my clit, Jason."

His lips and teeth bit into her neck just as his thumb pressed into her. This time he didn't make any pointed comments about her new vocabulary. And she was glad. Because Emma had never felt anything so good in all her life and she didn't want one single thing to spoil these wonderful new sensations.

Her body begged for more of his touch. Threading her fingers through his hair, Emma bit and sucked at his lips as the first waves of an orgasm crashed over her. She thought she tasted blood, and she didn't know if it was hers or his, but it didn't matter. She didn't care. All she could concentrate on, all she wanted to think about, ever again, was the incredible pleasure of Jason touching her.

Jason loving her.

Jason making her come like this again and again and again.

When her orgasm was on its final legs, Jason pulled off his boxers. His incredible penis jutted out at her beneath the water and she wrapped her fingers around it, sighing with satisfaction at the throbbing, hot weight of him in her hand.

Being with Jason like this, so close to him, gave her courage. She was no longer afraid to tell him what she wanted, not with the aftershocks of her incredible explosion still rocking through her.

"I've waited my whole life to feel you inside of me. Take me, Jason. Take me now."

He ripped off her bra, shoved her panties down her legs. She could feel the head of his penis, so hot, so big, pressing into her. Knowing she should wait until he had put a condom on, that she was being stupid and reckless, Emma was so desperate to feel him inside her she couldn't help but sink her weight down onto his shaft. Just an inch. That's what she told herself.

But an inch turned into two. And then three.

Unexpectedly, in the next breath Jason sank his entire length into her tight canal. Pain mixed with pleasure as his enormous erection stretched her so wide. Opening herself to him unconsciously, she rocked herself up and down on his shaft, using the water to buoy her hips up and down.

In a quick flash, he pulled all the way out.

"No," she cried, the voice in her ears sounding desperate and needy and horny. She tried to position herself back onto his penis, but then she realized why he had pulled out. Unlike her, he obviously had retained a modicum of sense as he somehow rolled on a condom under the water then plunged back into her oh-so-willing flesh.

Again and again he drove into her. She threw her head back, relishing the feel of his mouth on her nipples, his breath hot against the tight skin of her breasts. Water rippled around them, splashing against her incredibly sensitive skin, making Jason's body slip and slide on hers.

She was so close to coming again, just minutes after she had fallen apart in his arms, and she was amazed at how badly she needed this second orgasm. She'd die if she didn't . . .

Reading her mind, his thumb found her again. A feral sound came from her lips and he covered her mouth with his to swallow it. His tongue pumped in and out in perfect rhythm to his thumb on her clit. All of which was magnified a thousand times by the thick, perfect weight of his shaft spreading her, claiming her most private flesh as his own. He grew bigger and bigger inside her, then grabbed her hips and roughly pounded them together, bone to bone, cock to pussy.

This was exactly how she had always wanted to be taken but hadn't known it until right this very second.

With a roar that sounded all the way down the bottom of the lake he exploded into her.

Feeling like she had finally found the place she was supposed to be, the heaven she'd been searching for all her life, Emma let her orgasm spin her away into oblivion.

She had to have been lying.

It was the only rational, reasonable explanation for what she had said. *I've waited my whole life to feel you inside me.*

She'd probably said that to Steven every night before he slid inside her. The picture of Steven's big, lumbering, football-playing body impaling Emma in their bed filled Jason with rage.

But what really killed him, absolutely crucified him, was the fact that he had just experienced the most sexually fulfilling fuck of his life.

Hadn't he been with some of the world's most beautiful women? Underwear models that put Barbie to shame, movie stars whose perfection created the latest craze in nose jobs and cheekbones, lush women who made Marilyn Monroe look coltish in comparison.

So why was it that one too-thin woman, with enough lines around her mouth at thirty-two to prove just how uptight she was, had to be the only woman who had ever truly driven him insane?

Fortunately, he wasn't a dumb little twenty-one-year-old kid. He'd come to Stanford tonight for closure. Like hell if he was leaving without it.

Emma's limbs were wrapped tightly around his neck, his waist. Her face was pressed into his neck and she was panting. As a cold emptiness whipped through him, he efficiently disentangled her.

She came up sputtering, her perfectly straight, glossy blonde hair looking much more like it belonged on a mangy mutt than a society darling. Her eyes showed every ounce of her trademark fragility.

Granted, he'd just screwed her prim and proper bones raw in the middle of the Stanford campus. Who wouldn't be feeling less than steady?

Jason deftly reached for the hardness inside him and spoke quickly, before she could say anything that would throw him off or call to the man inside of him that believed women should be taken care of, protected. Whether they deserved it or not.

"We should get out of here right away."

"We should?"

Her voice trembled and Jason forced himself to ignore the softness that dared to creep into his heart. "Just in case the campus police are out and about. We wouldn't want anyone to find out about this, would we?"

"Actually, the funny thing is—" she began, but Jason didn't want to hear anything she had to say. Especially when he couldn't think of one single funny thing about his night so far.

Pulling her out of the water more roughly than he needed to, he said, "Wait onshore and I'll fish out our clothes." He dove to the bottom to pick up her bra and panties and his boxers. When he surfaced, Emma was shivering and holding her arms across her chest, and all he could focus on were her incredible naked breasts. The last thirty minutes played out in his head in brilliant Technicolor and he couldn't help but remember how amazing and beautiful and . . .

What was his problem? He needed to stop with the poetry and remember that Emma was nothing more than a lying, cheating woman. One who clearly had no use for him apart from what he could do to her clit.

Don't forget again, he counseled himself.

"Here," he said, throwing her wet clothes at her. Instead of catching the small wet ball of fabric and underwire, Emma let it hit her smack across the chest. Her mouth opened with surprise and she jumped back a step. Her lower lip began to wobble and as she stood there naked, and confused, and so damn beautiful, Jason almost forgot that tonight meant nothing more than hot sex to Emma. That she'd likely take a quick shower and run back to her perfect little suburban world to catch up on the latest gossip, their tryst completely forgotten.

Tamping down on his newly flared anger—both at himself and the woman he couldn't resist no matter how hard he tried—he barked, "Planning on putting your dress back on?" as he stepped out onto the shore.

He watched her struggle with his coldness. And yet, she still ate up his nakedness, need flaring up in her eyes.

Forcing himself to turn away from her obvious desire, Jason reminded himself that this was what he had wanted. For them to end their relationship once and for all.

Only this time, they were ending things on his terms.

Fighting his protective instincts every step of the way, he said, "Get dressed," pulling on his own pants over his naked, wet skin as if giving her step-by-step instructions.

But Emma was racked with shivers, as she held her arms tightly around her waist, hiding her breasts from him. "I . . . I'm all . . ."

Seemingly too cold and distraught to finish her sentence, Jason felt like she was imploring him with her big doe eyes to help her out.

No way.

He raised an eyebrow and waited.

Finally something inside the woman he craved *for no good reason* snapped. "I'm all wet!" she yelled. "Wet! I'll soak through my dress and my underwear is ruined and if you don't want anyone to find out about this you'd better think fast!"

Jason couldn't help it. He started laughing. He hadn't seen Emma this riled up since, well, ever actually. Judging by the look in her eyes, Jason guessed that Emma was pretty damn stunned by her outburst as well. If he knew her at all, she'd be apologizing in five, four, three, two . . .

"Sorry," she mumbled, at which point he threw her his sweater.

"Dry off."

Emma quickly rubbed the remaining droplets of water from her skin. *Such gorgeous skin,* he found himself thinking, wishing like hell that he could turn his damn sex drive off. He pictured greasy burgers, soggy, squeaky fries, withered salads. It usually did the trick, turning his stomach with disgust, but tonight even fast food wasn't quite the poison he needed.

Seconds later, Emma pulled her dress back over her head and Miss Priss was back in business. She finger-combed her wet hair, tucking it back behind her ears, and then slipped back into her heels. Folding his wet sweater with intense concentration, she held it out for him.

"I can't believe this happened," she said finally, a tremulous smile on her lips. "After so long . . . "

Forcing himself to hold tightly to his resolution to leave her without a backward glance, even though he knew she was trying to bridge the chasm between them, he ignored her opening to reminisce about the past.

"I have to get back to Napa."

Her eyes held his and he thought he saw a plea in them. Something caught in his chest and he nearly reached out for her, almost blurted out, *"How could you have left me? I loved you so much. I would have done anything for you. Been anyone you wanted."*

Everything went still as they faced off, a decade of emotion hanging in the air between them, and the only way Jason could find solid ground was to walk away.

Tonight had been a mistake, a beautiful mistake. One an intelligent man would never dare to repeat again.

five

U nable to return to the party looking like a half-drowned
rat, Emma drove home, replaying the evening's events
again and again in her head.

She had seen Jason again for the first time in ten years.
They had made love. In the lake. She had come not once, but
twice. Two incredible, mind-altering orgasms. They had finally
consummated their relationship in the most elemental way and
it had been so much better than anything she could have ever
imagined. Her skin felt hot and tight as she let herself into her
big, empty house, still feeling impossibly turned on.

Even though her heart had been broken all over again.

From the look in his eyes, the set of his jaw before he walked away without so much as a good-bye, Emma was certain that Jason thought he had made a mistake by being with her.

One that he wouldn't forgive either himself or her for.

She didn't blame him for feeling that way. How could she? She'd done all the wrong things in college, made all the wrong decisions, taken the one road that she knew would hurt Jason the most.

She could see that he didn't have one single reason to be rejoicing over their extremely sensual, private reunion tonight. Even though Emma could have named a thousand reasons to rejoice. Each one starting with Jason's touch and ending with his kiss.

Barely aware of what she was doing, her night having taken on a surreal glow, she locked herself into her opulent master bathroom and turned on the water in the bathtub. She'd never been this impatient to touch herself, never been this unashamed of finding her own pleasure.

Jason had given her that gift tonight. The gift of pleasure. Of satisfaction. Of finally knowing what giving herself to a man, body and soul, was supposed to be like.

Sliding down under the steaming water, Emma groaned with pleasure. Feeling so much bolder than she'd ever been before, she placed her hand over her mound and summoned up a picture of Jason in her mind.

Tell me what you want, he had said.

Emma's fingers trembled as she found her most sensitive spot and started rubbing small, light circles. Slick wetness flooded between her legs and seemingly of its own volition, her other hand found her breast.

What do you want me to do to your clit?

Heat rushed through her. Aching, desperate arousal.

Arching her body into her hand, Emma threw her head back and cried out his name as shudders racked through her.

Still in a daze, she dried off and crawled naked under her covers, falling into a deep, dreamless sleep. She woke to the insistent bleeping of her cell phone. It was Kate, it had to be.

But Emma didn't want to talk to her friend, didn't want anything to destroy her magical memories. When night came again she hoped she could retreat back into that special place where everything felt so good. So damn good. And she could pretend that she was still with Jason. And that he loved her.

Even though he didn't love her. Not anymore.

She was immediately overloaded with sadness as she slid out from beneath her duvet. Standing in front of the full-length mirror in her walk-in closet, she noticed that her eyes were bright and glossy, her cheeks were pink and hot, burning up, just like she had been last night.

Looking at the drab stick figure staring back in the mirror, Emma couldn't believe that she had done all of those naughty, breathless, incredible things last night with Jason.

Jason, the famous sex symbol.

Jason, the stunningly masculine man who had filled her so deeply, so completely with his huge erection.

Jason, the only man she had ever truly loved.

Emma sank back against a row of well-tailored business suits and closed her eyes. If she tried hard enough she could almost be back in the lake with Jason. She could almost escape from the boring, monotonous joke that was her life.

Almost, but not quite.

Emma put on a boring beige skirt and sweater set, slipped her feet into dull beige kitten heels, put on the small pearl earrings that her father had given her when she graduated from high school, got into her Range Rover and drove the half mile to her parents' house for their weekly Sunday brunch.

All the while trying to ignore how dead her heart felt.

⁓

Emma stood in front of her parents' front door for a long moment, taking a deep breath to compose herself before turning her key in the lock, stepping inside, and coming face to face with her mother.

"Emma darling," Jane said as she air-kissed Emma's cheeks.

Emma knew her plastered smile must look far more like a grimace, but it was the best she could do. Her mother peered closely at her face.

"Are you wearing blusher?" her mother said, through tight disapproving lips.

Emma frowned. "No, Mother."

But Jane obviously wasn't going to take her word for it, because she reached for a tissue from the nearby table and roughly wiped it over Emma's cheek. Staring at the unblemished white of the tissue, her mother was finally satisfied that she was telling the truth. "You know how vulgar blusher is."

Knowing her mother wasn't expecting a response, nor would wait for one, Emma merely nodded. It wasn't that she thought blusher was actually vulgar, but in her experience it was far easier to agree with her mother than it was to state her own opinion.

Having done away with makeup as a reason for Emma's new look, Jane asked, "Are you ill?"

Emma noticed that her mother took a step back as she asked the question, obviously more afraid of catching something from her daughter than she was concerned about Emma having an actual illness.

"No," she began, but then she realized that she did in fact look different. Her passionate, wild night with Jason—she could hardly say his name in her head without blushing and breaking out in a sweat—must have changed her on the outside, just as it had irreparably changed her on the inside. And if she didn't plead illness, what would she say?

Oh, you know how it is, Mother, when you spend the night having sex with an old flame in public, you just glow a little bit more than usual.

A wild giggle threatened to erupt from her mouth. If she ever dared to say something like that to her mother, the earth would surely open up and swallow her whole.

"Emma?" Jane said, her tone sharp. "I'm waiting for your answer."

Emma feigned a cough into her hand. "I might just be a tad under the weather."

"If only Steven were still here to take care of you."

Emma watched as Jane turned and headed into the kitchen, slightly sickened. As if Steven had ever taken care of her a day in his life.

If only her parents would learn to accept that Steven was gone. They were divorced and no amount of wishing and hoping would bring him back.

Not, Emma realized with sudden clarity, that she wanted him back anyway. Nothing she and Steven had shared during ten years of marriage had come even close to the passion and intensity of her stolen hour with Jason in the lake.

Emma felt as if a pin had pricked her. And it hurt. A lot. Until last night, she suddenly realized, she hadn't "felt" anything in years. She had, in essence, been walking around completely numb.

Dazed by the enormity of her discovery, her hand unclenched of its own volition and she dropped her purse and jacket in a heap on the well-polished hardwood floor.

"Emma, why are you dawdling in the foyer?" her mother called out from the covered back porch. "It's time to come outside and serve lunch to your father."

It took a moment or two, but the sound of her mother's voice, and the disapproval in it, helped Emma to refocus her blurred vision. She walked through the formal white and beige living room and out through the French doors to where her father was seated.

"Emma," her father said, his greeting as terse as usual. "Your mother's roast is getting cold. Please serve it now."

"Yes, Daddy," Emma found herself automatically replying, her tone as coldly polite, as emotionless as her father's. An image flashed before her of her passionate, heated, violent response to Jason's touch the previous night. It was such a contrast to the coldness all around her that she felt light-headed again and clumsily dropped the carving knife to the table.

She blindly reached out to steady herself on the back of a chair.

Jane immediately stood up and grabbed the knife. "Sit down, Emma. I'll do it," she added with a sigh.

Emma knew her cheeks had to be red, considering how the thought of Jason made her feel like she was burning up all over, and her father's eyes narrowed as she worked to regain her composure.

"I hope you didn't drink too much last night at your class reunion," he said. "That's no way to make a good impression on potential clients."

"You know better than that, Emma," Jane said as she slid the extremely sharp carving knife through the roast.

Jane finished serving the meal and Emma stared at the unappetizing plate of food before her. Without really noticing what she was eating she cut into a fatty piece of the roast and brought it to her lips.

"Emma!" her mother screeched. "What are you doing eating that fat? Don't you remember how plump you were as a teenager?"

Emma dropped her fork as if it were on fire. Every meal with her mother was a reminder of the year Emma had turned thirteen. Naturally thin as a child, once she hit puberty everything had changed. Her legs had gone from stick thin to slightly rounded and hips had appeared virtually overnight. Emma might not have thought too much about it—after all, all of the other girls at school had gotten their periods well before her and she felt almost scrawny and childlike next to most of them—but Jane had been horrified by her daughter's womanly transformation.

Ever since then, Emma couldn't remember not being on a diet. Food restriction and exercise were as much a part of her life as Sunday brunch with her parents.

She picked up her fork and small talk commenced again, mostly centering on how good Steven had looked last week when her father took care of some business with him. Her parents still fawned all over her ex-husband, and Emma sat as still as a rock, taking the familiar family scene in, not saying a word (no one expected her to, anyway).

Yet, at the same time, she wasn't really seeing her parents. Wasn't really listening to what they were saying. Because suddenly, Emma couldn't suffer through one more Sunday brunch. Not without rocking the boat at least once in her life.

Feeling reckless, she said, "The funniest thing happened to me at the reunion last night," she began, waiting for her parents to ask her to tell them more. But it was as if she hadn't even spoken. Her mother got up to refill her father's wineglass and he started another boring tale about golfing with some old cronies from work.

How long had she been living like this? With no one paying the least bit of attention to what she had to say? Dozens of Sunday brunches blurred before her, all exactly the same. With Emma playing the part of the quiet, good girl, who never did or said anything to upset anyone.

Well, not this time.

"I hooked up with an old boyfriend by the lake," she stated, knowing that this would have to get her parents' attention.

But again, it was as if she hadn't spoken.

Spying the bottle of ranch dressing on the table that only her father was permitted to eat, she picked it up and doused her salad with it. Spearing several leaves completely covered with the goopy dressing, she shoved them into her mouth.

Her mother turned to her then, noticing her presence for the first time in minutes. Emma knew then that while she might be invisible to her parents, Jane's "fat" radar could catch anything.

But Emma had already hit her limit. "Excuse me," she said to no one in particular as she got up from the table.

Walter continued eating his roast, carefully cutting bite-sized pieces off with his knife and fork, chewing them with great concentration, then starting all over again.

The pinprick of pain turned into a bullet hole in Emma's heart. Being with Jason, even if just for one fleeting night, had brought her this vision, this ability to see so many things she wished she could ignore.

She hadn't been just content with Jason. She'd been ecstatic. Full of passion. And delight. And life.

And fear. So much fear of doing the wrong thing. Of disappointing everyone. And losing their love.

"Good-bye," she said quietly. Thankfully, no one followed her out to the car. She hadn't thought they would, of course, given that the roast would just get colder.

⌐∾⌐

Emma drove away, in no particular direction, gulping air into her lungs. Drowning, she always felt like she was drowning in her parents' house. She remembered the summer she was thirteen and it felt like a watermelon was crushing her rib cage, all day, all night. She woke up gasping for breath, weighed down by the expectations of her parents, of their world, to forgo a messy adolescence. To be the perfect young lady. Now here she was, thirty-two years old, and she might as well be thirteen again for all that had changed.

Change. She had to make a change. And Emma knew exactly what she had to do. Exactly who she had to run to.

Jason. She had to see Jason again.

Just one more time.

She knew he might reject her. But for the first time in her life, Emma wasn't going to back down from a challenge.

She was going to drive ninety minutes to Napa to beg Jason for forgiveness. To ask him if they could start over.

Emma was thoroughly sick of her boring, whitewashed life. And if, along the way, she happened to make her parents angry enough to notice her existence, well, that would be a bonus, wouldn't it?

It was now or never.

And Emma was choosing now.

six

W hat's your problem, boss?"

Jason didn't bother acknowledging his sous-chef's question as he lifted his cleaver and hacked through a thick chicken bone, dispassionately splitting it in two clean halves. But Rocco was undeterred.

"I've never seen you get so twisted up over a woman," Rocco said, a note of laughter embedded in his words.

Jason carefully laid the cleaver down. "What makes you think my mood has anything to do with a woman?"

Jason was a fair boss, a phenomenal restaurateur, but never a man you could push around. Anyone else in the kitchen would have backed down. But not Rocco. They'd worked together for too many years, outrun too many fires while watching each other's backs. In truth, they were far more like brothers than boss and employee.

"Remember that summer I met you when you were washing dishes at that fleapit Mexican place in San Francisco? Must have been ten years ago. And that pretty little blonde came looking for you. You look the same now as you did then. Like you've been marinating in raw sewage."

"I'm good," Jason ground out before walking out of the kitchen into the back alley. He sat down on an upside down milk crate and stared out at what had to be the best, and most unexpected, behind-the-restaurant view in the world: a lush vineyard.

The best decision he'd ever made had been moving to Napa Valley to open his first restaurant. Cravings had taken off faster than Jason could have ever imagined. A four-star review in the *New York Times* coupled with positive online commentary from Thomas Keller, who owned one of the world's best restaurants, The French Laundry, in nearby Yountville, had turned Jason into an overnight superstar.

His worst decision . . . hunting Emma down at the reunion. And then kissing her and touching her and slipping inside her wet heat.

If he'd been smart, he would have left well enough alone. Shit, if he'd been really smart he never would have talked to her that first day of freshman year when she looked so scared. And so stunning she took his breath away.

"Hey, boss." Rocco stuck his head into the alley. "Someone's here to see you."

Emma. By the bemused tone of Rocco's voice, it had to be Emma. A part of him couldn't believe that she'd actually have the nerve to come to Napa, to his restaurant. But the other part—the stupid part—wanted it to be her.

Something simmered deep in Jason's gut. Lust and irritation warred with one another. Funny how one bad decision just kept coming back to bite a guy in the ass.

"She's still a looker," Rocco added as Jason pushed past him, knocking over a can of organic tomato paste. "Great legs on a classy babe have always done it for me."

Jason shot Rocco a look that had him backing up into the stainless-steel shelving, even though he outweighed Jason by a good eighty pounds.

"Hey, I meant that as a compliment."

"Get back to work," Jason growled, fighting back his instinctive protectiveness where Emma was concerned. Damn it, he wasn't supposed to care anymore. Regardless of how good she'd felt with her legs wrapped tightly around him last night in the lake.

Regardless of how tight her pussy was, how wet, how ready she'd been to take him in, all of him.

He paused at the swinging door that separated the kitchen from the restaurant and reminded himself that despite how attractive she was, and how much he wanted her, he wasn't a big enough idiot anymore to let himself fall for her game again.

Jason wasn't interested in being her gentle, concerned lover until she found her next Mr. Born on the Right Side of the Golf Course.

The truth was, he'd botched his plan Saturday night to erase her from his memory. He'd wanted one last look, enough impartial data to know that he was well and completely over her. But everything had backfired.

Because he'd gotten wrapped up in her. Her scent, her kisses, her beauty.

Rocco was right. Jason was all twisted up over Emma. And it made him angry at himself.

And at her.

The thought occurred to him that for her to have come here today, something must have pushed her to the brink. A part of him idly wondered what that final shove to the edge could have been. Her parents were no prize. Neither was her ex-husband.

A new plan formed in his mind, designed around getting payback. After all, wouldn't it serve her right if he reeled her in and then spit her out, just like she'd done to him in college?

And if she played right into his hands, what was the point of turning down more of the hottest sex he'd ever had?

Lord knew he'd greatly enjoy loving her before he left her.

Round 1 had been all Emma's back in college.

Round 2 last night had been a split.

But Jason was determined that Round 3 would be all his.

Emma stood in the middle of Jason's stylish yet comfortable restaurant. Another time she might have appreciated the colorful blown-glass lighting fixtures, the brilliant over-sized oil paintings hanging above the beautifully set tables, but anxiety was blinding her to everything but her own madness.

Was she crazy, driving to Napa Valley, invading Jason's world? Just because he had made love to her so passionately at the reunion didn't mean he loved her.

It didn't even mean he liked her.

Emma knew she should leave, get back in her car, go back

to her safe, boring life. But she couldn't. Not when she had to see him just one more time.

She didn't know what she was going to say. Didn't have a big speech planned, but even though something deep within her told her that running was her best option, she couldn't move.

Not until she saw him.

His face tight, but other wise devoid of expression, Jason swung open the door. Emma spun to face him, knowing her blue eyes were wild. Desperate. And yet, even though this pathetic need shamed her, she couldn't tamp down on the feelings he evoked within her.

She stared at him silently, taking in the rough stubble that covered his jaw, his stunning—if cold—eyes. Even covered with a bloodstained, jalapeno-print apron he was all man. And after last night, she would never be able to look at him again—whether it was on TV, or on the cover of a book or magazine—without feeling him sliding in and out of her all over again, making her scream with pleasure.

"Jason," she said, hesitantly, praying that he'd give her an opening, some sign that he didn't hate her. That he was at least a little bit glad she'd come to see him. Or would pretend to be for her sake.

"Emma." Her name was almost a curse on his lips and she would have turned and left right then, but something in his eyes made her pause. "Sit down. Have a drink."

"Thank you," she said, knowing that she should be saying so much more. And she would. Once she calmed down a little.

Glad for the sturdy weight of the leather bar stool beneath

her, she placed her purse down on the gleaming cherrywood bar top and watched Jason uncork a bottle of Pinot Noir. His hands were bigger, darker than she remembered. She supposed she was looking at the inevitable difference between a twenty-one-year-old boy and a thirty-two-year-old man.

Erotic images flashed before her eyes of all that those hands were capable of. On her breasts, between her legs.

Clenching her thighs tightly together as if doing so could lessen her elemental response to every single thing Jason did, every part of who he was, she reached for the half-full balloon glass. She tilted back her throat and downed the pricey Pinot like it was a beer bong.

"Hey now. You just guzzled a hundred bucks of fine wine in ten seconds flat."

Emma had the good grace to look chagrined. But then, she slid the glass back across the bar. The alcohol already working its magic, helping to dim the sharpness within her, she retorted, "You probably shouldn't waste the good stuff on me right now. 'Two-Buck Chuck' would be just fine."

It was the kind of banter they might have had back in college. Strangely, it still felt just right. Deep within Emma, hope bloomed. Was there a chance for the two of them after all?

Jason refilled her glass with the same vintage red. "I'm afraid you're all out of luck. The good stuff is all we've got around here."

Her mouth quirking up on one side, she said, "Figures." Just as quickly, her mirth disappeared. Nothing could come of endless small talk. No matter how much she longed to remain a wimp. To act as if nothing had happened.

"Jason, I need to apologize to you. I've needed to apologize for years. For how I behaved. For how I handled the situation in the quad."

He simply stared at her, neither encouraging nor discouraging. She knew her apology was ten years too late, that saying this today was more about her than him. But now that she'd begun, she couldn't stop. Not until the bitter end.

She looked down into her glass, finally taking another large gulp for Dutch courage. "I should never have kissed Steven that day. The quad was our special place. I mean, you and me, not me and him." She took another anxious mouthful. "Oh God, I can't say anything right. I should shut up . . . but I can't. Not this time. I'm just going to say it all. I have to."

She couldn't read his expression, but when Jason poured himself a glass and just as quickly downed it, she knew listening to her babble out a pathetic apology wasn't any easier for him that it was for her to get it out.

"I loved you so much back then, Jason. And I made all the wrong decisions. There was so much pressure, from everyone, and I crumbled beneath it." Her eyes remained dry even while her heart rebroke at the strain of having to go back to a time she wished she could forget. "I know there's no rewind button. Believe me, I've wished for one a thousand times. And I don't want to sit here, in your restaurant, making excuses. I want to take the blame. If you want to yell at me, call me names, kick me out—whatever you need to do—please, do it now, Jason. I want you to."

Jason merely shook his head. "You always worried too much," he said, the corner of his mouth quirking up into a faint smile. She tried to read his feelings, but nothing in his eyes, in his face, gave them away.

Still, he hadn't kicked her out yet and Emma's nerves settled just enough that she was able to let out the breath she'd been holding.

"I know," she said softly, holding his gaze, letting a small grin play on her lips. If only it could be like old times between them. Would he ever let that happen? And if he did, would she blow it again?

Without thinking, she gave voice to her crazy thoughts. "Do you think we could ever be friends again, Jason?"

He hesitated for a long moment, so long that she wished she could become invisible and creep out of his restaurant to find somewhere private to hide her hurt. Her humiliation.

 But then he reached across the bar and covered her hand with his. And as his warmth seeped through her cold bones, as she drank in his touch, he said, "I think we can definitely be friends again. And so much more."

Shock coursed through Emma only to be superceded by desire. Was he saying what she thought he was saying? That he wanted to continue where they'd left off last night?

Something about his quick acquiescence made her uneasy. Not to mention the new predatory look in his eyes. Last night she'd been vividly aware of how much he'd changed. Matured. But this morning she saw something else.

The man standing before her was no longer the sweet Jason Roberts she'd known back in college. A part of her was frightened by his intensity.

But the rest of her was incredibly attracted to it. She'd never felt quite this jumpy around him before. The way he was staring at her—like he wanted to rip her clothes off and devour her whole on the bar top—made her pulse race with anticipation.

A large blond man with multiple tattoos visible on his upper arms and hands stuck his head out from the kitchen. "Hey boss, I'm done with prep. See you in an hour."

She searched her brain frantically for something to say that wouldn't sound stupid or desperate, anything to keep Jason here with her for a little longer. "We didn't really get a chance to talk much last night. We have so much catching up to do. I want to hear all about your restaurant, what it's like to live in N—"

Her words died in her throat as he moved from behind the bar with a wicked gleam in his eyes. "Help me pull down the blinds."

Something in his tone sent another flood of moisture between her legs. Uncertainly, she slid off the bar stool and moved on shaky legs through the restaurant until all of the windows were covered.

He locked the front door, threw his apron to the ground, and then motioned to her with one finger. "Get over here."

She licked her lips. "There? Why?"

"Because I don't want to talk."

"You don't?"

"I want to fuck you. Here. Now."

Her body responded like he was in charge of her on-off switch. Slowly, she walked toward him, her heart beating faster and faster with every step.

Mere inches from him, she stopped, more afraid that she'd fail this test, that she wouldn't live up to being the wild woman he obviously wanted her to be, than she'd ever been of anything in her whole life.

No, she told herself, you can do this. The man you love is giving you another chance and you're going to take it.

As if he could read her mind, had faith in her determination to succeed, he reached for her. His mouth found hers then and she was lost to everything but the sensual pull that drew her deeper and deeper into him.

Threading her hands through his thick, dark hair, she kissed him like she always did in her dreams. Without holding anything back. Passion flooded between them and she felt Jason's control waver. She knew he was holding something back, but she didn't care. Maybe one day she'd break all the way through the thick emotional wall her own actions had built in him, but for now, she would take what she could get.

Because part of Jason was so much better than none of him at all.

He ran his hands over her hips and cupped her ass, roughly pulling her tightly into him. She felt his need to dominate her like a presence in the room and strangely, she found she didn't want to fight it.

Rather, she wanted to give in to it, sink into the power he held over her. She felt an insane urge to show Jason just how far she was willing to go, exactly how much she wanted him, and that all of her stupid "look but don't touch" rules from college were gone now.

Without words, she would show him that she would do anything, everything for him. Anything he wanted.

Dropping to her knees, she reached for the button on his jeans. "I want to taste you," she said, proud of how bold she was being, of how steady her voice was.

Hadn't she done this a thousand times in her fantasies? Taken Jason's thick cock into her mouth, throated him until he came in thick spurts?

His erection twitched in his pants and it felt good knowing that he wanted her. That she excited him. She wanted to make him feel as good as he'd made her feel the night before.

"I never knew you were such a risk taker."

His words held a slight rasp, and a huge challenge. She smiled as she ran one French-manicured nail down his zipper, taut from the pressure of his erection behind it.

No, she wasn't a risk taker. They both knew that. But now, just moments from pleasuring the man she loved, she wondered: What if she let herself be the Playboy bunny for once? What would it hurt?

Her life was already as bad as it could get, wasn't it? Long days at work, even longer nights on the couch with the remote at home.

She was so sick of being classy. Boring. For all Jason knew, she'd turned into a rampant sex kitten during the past ten years. And the truth was, she had—at least in her triple-X dreams.

And that's when it occurred to her: Here in Napa, with Jason, she could be anyone she wanted to be. No one knew her. No one could tell her she was being a bad girl, that she was a disappointment.

For the first time in her life, she could be the woman she'd always secretly dreamt of being.

A sexy, fearless, and very bold woman.

Suddenly excited about playing the sex goddess, going to a new, über-sensual place she'd never dreamed of allowing herself to go, she pitched her voice into a soft, sexy purr. "Are you kidding? I'm all about taking risks. Especially when it means I'm going to have your cock in my mouth in sixty seconds."

seven

Jason's thigh muscles jumped beneath her hand and Emma smiled, enjoying her newfound power, the feel of the word "cock" sliding from her tongue. Grasping the gold zipper on his jeans, she pulled it down and Jason's shaft sprang free from its denim confines.

She reached for the waistband of his boxer shorts. "Do you know how much I wanted to taste you in college?"

His huge, beautiful penis pushed out from his pelvis, and she couldn't wait another second to suck him inside, to taste his smooth, throbbing head, and then his shaft.

First one inch. Then another. And another.

Blowing him was as amazing as she'd dreamt it would be.

His penis twitched once, then twice in her mouth, and she pulled away, just enough to circle his engorged head with her tongue.

"Emma," he groaned, his hands in her hair, holding her against him as he stood in his empty restaurant, in broad daylight, letting her throat him with gusto. She'd never been this wet before and although she wanted Jason to come in her mouth, she *needed* him in her pussy.

Continuing to lick his shaft in long strokes, she undid the zipper on her skirt. She stood up and let it fall down her legs.

"I have a condom in my purse."

In a whoosh, he picked her up—God, how she loved to be manhandled by this man—and carried her over to the bar stool she'd formerly been sitting on.

"Get it. Fast."

Smiling at his rough, sexy command, she pulled out a long, newly purchased string of condom wrappers, ripping one off with her teeth.

"Put it on me," he demanded, nothing soft or loving whatsoever in his tone. Suddenly, even though it had been her idea to come here, to give him a blow job, to have sex with him, she felt completely out of control.

Jason owned her as completely now as he had ten years ago.

Only ten years ago she'd never allowed herself to slide a latex condom down Jason's erection. Which, she noted, was definitely one of the hottest sexual experiences of her life.

"Take off your panties."

Rather than being afraid of his bullying tone, she relished it, thoroughly enjoying being wicked with Jason. She stood up and slid her pink satin panties down her hips, past her thighs, finally letting them fall to the floor.

Never taking his eyes from her bare pussy, he ground out another delicious order. "Sit down and spread your legs."

His command gave her pause and a moment later his hands were on her knees, and she knew that he would have no compunction in spreading them for her. This, surprisingly, turned her on even more and she quickly complied.

Gasping at the sensation of her fully aroused vagina opening up to his hot gaze and the cool air, just inches from his throbbing penis, she struggled for breath as he grasped her hips, pulled her to the edge of the leather seat, and slid hard into her.

To the hilt.

She braced herself on the cool bar top with her hands and forearms as Jason pounded into her, again and again, harder and harder. His eyes were closed and she was glad for the chance to watch him surrender to ecstasy. This moment was what she had waited for her whole life. This chance to be with the man she loved. To give herself to him in the most elemental way.

All rational thought fled as everything tightened inside her. She gripped him tightly, and as he grew harder, thicker with each thrust, her need grew stronger, wilder, until she could no longer do anything but throw her head back, lean her weight fully against the bar, and be fucked into a crushing climax by the man she loved.

～

"Who are you?" Jason finally asked when they'd caught their breath and were reaching for their clothes.

The new, sex-goddess Emma—the woman who had taken everything Jason had demanded and given him back just as good, thank you very much—had no trouble looking him directly in the eye. "The same girl you knew back in college."

"No way. The girl I knew never would have fallen to her knees to throat me."

Hearing him say those words, about her, was a strange feeling. Instinctively, she felt bad, dirty. Exactly how she'd been taught to feel her whole life. Sex had always been clean and infrequent.

Suddenly, Emma hated those strictures with a fury she hadn't known she could feel. What was wrong with giving the man she loved a blow job? They'd both enjoyed it, and hopefully, her newfound sexual prowess would bring them closer. For once, she decided, she refused to feel shame at her own pleasure.

"Funny, seemed like you liked it to me," she found herself able to tease.

"Hell yes I liked it," he replied, wearing the look of men all over the world who just didn't understand women's minds. "Are you crazy? What guy wouldn't like it?"

She shrugged, enjoying her newfound confidence along with her evidently much-appreciated blow job technique. "So then what's the problem?"

"No problem. Except for the fact that my employees are going to start showing up in ten minutes. And I doubt any of them were planning on seeing their boss naked tonight."

"How many women work for you?" Emma asked, her voice all innocence.

"Three. Why?"

"I'll bet they wouldn't mind getting an eyeful," she said, hardly able to believe the flirty words were coming out of her mouth.

Seemingly against his better judgment, Jason threw his head back and laughed. Emma slipped her feet into her shoes and enjoyed Jason's laughter. Unfortunately, her pleasure didn't last long.

Evidently just because she'd given Jason a blow job in broad daylight didn't mean she could completely outrun who she was at her core.

Because she was already worrying about her next step. Mostly because she didn't have one. And after a lifetime of minute by minute planning she was far out of her element.

As if he could read her mind, he said, "What are your plans for the rest of the day?"

She bit her lip, finally admitting, "Actually, I don't have any. This was a spur-of-the-moment trip."

"Wow." He whistled. "Now I know something is up. You don't need to take your medication or anything do you?"

Emma was standing close enough to Jason to smack him with her purse. "I'm not on any medication, thanks," she said, forcing herself to turn his comment into a joke, rather than something more hurtful than that.

He held his hands up. "Can't blame a guy for checking. I don't know what's gone on during the past ten years. You could be having a breakdown for all I know."

She shook her head and a gave him a look that said *Don't be crazy*, but all the while she was thinking, *Is it that obvious?* Clearly, she needed to work at losing it more smoothly.

The thing was, if having a mental breakdown was synonymous with climaxing in Jason's arms once a day, she was all for it.

And then he said the most unexpected, wonderful thing. "I've got to get to work, but if you've got some time off and need a place to stay, you can hang with me for a few days."

Emma couldn't hide her surprise and delight at his offer, even if his mood seemed to be growing progressively colder with every passing sentence. Still, her extremely polite upbringing made her say, "Are you certain I won't be in your way?" even though she knew it was stupid to give him an out.

"Sure," he said, almost as if he didn't care either way, whether she stayed or whether she went back to Palo Alto.

"Great," she said, just as nonchalantly, even though her heart was racing at the thought of finally getting to see Jason's house. His private world.

His bedroom.

"1040 Second Street. White house. Black trim. Oversized Akita in the backyard. Door's unlocked."

He was pulling up the blinds as he spoke and Emma smoothed her hands over her skirt and top to make sure everything was where it should be. "I really don't need a key?"

"People are pretty honest out here in the country," was his reply and it seemed to Emma that he put extra emphasis on the word "honest." But the expression on his face didn't hint at hidden meanings, didn't give away anything beyond wanting to get back to work, so she tried to hurry up and gather her things while taking his words at face value.

"I'll be back around one A.M. And hey, if you wouldn't mind taking Marvin for a walk, that'd be great," he added as if she was nothing more than his new dog walker, rather than an old flame that he'd just pounded into sensual oblivion in the middle of his restaurant.

Emma stood in the middle of the restaurant and watched Jason disappear behind the swinging kitchen door. Forcing away her incredibly negative thoughts—after all, what did she possibly have to feel bad about given Jason's spectacular loving and his wonderful invitation to stay with him?—she still could hardly believe she'd actually come here. Actually left her suffocating life behind on a whim and knocked on Jason's door.

Had she really been the wicked woman half-naked on a bar stool being impaled by his huge penis?

She shivered with satisfaction. No one would ever believe it—Jason obviously barely did and he'd done it all with her—but ever since last night, Emma felt like a changed woman. And she was bound and determined to stick to her plan.

Playboy Bunnies had fun. Classy ladies hated their lives.

Her choice couldn't be clearer. It was Playboy Bunny all the way.

eight

Napa Valley?"

Emma held the phone away from her ear. Kate's voice was getting higher pitched with every passing moment. "That's right," she said, feeling extremely satisfied with her life for the first time in a long time as she swung on the white swing on Jason's front porch, with his enormous but friendly dog drooling at her feet. "I came to see Jason."

"Jason?" Kate screamed.

"Ow."

"You know damn well why I'm screeching," Kate said. "I can't believe you didn't call me this morning with all the details from last night. I only left you, what, twenty messages?"

"I wasn't ready to talk about it yet," Emma replied primly. Even though her recent behavior had been anything but prim.

"I'm your best friend. You don't need to be ready to talk to me."

Emma smiled. "You're right," she said, but she still didn't want to share any of the erotic details with Kate.

Jason wasn't just some guy she'd picked up in bar. Not that she'd do that in a million years, of course. He was special. And she didn't want to cheapen their lovemaking by gossiping about it. So instead of dishing about sex, she said, "Jason invited me to stay with him for a few days."

"Are you kidding me?"

"Isn't it amazing? I apologized to him for everything and he's not even mad at me."

Kate was silent for a long moment. "Honey, I know I'm the one who encouraged you to leave the party with him last night. But maybe you should be careful. Take things slow."

"You don't understand," Emma said, angry with her best friend for trying to bring her down from the high she was on, especially since the same thoughts had been floating around her head ever since Jason had told her that, yes, they could be friends again. Just like that.

Working to not only convince Kate that everything was fine, that she was only imagining dark clouds of danger, but herself as well, Emma said, "Being with Jason again is the best thing that's ever happened to me."

But she could tell that her best friend wasn't convinced. And neither, to be perfectly honest, was Emma.

"You know I just want you to be happy. And I'm not trying to be a big downer, I swear. You've never once told me to stop sleeping around and settle down with one guy, even though I've given you plenty of reason." Kate paused for a beat, then added, "A lot can happen in ten years. You and Jason are different people now. That's great if he's really forgiven you. But try to keep your eyes open to what else could be going on. At least think about what I'm saying, okay?"

Emma couldn't stay mad at Kate for more than five seconds, even if the subtext of her words was that there was no way Jason could have forgiven Emma so quickly. And that he must have an ulterior motive to be acting so nice so suddenly.

But Kate was only trying to be a good friend, just like she'd always been. "It's just that I'm so happy," Emma said. "For the first time in such a long time. Ever, really. It's like you said last night. I want to take risks. I want to buy sexy underwear and wear too much makeup."

She could practically hear Kate smiling over the phone. "In that case, I say go for it. And give Jason my best. He was certainly looking good last night."

Emma closed her cell, ready to put part two of her new impromptu plan into action. Seducing Jason in his restaurant had been a very successful part one. Seducing him in his bedroom clad in the naughtiest lingerie she could buy was round two. No matter what she wasn't going to wimp out. Not after the ecstasy she'd read on his face this afternoon when his eyes were closed and he was loving her from the inside out.

Clipping the leash by the front door onto Marvin's enormous collar, she said, "We've got some shopping to do."

It had been a great night at Cravings. The tables had been full, the wine had flowed freely, and Jason's staff, both in and out of the kitchen, had worked like a well-oiled machine.

Still, the whole night, Jason had been just left of his game. He'd burned the scallops, cut his wrist, and finally bowed out altogether to work on next month's menu and inventory. He'd stared at the spreadsheet for hours, chomping at the bit for everyone to go home so that he could down a bottle of Grey Goose vodka.

Finally, the last customer cleared out and his staff restored the kitchen and dining room to order. Like an animal that had been pent up in its cage with no food or water, he burst out of the small office and hightailed it to the bar. Forcing away the image of Emma spread wide on the bar stool, impaled on his cock, he poured a hefty shot of vodka and downed it in one gulp.

Rocco emerged quietly from the kitchen and Jason nearly groaned. He needed to be alone with his thoughts for a while. When Emma had walked into his restaurant that afternoon, *Holy shit, I still love her,* had kept crowding his brain.

Somehow, he'd realized as she moved toward him and he barely managed to keep it together by pouring her a drink behind the bar, seeing her again, finally having sex with her, was making him crazy.

Because although he hadn't been able to stop thinking about her since he'd left her shivering and wet by the lake the night before, he'd hoped that over time, the insanity of his need for her would recede. But seeing her again in the flesh, not twenty-four hours later . . . shit, he needed to crack down on his pathetic, useless feelings for her.

So when she'd offered to suck his cock and he'd realized

that she'd traveled all the way to the wine country for some good fucking, he was perfectly willing to acquiesce. But this time, he'd decided, it was going to be on his terms, on his timetable. Hot and heavy screwing was *all* she was going to get. He would put his mouth on her, his dick in her, but he wasn't going to let himself get emotionally involved.

Not this time. Not ever again.

Jason had never been a vengeful person. But knowing he couldn't keep his hands off of Emma meant he'd have to figure something out to keep from getting stuck in Emma's web of lies again.

It meant he was going to have to take the opportunity that she was handing him on a platter for payback. So before he headed back to his house—and Emma—he needed some quiet time with the Goose to figure out exactly how he was going to stick to his newly hatched plans for revenge, not shoot the shit with a buddy.

"Pour me one," Rocco said as he slid onto a bar stool. Jason filled Rocco's glass, then refilled his own, more than ready to get from conflicted to numb. "Never did get a chance to ask you how it went with the hot blonde this afternoon."

"Fine."

Rocco nodded, sipping his vodka slowly, appreciating the flavors the way they were meant to be savored, rather than the way Jason was gulping it down.

"Could have fooled me. You were a greenhorn in the kitchen tonight."

Jason gave up. He came around the bar, bringing the bottle with him. Maybe Rocco would help him see sense. He'd never taken any bullshit where women were concerned.

"We used to date. Ten years ago."

"Figured she was the one."

"She was only slumming it with me while trolling for a bigger prize."

"I take it she found one?"

Jason nodded. "What an asshole. Quarterback, homecoming king, pre-law."

"They got married?"

"Of course they did. Figured there'd be two-point-four children by now, too."

"Got divorced instead, I take it."

Jason sucked the last drop from his glass and studied it for a long moment, before deciding, what the hell, he was a long way from drunk. Might as well have another.

"Seems like you already know the story. Why don't you go home and let me get drunk in peace?"

Rocco ignored him. "So you think she's on the rebound from football boy?"

Jason ran one hand through his hair. "Maybe. Or it could have something to do with the fact that I stupidly attended our ten-year reunion last night. Couldn't leave well enough alone."

Rocco nodded. "That's the thing about hot blondes with legs up to here." He pointed to his neck. "Even when they've screwed you, you can't help coming back for more punishment."

Halfway through his fourth shot, Jason felt compelled to confide his plan to Rocco. For backup, if he needed it. "I want payback," he said simply, enjoying the sound of the word as it left his mouth. "Payback," he repeated, letting it sink down deep as a reminder of his ultimate goal.

"Hmm," Rocco said, setting his empty glass down on the counter. "How do you figure on getting that?"

"I've invited her to stay with me for the next few days. While she's here I'll have the perfect opportunity to reel her in. Then spit her out. Just like she did to me."

Sliding off the bar stool, Rocco grabbed his coat. "Good luck with that, boss. See you tomorrow."

Unwilling to take Rocco's parting words at anything but face value, Jason pushed back from the bar. It was time to go home.

To Emma.

⌒⌒

The door opened and Emma nearly shot off of Jason's couch to run and lock herself in the bathroom. Hours ago, when she'd come up with her brilliant plan to be sexy and fearless, she'd felt bold and reckless. Up to the challenge. But as the hours wore on, no matter how much wine she pumped into her system, her anxieties kept growing. If she moved quickly, she'd still have time to do the smart thing and run back to her clothes, to the safety of Jason's guest bedroom and the shiny lock on the door.

No. She didn't want to be that girl anymore. This was her chance to be wild and spontaneous—to unleash the bad girl inside who was dying to get out—and she was taking it.

Kicking her newly stilettoed feet up onto Jason's coffee table, she lay back against the cream pillows on his plush couch, trying to show off her new lingerie to its best advantage. She felt daring and sexy, but at the same time she was afraid of being too bony, too pale, too-dried up to ever attract anyone again.

Please, she prayed, *all I want is for Jason to drool when he sees me. Not laugh.*

Just then, he rounded the corner from the foyer and stopped dead in his tracks. His eyes roved the room, first taking in the lit candles on every surface, the two glasses of wine on the coffee table, and then, finally, Emma in dishabille.

"You're still awake?" he said, sounding angry and tired. And the tiniest bit uncertain.

"I was waiting for you," Emma purred in what she hoped was a sensual, inviting tone, even though she was freaking out. Oh no, she hadn't expected him to regret inviting her to stay with him already. After the wild sex they'd had that afternoon in his restaurant, she'd thought . . . well, that he'd be happy to have her around a little while longer. At least in his bed, if nowhere else.

He took another step into the room, rubbing his hands over his eyes. "You went shopping."

She smiled and nodded wishing he could have said something slightly more welcoming, like *I'm so glad you're here,* or, *I've been waiting for you too.*

"I wanted to surprise you," she said, hoping that by gesturing to her nearly naked body as if she were a spokesmodel on a TV game show showcasing the evening's prize, she could distract him from the wobble in her voice. "Surprise!"

Jason stared at her, his expression unreadable, and Emma nervously bit her lip. She'd had visions of his walking in the door and being so overwhelmed with passion that he jumped her without so much as a hello. Unfortunately, it looked like she was going to have to try a little harder to get to the bone jumping part of the evening.

If there was even going to be one.

Shifting on the soft cushions, she lowered her lashes. "I must have tried on nearly everything in the store. Every time

I slipped into a silky bra I thought about you looking at me. Taking it off of me." She paused and raised her eyes to Jason's hot, steady gaze, then stood up to reveal her lingerie in full detail, forcing herself to do a slow, seductive spin. Over her shoulder, she said, "I never knew thongs were so sexy. Did you?"

He didn't say anything, but by the tightness around his jaw, the heat in his eyes, Emma knew she was on the right track. "All night, I've been waiting for you wearing this, thinking about what we did this afternoon, what we did last night." She lowered her voice to nearly a whisper. "Thinking about what we were going to do tonight when you came home."

She'd barely finished her sentence when Jason lunged for her as if he'd been straining against shackles that had just broken free.

"I don't know what you did with the Emma I used to know," he said. "And I don't care. Just one thing I'd like to make clear first."

Emma nodded, thrilled that he was about to kiss her again. Touch her again. "Anything."

"I don't want to talk tonight. You came here to fuck. You dressed to fuck. So that's what we're going to do, Emma. We're going to fuck each other's brains out."

⌐∾

Jason's mouth was hot and hard as he cupped her head with his hands to better capture her lips, his tongue branding her, filling her senses. She felt naughty, her nearly naked skin brushing against his clothes, his thigh grinding into her wetness.

Being with Jason like this was everything she'd ever dreamed of. And more.

Only, in her fantasies when he talked dirty to her, there was always an undertone of emotion, of caring to his words. Unlike tonight, when he made it perfectly clear that he wanted her body. But nothing else.

Emma told herself that she was okay with his 100 percent sexual focus. Wasn't making love with Jason a step in the right direction? It had to be better than continuing their decade of utter silence and noncommunication. They could work on their personal relationship later, couldn't they?

He dragged her down the hall and she stumbled in her unfamiliar spike heels through his bedroom into a truly luxurious bathroom. He pushed a few buttons on the wall by the door and not only did several dim lights turn on, but water began to pour from the bathtub faucet.

"You know what I always wanted to do with you?"

Emma shook her head. "Tell me."

"Take a bath."

She reached for the clasp at the back of her bra, but he cupped one strong hand over hers. "I want you all wet. Looking like this."

Emma nipples hardened as his words sank in. Tonight was turning out to be an even more sensual experience than she could have ever imagined.

He knelt down and began to undo the ribbons of her new pink heels. "These are the sexiest shoes I've ever seen. I want you to wear them again for me later. When you're completely naked."

Emma shivered as his fingers brushed against her ankle through her fishnet stockings. Looking up at her as he slid one heel off and began working on the next, he mused, "I never thought I'd get to see you in a garter. Or fishnets. Or a thong."

Her words came out more uncertain, more breathy than she intended. "What do you think?"

He smiled, but it was a look of desire, rather than happiness. "I think you were born to wear them."

Something inside Emma bloomed at his words, some newly discovered femininity. She felt beautiful and desired in Jason's eyes. Just as she always had. *How could I have willingly given him up?*

"The water's ready," he said, standing and leaning against the sink.

"Aren't you going to join me?"

"Not yet. I want to watch you first. Getting wet. Everywhere."

A flush stung Emma's cheeks. Somewhere in the back of her head she'd thought that Jason might want a show, a striptease, but she'd pictured a backdrop of candles in a dimly lit room. Not in a bathtub, with water streaming over her.

But dressing like this for him tonight, surprising him with her boldness, had been her idea and she was going to see it through. The intense arousal coursing through her was going to help her push past her innate apprehension.

"I didn't know you liked to watch," she said, trying her best to play along, not wanting Jason to think she was a clueless, unadventurous lover. Even though she was. Quick in and outs with Steven in the dark had done nothing to prepare her for the kind of kinky sex that Jason obviously preferred.

Emma wanted desperately to be up to the task, though,

and when he said, "I only want to watch *you*," his words propelled her toward the tub.

She dipped her toe in the water. "Mmmm, it feels so good," she said, hoping she was saying what he wanted to hear.

He didn't smile, didn't shift his rigid posture, but still, Emma felt that she was getting to him, slithering her way under his skin. The newly sensual woman in her knew it with every fiber of her being.

Stepping into the tub, she shifted to face him and slowly lowered her long, lean limbs into the water. The warmth felt good as it washed over her, though nowhere near as good as Jason's touch.

The thin black lace of her bra and thong grew translucent beneath the water. Emma felt as if she had gone a step beyond naked, straight to transparent. Could he see her heart beating beneath her skin and bones?

"Come into the tub with me, Jason. I'm all wet and ready for you."

He didn't rush, and yet, moments later he was stark naked, his glorious erection bare and perfect. She longed to lunge out of the tub to wrap her lips around it again, but hopefully there'd be time for that later. Right now, she was ready for a new experience.

Like making love in the bathtub.

Life with Jason was one wonderfully novel experience after another. Just as she had always known it would be.

He climbed in between her legs, then wrapped his hands around her thighs, pulling her deeper into the water, yet lifting her higher at the same time. Floating near the top of the water, Emma should have been chilled. But that was impossible when Jason was touching her like this, looking at her with such need.

"I can see through your bra and panties, Emma. I want to rip them off you. Take you hard and fast until you're screaming."

She bit her lip. Any moment now she knew he was going to touch her, going to pull her panties down, slip a finger inside her slick pussy, slide his penis inside and stretch her wide again.

But his actions were at odds with his words as he took his time to look, rather than touch. His gaze seared her nearly as much as his touch would have and she gasped with awareness.

Finally, he ran his thumb down from her belly button to the lace on her panties, over her swollen clit, to the entrance of her cunt. More than anything she wanted him to slip his thick digit inside, to fill her up. Instead, he repeated the slide of his fingers, using two fingers now. And then three. Then four. Until his whole hand pressed against her and she was crying out as she pushed into him.

Her orgasm was quick and sweet and she was barely aware of his fingers moving over her bra, over her hard nipples.

"Take it off," she begged, but he shook his head.

"No. You're beautiful in your lingerie."

The words "you're beautiful" echoed through Emma's brain and she desperately wanted to give Jason as much pleasure as he was giving her. Taking him by surprise, she shifted in the water, pushed her thong aside, and slid onto his hard length, gasping for breath, slipping up and down on his penis.

"You said you wanted it hard and fast," she said. "You said you wanted to hear me scream."

"Emma," he groaned, and then again, "Emma," as her

climax began anew. She could take him deep, so deep in this position. His hands were on her breasts again, his thumb on her clit and he was pushing higher and harder in her, making her orgasm impossibly intense. She screamed out, for the first time in her life giving voice to her pleasure, and he pulled out and shot into the water, but she was too far gone to notice.

She lay back against the tile rim of the huge tub, her eyes closed, her chest heaving as she tried to regain her breath. She was vaguely aware of being wrapped in a large, plush towel, being carried out of the bathroom, and finally curling into Jason beneath a warm, thick duvet.

And even in an exhausted sleep, the joy of being with Jason colored all her dreams.

nine

Sunlight streamed across the bed, and Emma blinked in confusion as she looked around the unfamiliar room. Her bedroom in Palo Alto was shaded by a huge elm and she'd never heard so many birds singing all at once. She inhaled Jason's spicy, delicious scent and warmth spread through her from head to toe. Now she remembered. She was in his bed. In his house.

Just hours earlier, she'd been in his arms.

The rational part of her brain told her that he had left without so much as a "good morning" or "good-bye" because he had to open his restaurant. But inherent insecurity had her wondering if the real reason he'd crept away in the early morning hours was because he couldn't stand the sight of her, didn't want to face up to sleeping with her again.

Sliding out from beneath the duvet, Emma opened the French doors that led out to a large redwood deck, complete with a hot tub and a view of grapevines. She took a deep breath, inhaling the sweet scent of nature into her lungs. The beauty all around her refused to let her wallow in negative thoughts. Besides, what did she possibly have to complain about? She'd not only reconnected with Jason, but he'd made passionate love to her three times in two days. All of her dreams were coming true one by one, and now, the only thing she needed to do was make sure that she remembered to act like a fun sex goddess, rather than a sophisticated, yet desperate, suburban divorcée.

Maybe, Emma mused as the sun warmed her skin and a squirrel skipped from an oak tree limb onto the wires that held up the grapevines, if she could just keep Jason on his toes with increasingly wild and sexy antics that he couldn't refuse, she could break through the wall around his heart that she herself had been so instrumental in constructing.

On any normal day, the first thing she would have done upon waking was go for a long run. She'd learned back in high school that running was the best way to stay thin. She'd never been fast enough to join the cross-country team, but she had the will to keep pounding the pavement, mile after mile.

But nothing about being here, in Napa, with Jason was normal. She felt like she was living in a fantasy world where she was having enough sex to easily offset her lack of exercise. Besides, in her rush she hadn't packed her running shoes.

After a quick shower, she wrapped herself in his thick, extra-large robe and rummaged through her overnight bag for something flirty to wear, something that would make

Jason's eyes grow big with appreciation. But she already knew all she would find was a standard beige knee-length skirt and sweater set.

How had she lived thirty-two years in these clothes? No wonder her office assistants always rolled their eyes at her outfits. Could they be any more boring? Yes, it was definitely time for a change.

Marvin came trotting up from behind a bush in the backyard and she smiled at him as she scratched his big, furry head.

"You were such a great shopping companion yesterday. What do you say we head out this morning and do it again?"

Marvin wagged his tail in response. It was all the encouragement she needed.

By lunchtime, Emma planned on being an entirely new woman.

Or, at the very least, looking like one.

～

"How'd it go last night with the hot ex?" Rocco said, as he helped himself to a large serving of white truffle frittata.

Every Monday morning, Jason and Rocco met to discuss the previous week at Cravings and to plan the following week's menu.

Without giving Jason a chance to reply, Rocco answered his own question. "Must not have been that good, or else I would have expected you to blow me off this morning. Lord knew, if I had a hot babe in bed with me, you'd be yesterday's news."

Jason glared at his crass friend. "Call Emma a hot babe

one more time and I'll make sure you are blowing me off. In a hospital bed."

Rocco blew out a low whistle. "So that's how it is, huh? I can take a hint, boss. I know when things are serious with you."

"Nothing's serious," Jason growled, then added, "And lay off that boss stuff. Before I make you."

Rocco grinned, clearly enjoying getting under Jason's skin. "You pay the bills, I call you boss. Deal with it. But if you're sure you don't want to talk about . . . Emma. Nice name. Classy."

What was there to say? Jason thought darkly. She'd been waiting for him in the barest of lingerie and he'd pounced on her without a second thought. Even let her sleep in his bed.

Rocco took Jason's silence as leave to ask more annoying questions. "I was thinking about that revenge plan you've got going. I don't know. I think it's gonna get messy."

"Everything's under control," Jason said, quickly changing the subject by sliding last week's numbers and a new review across the table, straight into the Tabasco sauce dripping from Rocco's eggs. Rocco dropped his eyes to the figures on the page, leaving Jason alone with his thoughts again.

He knew he was completely full of shit. Nothing was under control where Emma was concerned. And that was exactly his problem.

Truth be told, he'd never felt like he held the reins of control less than he did right now.

One look at her, one taste of her, and he lost hold of his senses. Control over his own mind. Control over his cock. She was driving him insane.

And the problem was, a large part of him would rather be crazy with her than have things make sense without her.

Which meant that he was royally fucked.

Somehow, some way, he needed to take back the reins and not let go. The only way he could think of doing it was to continue to push her sexual boundaries as far she would let him. Farther, even.

Hopefully, he'd succeed in pushing her all the way out of his life. Because he wasn't entirely sure he'd be able to let her go. She needed to make the decision to leave him on her own. And he was going to have to help her do that by being the kind of kinky, ultra-inventive lover she could never handle in a million years.

~

Emma strolled down Main Street with Marvin trotting happily behind her leaving drool spots every few feet on the sidewalk. It really was wonderful having a companion who was so cheerful, who didn't want anything from her but to go for a walk and get pet on the head every so often.

What a contrast today was to all those years with Steven when she'd felt so cold. Her house had been cold, her bed had been downright frigid, her heart had been frozen solid. But two nights with Jason, this warm wine country sunshine, and a big silly dog were melting her frigidity away in sheets.

Her brand-new, very expensive pink-and-white print sundress floated around her thighs. She felt pretty, truly pretty, for the first since freshman year in college when Jason had kissed her. She felt unbearably sad at the realization that she'd spent more than ten years being unpretty, unwomanly, and unsexy.

She truly had been living in an igloo.

Two kids skipped by with enormous ice cream cones dripping down their arms and suddenly, desperately, Emma wanted one. Yes, all her life she'd watched her weight fanatically, but what was the point of being bony and dried-up? The Playboy Bunny hanging on her ex's arm at the reunion certainly hadn't been a stick.

Plus, a little voice in Emma's head told her, "Maybe Jason will want you even more if he's got something soft to hold on to."

And that's what this was all about, wasn't it? Making Jason want her. It was all the push she needed to get the ice cream she hungered after. That she'd hungered for her whole life.

Tying Marvin's leash onto a pole outside the old-fashioned ice cream parlor on Main Street, Emma purposefully walked inside and spoke before she could wimp out and change her mind.

"I'd like a scoop of vanilla."

But that wasn't nearly decadent enough, was it? It was something the old Emma would have taken one spoonful of then thrown the rest away, vowing to work out twice as long on the elliptical trainer the next evening at the gym.

"No, make that chocolate fudge brownie."

"Single or double?" the young man behind the counter asked her.

Emma could have sworn he was looking appreciatively down the low-cut top of her new dress. Feeling bolder than ever, trying desperately not to calculate fat and carbs, she said, "Double."

"Cone or cup?"

"Cup," was her automatic response. Who needed to waste calories on a cone? She caught herself just in time. God, for the first time she actually felt like her constant need to diet was a sickness. One she wanted to conquer, if nothing else, to prove to her mother that Emma, and Emma alone, was in charge of her body.

Well, that wasn't exactly true. Jason certainly had a heck of a lot of control of her body. No one could make her feel as good as he did. No one.

"Excuse me," she said as the boy reached for a cup. "Could you change that to a cone please?"

"We make our own waffle cones," he said, and she knew getting the enormous homemade, sugar-laden cone was her only option. It was what a secure, happy woman would have done, one who was more worried about her own pleasure than in making everyone else happy.

"Then a waffle cone is what I'd like to have. Thanks so much."

A few minutes later, Emma walked out of the parlor with the world's largest ice cream cone. She laughed out loud at the sight of herself in the window, an extremely slim woman grasping a huge dessert. Bringing the decadent treat to her lips, she licked the chocolate fudge into her mouth. Her eyes closed on a groan. My God, what had she been missing all these years?

"Marvin? Emma?"

Emma spun around to see Jason in all his masculine glory striding toward them on the sidewalk.

He was what she'd been missing all these years. Jason was the one person she hadn't let herself be close to. The one person she needed more than anyone else. Yes, she hadn't let herself indulge in chocolate ice cream, but that deficiency paled to her need for Jason.

Her tongue moved to lick a drop of chocolate off her upper lip. "Good morning," she said, suddenly shy, worried that she looked like a ridiculous glutton with her huge ice cream cone. Making excuses she said, "I figured you had to work this morning so I decided to take Marvin for a walk and do some shopping."

"And eat ice cream?"

She glanced guiltily at her cone. "I know I shouldn't have."

"Are you kidding me? The Chocolate Cow makes the best ice cream in the country. I've been trying to get them to work up a plan for national distribution, but wouldn't you know it, they want to remain a small family business."

Nodding stupidly, she said, "It's the best ice cream I've ever had."

Something in his eyes softened. "I'm glad you're enjoying it. When I think back to all those times in college that I tried to get you to eat ice cream." His words fell away then, and Emma remembered how concerned he'd been in college, always trying to get her to eat something besides Diet Coke and fruit. He was one of the only people who had cared enough about her to point out that her eating habits were troubling.

In fact, it was during those years with Jason that she'd actually gained a little weight. Her mother had been on her constantly, and Emma had grown frightened of the way love could take away her self-control. Being with Jason, in some ways, was equated with the danger of being fat. It was yet another way she'd thought he was bad for her. She'd hardly known herself when she was with him. The only difference now was that she *wanted* to change into someone new. Perhaps flirty clothes and ice cream cones were only the beginning.

Plus, now that he'd finally brought up their past she didn't know how to respond. So she didn't. She just stood there clutching her cone like a lifeline, chocolate beginning to run down her arm. Finally, Jason broke the tension by saying, "How about I get a cone and join you?"

Emma spoke before she could rethink her words. "You can share mine."

He raised an eyebrow. "I wouldn't want you to feel deprived."

Heat shot through her. She felt anything but deprived. Not with the things he did to her body. "I don't." She realized what she said and stuttered, "I mean, I won't. Please. I can't eat it all. My eyes were way bigger than my stomach."

As if on cue, a huge chunk of fudge began a slow slide down her hand to her wrist. Jason moved quickly, running one index finger up the sensitive skin at her pulse point, making her shiver even while standing in direct sunlight.

He sucked his finger into his mouth, holding her gaze. "Delicious," he said, and she wasn't sure if he was talking about the ice cream. Or her.

Shocked to be feeling so aroused while standing in the middle of a bustling main street, she lowered her mouth to the ice cream cone. Jason grabbed Marvin's leash and together the three of them walked across the street to a lovely town park. Anyone who didn't know better would have thought that they were a happy couple taking their dog for a walk and sharing an ice cream on a warm summer day.

But Emma did know better. And no matter how much

she wished that was exactly what was happening, it wasn't. Not with so much pain still lingering between them.

Three hot lovemaking sessions couldn't change ten years of silence and betrayal. Suddenly she realized that if they were ever going to work through their past they'd have to acknowledge it. Later, when the time was right, she would try to get them to laugh together over old times. Good times.

Having a real friendship with Jason again, having him love her again, was her greatest wish. She didn't want money. She didn't want power.

All she wanted was Jason.

Silently, Emma vowed to do everything in her power to make it happen. She might have been frigid for most of her life, but she wasn't stupid. And she knew damn well that taking a trip down memory lane wouldn't be enough to break through Jason's walls.

Continued seduction was her best bet. She felt certain of that after his passionate response to her last night, his lack of control in her arms.

The question was, what could she do to seduce Jason today that he wouldn't expect?

And couldn't refuse.

What the hell was he doing sharing an ice cream cone in the park with Emma? Sure, he'd planned on stringing her along before he dumped her ass to the pavement as hard as she deserved, but acting like the happy couple had certainly not been on his radar. He'd taken one look at her standing on the sidewalk with the ridiculously big ice cream cone and been so glad to see her—so glad to see her actually eating too, something he'd worked so hard to get her to do in college—that he temporarily lost grasp of the blackness within him. The part of him that wanted Emma to hurt, rather than be happy.

He was behaving like a fool. A lovesick fool. Somehow he needed to figure out how to walk the fine line between stringing Emma along and being lovey-dovey. Wherever the hell that was.

"Are you off on break right now?" she asked between licks, and it took everything in him to fight the urge to kiss the chocolate off her lips.

He nodded, even though Cravings was closed on Mondays and he usually took the afternoon off to recharge for the busy week ahead.

"I was hoping I could steal you away for an hour or so," she said and he could hear the apprehension in her voice. It made him feel sorry for her, which he hated, and his voice grew hard in response.

"I don't know if I'll have time," he said. "You caught me off guard with your visit. It's the busy season."

While everything he said was true, the real truth was that he couldn't control himself around her, and if he admitted to having the entire day off, he'd likely spend the next twenty hours worshipping her with his hands, his mouth, and especially his cock.

Instantly, Emma reverted back to the prim and proper, not-a-hair-out-of-place girl he'd known so long ago. "Of course you're busy. I should never have presumed that you would be able to give up more of your valuable time." All of her lush, expressive sensuality disappeared as if it never existed. "I should probably get back to work as well," she said, her lips tight, her eyes dead.

Disappointment rushed through him. He'd wanted her to beg him to spend time with her, but that just wasn't Emma. Her whole life she'd had it drummed into her head to always do the right thing, so if he actually wanted to see his plan for payback through, he'd have to convince her to throw caution to the wind.

Just like he always had done. The same old roles, repeated a decade later. Clearly, people never changed. Even when you wanted them to.

Besides, if he didn't convince her to stay, he would miss out on another chance to sample what she was so clearly offering in her stunning low-cut pink dress, those strappy sandals elongating her fabulous legs.

"You know what, on second thought I can shuffle my schedule around. We haven't seen each other in so long and who knows when you'll get the time to visit me again."

A shadow crossed Emma's face and he wondered again what had brought her running to Napa, away from the safety of her perfect suburban life. Once she trusted him with her secrets, he'd have one more weapon against her. It likely wouldn't take much persuasion to get her to open up to him. He sensed, as he always had, that Emma was simply dying to unburden herself of all her fears. But she'd surely grow skittish if he moved too soon. So he backed off, saying, "How would you like a personal wine country tour guide? If the restaurant hadn't worked out, that's probably what I'd be doing today."

Her smile lit up not only her face, but something deep within Jason. Forcing away the good feelings, he threw the rest of the dripping cone away, grabbed her hand, and said, "Let's get on with the tour," racking his brain to think of the best possible backdrops for more erotic adventures.

ten

I can't do it." Emma took a step back in horror.

"Sure you can. Besides, you can hold on to me if you get really scared."

While wrapping herself around Jason sounded wonderful, doing it hundreds of feet in the air courtesy of a hot air balloon wasn't exactly the venue she had in mind.

"Can't we just go for a walk through the vines instead? I don't need to see what they look like from the air. The ground is just fine." Flicking him the big-eyed look he'd never been able to resist in college she said, "And then we could talk. About old times. Remember what fun we had together?"

She knew the minute she'd said it that she was moving

too fast, had taken exactly the wrong approach. So she tried another angle. "I thought hot air balloons could only fly first thing in the morning," almost adding, *We don't have to talk about the past if you don't want to,* but managing to keep her mouth shut before she jammed both feet into it.

Jason climbed up the stairs into the huge basket and reached for her hand. "My buddy says the air is still enough and hot enough. We'll be just fine."

She looked around the deserted field in desperation. "We're not going up in this thing alone, are we? Isn't your friend going to come with us? Don't we need a licensed pilot?"

"Emma," Jason said, a wicked gleam in his eyes, "don't you trust me?"

"Of course I do," she practically shrieked, "in the kitchen and the bedroom!" She flushed as her words hurtled back toward her. Had she actually just said she trusted him in the bedroom?

Grinning wolfishly, the hardness her "talk about old times" speech had conjured up finally gone again, Jason effortlessly lifted her into the balloon. "Good. Then you'll just have to add one more location. A hot air balloon."

She had to make one last try to get out of this death trap. As far as she could tell, there was one thing Jason couldn't resist. And neither could she.

"Couldn't we just go back to bed instead?

"Very tempting," he said as if he were considering her suggestion, "but then what kind of Napa Valley tour guide would I be?"

With that he lit the wind-protected propane tank in the middle of basket and they began to float up in the air. Emma gripped the thick rim of the oversized basket so hard her knuckles cracked. Jason's arms came around her waist and he hugged her tightly to him.

"Try to relax and enjoy the ride."

His words were coaxing, but she was so wound up at the vision of the two of them falling from the sky and crashing to their deaths in the middle of a picturesque vineyard that she could barely appreciate the hard planes of his body pressing into her.

"Do you need me to help you relax?" he murmured into her ear.

She spun her head to face him. "Don't be crazy," she hissed. "We can't fool around up here."

"Give me one good reason," he said as one of his hands moved up to cup her breasts.

A soft wind blew across them and she shivered with the beginnings of desire. "Because you're driving this thing."

Her protest sounded slightly wimpy even to her ears. She was still afraid they were going to die, only it was increasingly difficult to concentrate on their impending demise when he was touching her like that.

"Piece of cake," he said and she no longer knew if he was talking about piloting the hot air balloon or getting her all hot and bothered.

His free hand gently pulled the thin, soft cotton of her dress up her thigh. "We can't do this," she said again, her objections growing weaker and weaker. "Not here. Not now. It's too dangerous."

"Of course we can," he said, a man who was 100 percent certain of his decision to pleasure a woman hundreds of feet in the air. "I thought you wanted to live dangerously."

Barely aware of the way her limbs and muscles were relaxing beneath his touch, she leaned her head back into the space between his chin and shoulder. He cupped her more closely to him, his thumb and forefinger on one very erect nipple, his other hand just now reaching her silk thong panties.

She was already impossibly aroused by his touch, even when she was more than a little hurt that he'd much rather have sex than reminisce about old times. But for now, if hot sex was all she could get, she told herself to be happy about it. Better some part of Jason than no part at all, right?

"Yes," she whispered, "that's exactly what I want. To live dangerously. With you."

The bold words had barely left her mouth when his hand was cupping her mound and she could feel how wet she already was, utterly desperate for him to slide one of his thick fingers into her.

"I know what you want, Emma," he said as she moved her legs apart to give him better access and then he was inside of her, stroking her.

"Jason," she cried, his name merging with the blue sky and clouds.

"Come for me," he urged and as she moved rhythmically into his hands, she was already there.

Her breath came in shallow gasps and she forgot everything except Jason's hands, his tongue and teeth on her neck, his fingers slipping over her clit, into her pussy, across the tight buds of her breasts. Her climax was wondrous and comforting all at the same time.

And as she floated back from the heavens into his arms, Emma knew that was exactly what he intended. To relax her worries away via an orgasm. To make her forget about revisiting the past, opening up old wounds.

"Feel better?" he asked, and if she hadn't felt so darn good she would have retaliated against the smug satisfaction fairly emanating from him.

Slightly embarrassed by how willing and easy she was for him to sexually manipulate, Emma said, "Yes," in a crisp voice and pulled away. She felt his grin at her back as she adjusted her bra and panties and dress.

"Nice dress, by the way," he said and she was thrilled by his compliment.

She decided to get over herself already. After all, hadn't he just done a bang-up job of not only making her come but getting her to forget that she was terribly afraid of heights?

She turned back to him and smiled. "I'm glad you like it."

Realizing she finally felt stable enough to look over the edge of the basket, she slowly peered at the ground below. Her breath was taken away by the lush green vines and gorgeous mountain vistas.

"I've never seen anything this beautiful before."

Jason moved beside her at the rail, putting a hand over hers. "I know. That's why I wanted to bring you up here. And make sure you were relaxed enough to enjoy it."

Just like they were college kids again, she elbowed him in the ribs. "Like that was your only reason for wanting to feel me up."

He grinned and kissed her forehead and she hoped things between them were going to be all right after all. Why else would he be this affectionate with her, this easygoing and fun?

"I don't need a reason to touch you other than wanting to," he said and she loved the possessive tone of his voice, the way he didn't ask if he could touch her, he just took her body in his hands and had his way with her.

Feeling giddy as they flew through the sky, she said, "As long as it's fair game for me to attack you any time I want."

His words, "I was hoping you'd do just that," were like warm sun pouring through her veins. Emma's head was immediately filled with X-rated visions of Jason pumping into her as she leaned over the rail of the balloon's basket.

Reading her mind again, he said, "I want you to enjoy this ride first, and then I promise I'll take you on another one. Very soon."

She smiled and took a deep breath of the cool, clear country air. Every day with Jason just got better and better. She had to hand it to him: the anticipation of riding him later in the day, wherever he took her next, was so good that it only made her appreciate the hot air balloon ride more.

Still, while Napa Valley was beautiful, it had nothing on Jason himself.

⁓

He was enjoying himself. A lot. So much so that he didn't want to think too much about it. He'd decided to spend the day with Emma, to introduce her to new sensual delights, and that was exactly what he was doing. Sure, since he was ultimately out for revenge perhaps he shouldn't be having this good of a time, but what the hell. All he was doing was taking what she was giving and getting his rocks off while he was at it. That was his story and he was sticking to it.

After a delicious lunch at a gourmet deli that some good friends of his owned in Yountville, they'd driven up to the natural hot springs in Calistoga and were standing at the edge of an outdoor rock mineral bath. On the middle of a weekday, it was unlikely that many tourists were bound to find this spot.

In under sixty, his clothes were lying on a pile of rocks and he was getting into the water.

Emma looked around the deserted forest uncertainly. "We're going in naked?"

"It's the only way to get the full benefits of the hot springs," he exaggerated.

"Oh," she said, biting her lip in that sexy way of hers. "But what if someone walks by?"

He wrapped one hand around her ankle. "Then I guess they'll get a really good show, won't they?"

She pulled her ankle away as if he'd burned her. "Don't be ridiculous," she said, once again the prim and proper girl that he knew so well.

He shrugged, intent on seeing how far she would try to take the new bad girl persona she'd been trying on these past few days with the new lingerie and willingness to have sex in kinky places. He wasn't stupid. He knew she hadn't changed in the past ten years. Her coming to Napa, her acting like a bad girl, it was all connected. At some point he'd find out what was up.

Or not, he thought, trying to convince himself that he really didn't care, that payback didn't have one single thing to with understanding the woman Emma had become. Revenge, he knew, didn't have anything to do with being gentle and nice to Emma. Not when it would be so much easier in the long run to let her go if he kept her at arm's length.

"I should have known you'd be too uptight to skinny-dip." He purposely made his words a challenge.

Instead of meekly backing down, she retorted, "After what we just did in the hot air balloon, I can't believe you have the nerve to call me uptight."

He merely shrugged and said, "That was earlier. This is now." Upping the ante, he added, "Besides, if strangers show up either they'll run screaming . . . or they'll want to join us."

Jason enjoyed watching Emma's eyes grow huge at the thought of a ménage. Continuing to push at her innate propriety, he said, "Ever thought about a threesome? Or a foursome?"

She shook her head so quickly, her blond hair went flying and a strand got caught on her lips. "No," she gasped. "I haven't."

He knew what was coming. Of course she was going to be curious. How could she not be?

Finally she said, "I'll bet you have though, haven't you?" her tone clearly defensive, rather than simply curious.

But he wasn't going to let her get away with being too embarrassed to say what she really meant. "Done what? Gone skinny-dipping in a mineral bath? Sure. Lots of times."

Her frustration at the way he'd purposefully misunderstood her question was crystal clear in her blue eyes. "No. That's not what I meant. I was asking if . . . " Her lips were plump and juicy as she nervously licked at them. "You've been with more than one person. More than one woman. At the same time. Have you?"

He grinned at her erotic accusation, rather pleased with himself for getting her all in a dither. She was so much fun to toy with. Always had been, come to think of it.

"Do you really want to know the answer, sweetheart?"

She stared at him for a long moment before nodding.

"Come in the water, then, and I'll tell you what you want to know."

She warred with herself, standing there in front of him, and he was pleased when she began pulling her dress up over her head and kicking off her shoes. Still in her panties, she dipped a toe in.

"Not so fast, Emma. Naked mineral baths only. Those are the rules."

"The rules?"

She looked around for a sign, the cutest rule follower he'd ever met.

"My rules," he said, his voice suddenly husky as he took in her incredible beauty in pink silk.

He could tell she was still upset with him for accusing her of being uptight, but he wasn't going to apologize. Even if he wanted to.

Her tone petulant, she demanded, "What are you going to do if I don't obey you and your stupid rules?"

"Spank you, of course."

That stopped her in her tracks, just as he'd known it would. Her eyes grew big again and her nipples hardened. He made a mental note to add spankings to his list of games to play with her before she left.

"I don't believe you," she said with false bravado, but at least she'd forgotten her irritation and stripped off her pink silk panties, giving him a full-frontal view of her beautiful pussy.

Gingerly, she put one foot in the water. "Mmm," she said, unconsciously sensual, "this does feel good."

As far as Jason was concerned, she hadn't even begun to feel good.

She sank into the natural stone hot tub and once she was settled across the tub from him, she raised an eyebrow and gave him her most world-weary perusal. "Back to all that kinky group sex you've had. Do tell?"

He would have laughed at her bravado had he not been so turned on by it. "Did I say anything about kinky?"

Her smile said, *You didn't have to.* "Call it an educated guess. A good-looking guy like you, bestselling books, award-winning cable show. I'm guessing plenty of girls have thrown themselves at you." She paused and licked her lips. "As a package deal."

Oh shit, he hadn't thought he could get any harder. She might have just been playing at being a bad girl, but damn if she wasn't good at it.

He waited until he knew he could keep his voice steady. "I can't tell you all my secrets, can I?"

She pouted with those delicious, soft lips. "You used to, remember?"

But he didn't want to remember. He wasn't interested in revisiting their history. Too many minefields. He simply wanted to screw her again with no thoughts of the future, and absolutely no remembrances of the past.

"Do you think you can handle it?"

Silently, he dared her to say yes.

That stopped her. He guessed she was starting to really imagine him with two women at a time. Or more.

Bravely she lifted her chin. "Of course I can."

"Of course," he murmured, still utterly unconvinced that she had any idea at all what her threshold for kink was. "So then there's no reason not to tell you about my first three-some, is there?

Her mouth opened ever so slightly in surprise, but she quickly clamped it shut. He pretended not to notice.

"I knew it. You actually have had sex with two girls at once."

He grinned and threw himself into his role. The role she evidently wanted him to play. "It wasn't exactly in my plans, but how could I turn both of them down? They were so insistent. Like you said, they *came* as a package deal."

Her eyes dropped from his face to his enormous erection poorly hidden by the clear water. "I'll bet they did," she muttered, and he wasn't sure if she knew he could hear her.

"It was after my first TV special had aired. I was in New York City, and the cable execs took me out to celebrate. They'd invited two gorgeous girls. One brunette, one redhead. Legs up to here . . . " He paused for effect. "You know the kind of girl I'm talking about."

She raised an eyebrow as if she could have cared less what he was saying, but he could tell she was riveted. "The slutty supermodel type who plans on sleeping her way to the top," she said rather uncharitably. "Go on."

It took everything he had to hold back his grin. She was too easy. She really was. "The champagne was flowing and I was happy and then we were back in my hotel. All three of us." Her chest was rising and falling rapidly now. "Before I knew it they were taking off my clothes. And then they were taking off their clothes."

Her words were barely a whisper. "And then what happened?"

Jason weighed his words, trying to decide how far he should take this game. He knew he was being mean to her, but as far as he was concerned, the small ways he'd been toying with her were inconsequential against the backdrop of her past betrayal. Just thinking about watching her sweetly sensual lips be taken by that jock asshole in the Stanford quad, ten years ago, was enough to send an invisible fist straight into his gut.

His mouth twisting with mockery, he said, "I never knew you were such a voyeur, Emma. That you'd get such pleasure from hearing about me having sex with other women."

"I'm not," she protested, but he knew how disappointed she would be if he stopped now.

"One of them starting kissing me and the other one dropped to her knees to take me deep into her throat."

"She didn't!"

"Oh yes she did." He smiled and closed his eyes as if he were remembering this very event. Only, all he could think about was Emma dropping to her knees in his restaurant, sucking him in her delicious mouth.

"You liked it, didn't you? Being showered with all of that attention. Men are so disgusting."

He shrugged as if it were no big deal. "Who wouldn't?" Going for the gold, he added, "The only time it got difficult was trying to figure out who to make love to first when they were both begging for it."

Something in her eyes changed then, turned from unexpectantly aroused to painfully foolish.

"Emma?" he asked, knowing he was a tool for pulling her gently onto his lap, "are you all right?"

She looked up into his eyes, more defenseless than he'd ever seen her. "No, I'm not all right. I'm jealous," she admitted in a small voice.

Without letting himself dissect his actions, not willing to admit that his urge to comfort her was at odds with his desire for revenge, he ran his thumb over her lush lower lip. "Don't be."

She shook her head. "How can I not be? You've not only had beautiful women, but two at once. How can I ever compete with that?"

Jason hated to watch her new self-confidence fall away like this. It wasn't what he'd intended.

Not yet, anyway.

"You don't have to," he said, unable to be anything other than honest with her in this moment, even if she didn't deserve it. Even if she hadn't been the least bit honest with him ten years ago.

"None of that actually happened, Emma," he admitted. "I was just playing with you."

"You don't have to deny what you did to make me feel better. I can handle it. You're entitled to your own life." Her voice breaking, she said, "I stupidly gave you up to other women a long time ago."

Jason spoke quickly before Emma went any further. Before she delved any further into the past.

"I've never done a ménage. I swear. You just seemed to want to hear about one so badly." Working overtime to change the tenor of their skinny-dipping session, he gently teased her. "A ménage is one of your fantasies, I take it?"

Her smile came back then. Not as quickly as Jason would have like, but there nonetheless.

"No," she protested, but judging by the excited way she'd begged for details, he didn't believe her.

Not that he could ever share her with another man. Or another woman, for that matter.

It might have been stupid, emotional suicide even, but now that he was with Emma again, Jason couldn't deny the truth any longer: He wanted her all to himself.

eleven

Emma could hardly believe he'd toyed with her like that. Then again, she'd asked for it, hadn't she? Had been dying to hear about his threesome. She'd been trying to be so brave, so blasé about it all, but she'd only ended up feeling foolish. Inadequate.

But now that she knew he'd only been playing with her, teasing her, she felt both relieved and hornier than ever. Buoyed by the water, she shifted until she was straddling him.

All she wanted was to have fun with him again. To explode in his arms. To feel beautiful and wanted.

"I can't let you get away with that, now can I? You're going to have to pay the price for telling fibs."

"I hope so."

"Bad boy," she whispered as she sank down on his erection, taking him all the way into her without preamble.

"Emma," he groaned as he pulled her lips down to his and ravaged her mouth.

She rode him with all of her pent-up desire from the hot air balloon, letting loose all of her jealousy at the thought of him sleeping with other women, taking and taking with no thought of anything but finding her pleasure.

The sun was fading by the time they parked in front of Jason's dark and empty restaurant. He held open the door for her and helped her out onto the sidewalk, the perfect gentleman as always. Well, maybe not always, she thought with a secret smile.

She wouldn't want him to be too much a gentleman in bed, now would she?

"Hungry?"

Her stomach growled in response. "Starved."

"Since we're closed tonight, think of Cravings as your own private restaurant."

She followed him inside, memories of their naughty romp in the dining room flooding through her as they headed for the kitchen. Jason flipped on some lights and she looked around, utterly amazed by his lair.

"Very impressive."

He shrugged. "Your standard restaurant kitchen."

"If you say so," she said, doubting that other restaurants bothered with aesthetics in the private space that was off limits to customers. "The colorful tile backsplash is a nice touch," she said, running her fingers over the mosaic inlaid to look like tropical fish were swimming in a lagoon.

"The artist owed me a favor."

"Sure. Or maybe you just like working in pretty environments."

"Sounds kind of girlie to me," he joked, but the look Emma gave him made it clear that she thought he was anything but girlie.

Jason turned and pulled out pots and ingredients for their meal and Emma started to feel more and more out of her element. Useless, really. All those years of dieting hadn't really inspired her to learn how to cook. But after two days back in Jason's world, she realized how much she'd been missing all her life.

Taste.

Flavor.

The excitement and pleasure of truly enjoying a meal. And a man, for that matter.

"Teach me to cook," she said impulsively.

Jason snorted. "Sorry. I don't know how to make rice cakes."

Emma instinctively lifted her hand to cover her heart. "That's not fair," she protested hotly. "I've eaten everything you have today." Didn't he know what an effort she was making to change? Perhaps if he'd made the rice cake comment in college she could have rolled with it, would have known that he was only teasing her because he was concerned about her. But they were on such weird ground and she wasn't sure how to take his comment. Other than to know that it hurt.

He raised an eyebrow, clearly intent on calling her bluff. "Sure, you've been a wild woman for one whole day. Come tomorrow you'll probably go on a ten-mile run to burn off the calories and insist that you're full after half a grapefruit."

She hated the way he was mocking her.

Hated even more that he was right.

"You're wrong," she stated, hoping that her words would be true one day, even if they weren't right now. Her face falling, she admitted, "No, you're not wrong. But I wish you were. I'm sick of working so hard all the time to be skinny." Feeling scrawny and lacking as a woman, she gave voice to her fears. "Do you really think of me as just a bag of bones?"

"No," he said, pulling her against him. "God no. You're right, I'm just being an ass again. Us guys are stupid about women and food."

But that was just it. Jason had never been stupid about her feelings before. He wasn't deliberately trying to hurt her, was he?

No. She pushed that thought away as quickly as it had come. She was being ridiculous. Reading too much into every word. Every look. Every touch.

"It's made me happy, today," he said, "watching you eat without picking at your food. I hate to think of you dieting, Emma. You don't need to."

"Yeah right. I dare you to say that after I've gained twenty pounds from all this rich food."

His face utterly sincere, he said, "You'd look fantastic. I mean, you're beautiful now just as you are, but I can see you with curves, lush curves."

Yet again, he was making her feel like the most attractive woman in the world, and, at the same time, giving her permission to enjoy her life. To eat like a normal person. Both were gifts that he, and he alone, had given to her.

Truth be told, she'd never given herself permission to eat, drink, and be merry. She'd always been too afraid of the consequences. Too afraid of her mother's nagging. Of failing.

"Please teach me to cook," she said again, suddenly certain that her issues with food were another roadblock she needed to smash down on her way to figuring out how to really and truly be happy.

He studied her for a long minute. "It would be my pleasure."

Of course a lifetime of habits was not easy to forget all in one night. "Do we really have to use that much butter?" she exclaimed in horror as he dropped an entire stick into the Dutch oven.

The look her gave her smacked of *I told you so*. "Can't make cream sauce without it."

He stirred the rich sauce then held the spoon up to her lips.

"Taste." She hesitated for just a moment too long and he teased, "Guess I'd better taste it myself, huh? Only I have a feeling it would be much better if I lick it off you instead."

Without so much as blinking, he dropped a dab on the curve of her breast that was visible above her sundress. And then his mouth was on her and she was desperate for him all over again.

He raised his head and the heat in his eyes took her breath away. "Delicious."

Suddenly, Emma wasn't hungry anymore. At least, not for food. He dipped his finger in the pot and held it out to her.

"Your turn."

She sucked his finger into his mouth. He was right—the cream sauce tasted like heaven. Just like Jason.

"What do you think?"

She shivered as her tongue dragged across the pad of his index finger. "I love it."

His eyes changed from molten heat to ice-cold steel. "Let's get on with this cooking lesson so we can eat."

In the blink of an eye he'd gone from playful to crisp and utterly detached. Emma felt as if he'd punched her in the stomach. What had she said that had been so wrong? He didn't think "I love it," meant "I love you," did he?

Oh God, she thought with a sinking heart. That was exactly what he thought. Here he thought they were merely having fun in the sack and he was obviously afraid that she was reading more into his sensual attentions than he intended.

The small hope that had been building within her all day died. She knew better than to dream of building a new, better relationship with him. He might have accepted her apology but she had a feeling he was never going to trust her again.

But even though Emma's heart was in a million pieces— and it was her own damn fault, of course, for not only betraying him in college, but for acting like such a hopeless romantic—she was determined to make the best of this precious time with Jason. After all, she certainly wasn't suffering in his arms, was she? Just because he wanted to keep things light and fun didn't mean she had to go back home to her awful life with her tail between her legs, did it?

From here on out, she'd remember to keep their relationship carefree and sexy. And she definitely wouldn't use the word "love" again under any circumstances. She'd get as much pleasure from being with Jason as she could, and then when it was time for her to finally return to real life, she'd have lots of truly wonderful memories to savor for the rest of her boring existence.

"I have an idea," she said, forcing flirtatious banter that she didn't really feel. "How about we scrap the cooking lesson and move straight to the eating strawberries and whipped cream off each other in bed part of the evening?"

He blinked once and then she visibly saw him relax as he bought her "I just want sex" act. She reached for him and the way he captured her mouth let her know exactly how much he wanted her body.

Even if he didn't want any part of her heart.

He was getting in too deep. Jason knew it, and yet he'd found it impossible to pull away from Emma. Until she said the L-word, that is. Just hearing it fall from her lips had knocked sense into him, like a ten-ton truck driving over his heart. What the hell was he doing? He was supposed to be fucking her raw, not falling for her charming banter, her pretty smiles.

The problem was, no matter how he tried to keep his distance, he was sliding deeper and deeper into the quicksand. Falling for Emma all over again. Hard. Everything between them continued to change by the second as he slipped deeper and deeper into the woman he'd never stopped loving.

He wasn't sure he could ever forgive her. But suddenly he wondered if he wanted to be with her badly enough, then perhaps he didn't need atonement after all?

Breathless as he lifted her up onto the stainless-steel counter, Emma asked, "Have you ever made love here?"

"Well, there was this dame yesterday who wouldn't leave me alone until I let her blow me in the restaurant."

Emma blushed at the wicked memory, but even more so because she had so enjoyed being that dame. "Lucky girl," she murmured, playing along. "What about in the kitchen?"

"Do you mean have I ever had a hard time keeping my hands off the staff?"

She shook her head. "I know you wouldn't do that. I was talking about bringing your dates here."

Jason laughed at that, but since he was also running one hand up her bare thigh, she was having a hard time figuring out what was so funny.

"You don't honestly think any of the women I've been with would want to so much as set foot in here, do you?"

Frankly, Emma wished she'd never asked the question, because all of a sudden she really, really didn't want to hear any more about all the perfect, exotic women he'd been with.

"Forget I asked."

"Are you sure you don't want to hear about the threesomes I've had back here?"

She smiled then, relieved that he was making light of her silly question, rather than launching into a full-scale description of the perfect breasts he'd sucked and wet pussies he'd impaled on this very countertop.

"You're the only woman I've ever taken into my kitchen," he admitted.

Emma wanted desperately to believe his words meant something, that she was special. But that was exactly the kind of thinking that was leading her down the road to heartache. Sexy and fun, that's what she needed to keep in mind at all times.

"In that case," she said, licking her lower lip and enjoying the way his hungry eyes followed the path of her tongue, "I'd better make sure you don't regret it."

He raised an eyebrow in silent challenge.

Wrapping her legs around his waist, Emma pulled Jason against her. It was all the encouragement he needed, because seconds later, his hands were threaded in her hair and his mouth was on hers. As his tongue swept into her mouth she gave in to her very intense, very real feelings that had been growing stronger and stronger with every hour that passed in his amazing company.

She could pretend to be someone else everywhere but when she was in his arms.

She rubbed her sensitive breasts against his chest, giving silent thanks for her skimpy sundress. No doubt about it, a bra would have definitely gotten in the way.

He nudged her head slightly to the side and ran kisses down her neck, her earlobes, her collarbone. Through the thin cotton her nipples grew taut against his hard chest. He slipped his fingers under the straps across her shoulders and slowly slid the dress off. It fell to her waist, a pile of pink-and-white cotton at the base of her naked breasts and stomach.

Jason leaned back and looked his fill. Swallowing, he took a long look at her bare and puckering nipples. "You are so beautiful, Emma," he said, his warm words at odds with his cold reaction to her inadvertent use of the L-word.

His reverent statement warred with Emma's insecurities. Sure, she'd had wild sex with him again and again during the past three days, but suddenly, she felt horribly shy and insecure about what they were doing and where they were doing it. Especially after the rice cakes comments, which still smarted.

"Could someone walk in on us?" she whispered, unable to shake off her innate sense of propriety.

It wasn't that she didn't want to make love to Jason in his restaurant again, of course she did. But they'd already gotten away with it yesterday and she wasn't sure how long their luck would last.

Sensing her apprehension, Jason took her mouth again in another toe-curling kiss. "If anyone walks in they're fired," he said and her insides liquefied as their lips mated and his fingers played down and around her rib cage as he cupped her breasts.

He rubbed his thumbs over her tight nipples and she gasped as pleasure shot through her. "I need to taste you," she heard him say as if through a thick fog.

The next thing she knew his warm lips were suckling her breasts, first one and then the other. Emma gave him even better access to her tits by arching her back and pushing up into his mouth.

Laughing softly, obviously pleased by her intense arousal, he pushed her breasts together and nipped at her incredibly sensitive skin. She couldn't believe that she was actually whimpering, but there was nothing she could do to stop it.

She took in his wild eyes and the erection straining at the zipper on his jeans. She reached for his belt, desperate to see him naked again, but he had other plans as he kneeled between her legs. Emma felt how wet she was as he pushed the dress up her legs, exposing her damp, silk-clad pussy to his hot gaze. She would have been embarrassed at how much she needed him were it not for the reverent way he slid his hands to the edge of her hips, lightly brushing his fingers across her almost exposed mound.

God, she loved the way he looked at her, loved the way he was about to devour her. With his tongue. His teeth. His lips.

She shivered as he slid his thumbs beneath the thin band of her panties. She shifted her hips to give him better access and it was sweet torture as he painstakingly drew the pink silk past her thighs, over her kneecaps, and finally down past her calves and feet. His fingers set every inch of her body aflame and she writhed beneath him, wanting more.

Much more.

Sitting back on his heels, his breathing labored, Jason cupped her slick pussy in the palm of his hands.

"Your skin is so soft and warm. And smooth. And wet."

She nearly bucked up off the stainless-steel counter, she was so inflamed by his intimate touch. She wanted to do something, anything to let him know how good he was making her feel, but she was captive to his touch.

With his hand still pressed into the sensitive flesh between her legs, he said, "I want to make you feel good, Emma. That's all I want." She believed him, believed that he was looking out for her, just as he always had.

Holding her breath, she nearly exploded right then and there when he added, "Do you want to come?"

"Yes," she moaned, surprised that she was still able to speak as he rose up from his knees and ran kisses down her neck, across her collarbone, over the tight peaks of her breasts. Overwhelmed by the feeling of his tongue licking and teasing her nipples, she was caught completely off guard when he slipped his middle finger into her.

Every nerve in her body was on fire, the rhythmic pattern of Jason's hand slipping in and out of her matching the insistent beating of her heart. He ran kisses over her stomach, and she felt as if every last bit of blood in her body had rushed between her legs. And then, suddenly, he focused every last bit of his attention on pleasuring her.

His tongue alternately swirled over her clit—first soft, then hard—then swept between her pussy lips and dove into her cunt. She arched against his mouth, rocking back and forth against him frantically as something inside of her swelled and then exploded into a glorious rainbow of pleasure.

Thoroughly dazed from her incredible orgasm, by the time she opened her eyes, Jason had unzipped his jeans. Emma drank in the sight of the most beautiful man she'd ever seen standing in front of her, his erection proudly jutting out. She reached out to touch his hard, throbbing shaft and he groaned as her fingers wrapped around him.

Feeling incredibly bold and very sexy, she ran her thumb over the velvety skin on the head. Quickly slipping on a condom, he positioned himself between her thighs. Emma eagerly opened her legs for him and cried out her pleasure as he began to slide into her one slow, mouthwatering inch at a time. But she was all out of patience and grabbed his hips, driving his cock all the way into her.

Their hips bucked and rolled together as he pumped in and out of her wetness. He pressed his thumb to her clitoris again and as her muscles began to clench around him she was so overwhelmed by the power of her second orgasm that she was barely cognizant of Jason finally experiencing his own equally violent release.

As their breathing slowed, Emma somehow found the wherewithal to keep from declaring her undying love. Fun and sexy was all he wanted, so that's what she was going to give him.

Emma knew she was sticking her head in the sand and that at some point in the very near future they would have to actually talk instead of just having more hot sex. But she was afraid that that future conversation might break apart their new and fragile bond.

Plus, she told herself, hadn't something about their lovemaking just now been different?

Yes, it had been hot and out of control, like always. But Jason hadn't been quite as aggressive, quite as focused on dominating her. She certainly wasn't complaining about the sex they'd had during the past three days—it had been beyond her wildest dreams—but it was nice to finally feel like she was contributing more than just her naked body, that Jason was getting something emotional from her that he couldn't get from anyone else.

"Ready for dessert yet?" she murmured into his ear, wanting more of his touch, hoping that each orgasm would bring them closer together.

When he pulled back, he was grinning. "You're insatiable, woman."

Matching his grin with her own, feeling that somehow he'd just given her a big compliment, she smiled a very feminine smile. "I know."

twelve

Thirty minutes later, they were sitting cross-legged on the colorful rug on Jason's living room floor, a bowl of plump red strawberries and a smaller bowl of freshly whipped cream between them.

"I hope you're planning on feeding me some of these. A guy needs to keep his strength up, you know."

Laughing, Emma shoved a strawberry into his open mouth. Juice dribbled down his chin and she leaned forward to lick it off.

"You know what?" he asked in a low voice.

"What?" The word came out barely loud enough to reach him.

"I never thought I'd say this, but food can wait. This can't."

His mouth claimed hers as he greedily demanded more of what she was dying to give him. She wrapped her arms around his waist and clung to him, desperate as always for his touch.

He pulled her on top of him and then as he kissed her senseless he rolled them over. She moaned as his hard, muscular heat enveloped her. He made a growling sound deep in his throat as he grasped her cotton dress with both hands and ripped it open down the middle.

Emma was secretly thrilled at his loss of control. "You'd better be planning to buy me a new dress."

"I'll buy you a hundred new dresses if you want," he replied, "but right now that one was in my way."

Emma couldn't fight back her grin. It felt so good to know that he wanted her enough to rip the clothes from her body. She was about to say something cute and witty, when all of a sudden, she felt something cool and wet on her lips, quickly followed by his tongue. He gently nipped at each sensitive patch of her lips, dipping his tongue into the corners to get at the whipped cream, taking small bites at her lower lip, running the tip of his tongue over the arch of her upper lip.

"Good?" she barely managed to ask.

"Very sweet."

The next dollop landed on her nipples and as he bent down to clean her off, the light stubble on his cheeks brushed against the underside of her breasts. He ran his fingers over her hard sticky breasts.

"You have the most amazing tits."

"I do?" she said, sincerely doubtful that her natural B-cups could ever compete with the silicone wonders she'd seen him photographed with over the years.

"Oh yes," he replied, cupping each of them in his hands, sliding his thumbs over the taut tips. Running hot kisses down her stomach, he kissed the upper seam of her panties. "It would be a shame to have to rip these off." Spooning whipped cream onto the lace he sucked at her mound and an orgasm whipped through her, from zero to ninety in under a second. And then he was naked and rolling onto his back, pulling her up to straddle him. Slipping on a condom, he slid her sticky panties to one side and positioned her above his hard shaft.

She moved with an instinctive rhythm above him, slowly up then down on his shaft, then faster and more insistent as the wonderful pressure built up inside of her.

On the verge of release, Jason pulled her into a kiss and as their mouths connected he plunged his tongue in and out in the same rhythm that he was rocking his pelvis against hers, both of them losing control. Gasping, he ground himself against her as he pulsed deep inside.

Minutes later, on the verge of falling asleep in the middle of his rug, Jason picked Emma up and carried her to his bed. Wrapping his arms around her, she closed her eyes, happier than she'd been in a very, very long time.

⟡

Emma woke up the next morning just as Jason was tucking his shirt in and fastening his belt. He was freshly showered and smelled so good that she wanted to pull him back down to the bed to make love again.

"Do you have to go?" she asked, hating the whine in her voice, but unable to keep it at bay.

"Duty calls," he said on a grin, but she could see in his eyes that he didn't want to leave either and that made everything all right.

The perfect day they'd had made her feel confident enough to tease him. "You world-famous chefs are in such demand." She licked her lips, remembering just how in demand he'd been yesterday. First in the hot air balloon. Then the hot springs. Followed by a "cooking lesson" she'd never forget. "Having sampled from your menu I know exactly why."

Suddenly she was halfway out of bed, in Jason's arms, her naked breasts pressed against his crisp button-down shirt.

"If I didn't have to meet with my publisher, you'd better believe I'd have you tied to the bed, your long legs spread for me, begging for me to fuck you again and again with my tongue." He ran his hands over her breasts, past her waist, between her legs. "With my fingers." He pressed her hand to his erection. "With this."

Emma shivered, the image he painted so close to the vividly erotic dream she'd had less than a week ago in which bondage and begging had played a major role. At the same time, she was slightly disappointed that, yet again, he felt the need to make it perfectly clear to her that she was nothing but a sex toy to him. After last night, she'd nearly convinced himself that they were moving beyond pure sex into a more emotional bond. Like the one they'd had back in college. Obviously, she'd been mistaken.

Still, that was what she had signed up for and since she wasn't ready to leave yet, she refused to betray her disillusionment.

"Cancel your appointment," she whispered. "Stay here with me."

But evidently, Jason had a heck of a lot more willpower than she did. And was a great deal more committed to his career than she was, considering she'd dropped her business like a hot sack of coal with barely a second thought.

"Sorry, babe," he said, dropping her back to the bed rather unceremoniously.

She tried not to feel hurt by how easily he could shove away his need for her. After all, hadn't she burst into his world unannounced two days ago? What right did she have to claim his time wholly and completely?

And hadn't he already given her so much pleasure?

"You're right," she said, pulling the covers up over her bare breasts in an effort to regain some control. "You need to take care of business. And so do I."

He turned to her, his hand on the doorknob. "Aren't you on vacation?"

She bit her lip guiltily. "Not exactly."

Jason frowned, but didn't ask for clarification. On the one hand Emma was relieved that she didn't have to explain herself. But at the same time, she hated that he didn't care enough to ask.

"I'll call you tonight."

Emma's smile returned. *I'll call you tonight* was exactly the kind of thing a boyfriend would say, rather than a part-time lover who couldn't wait to get her out of his hair. "Great!" she chirped. "Have a fantastic meeting."

He closed the door behind him and she propped the pillows behind her back, enjoying the view out the French doors. She could lie here all day doing nothing.

Only, she couldn't. Because lying around eating bonbons wasn't her thing. She was a worker, a doer, and now that she knew Jason was going to be busy all day, now that he'd reminded her that work needed to be done, she already felt lost. Empty-handed. They'd been tourists yesterday and it had been the most wonderful day of her life. The thought of venturing out to wineries, to galleries, to shops without him felt impossibly lonely. But she couldn't just sit around his house all day either, waiting for him to come back and make everything okay.

A girl could only fool herself for so long. Real life awaited and the best way to start her day was to check her voice mail and e-mail in Jason's tidy home office. She did have clients who depended on her, after all, and even if she was busy running away from her life, she acknowledged that it wasn't exactly fair for her to run away from their business affairs as well.

Five minutes later, Emma was knee-deep in more than a hundred messages that had accumulated since Saturday night. Oh God, what had she been thinking? She couldn't just turn off a switch and escape. Not when all these people needed her, depended on her. Just because she'd had two fantastic days and three hot nights with Jason didn't mean that she wasn't still stuck. Because she was.

Depressed again, her eyes blurring as she read and re-read the same e-mail, she pushed back from the desk and hit the off button on Jason's computer.

No! She couldn't go back to her awful life. Not yet. Not when she'd barely begun to live again.

She dialed Kate's cell phone and walked outside, hoping the warm sun and her best friend could put her to rights again.

"Emma, honey, are you still in Napa?" Kate asked.

"I am," she said, trying to sound normal and upbeat and failing miserably.

"What's wrong?"

Emma's throat grew tight. "Jason's been wonderful. Amazing. I feel so free in Napa. You wouldn't believe the people we met yesterday. The vintners, the painters, the farmers. Everyone is so happy here. Living their passion."

Everyone but me, she thought, the weight of her e-mails and voice mails and untold numbers of faxes piling up on her slim shoulders.

"It sounds amazing, Emma. Just what you needed, right? Just what you were hoping for."

"Oh yes. I need it so badly." Emma lowered her voice. "I'd completely forgotten what it's like to have fun." Knowing Kate would understand, on a whisper she added, "To be a passionate woman. To crave a man's touch."

"Don't blame yourself, honey, with a husband like Steven how could you have possibly felt passion? Or craved his touch? Yuck."

"But that's just it. I do blame myself. I chose him. I chose my life."

"So change it. Just like you're doing right now."

Emma shook her head. "It's not that simple, Kate."

"It is that simple. You screwed up in college. You know it. Jason knows it. Fine. But now you've got the chance to live the life you should have had all along."

Emma insisted, "You wouldn't believe how many clients are trying to reach me regarding loans and refinances. My parents have left half a dozen messages. Who am I fooling? I'm never going to be able to change my life. Never."

Kate snorted. "Do I need to come up there and smack some sense into you? Of course you can change your life. You already have. You're in Napa, aren't you? With Jason. This is only the beginning."

Sensing her dismay, Marvin jogged over to her side and Emma sat down on a low rock wall to stroke his fur. Yet another thing she didn't want to have to leave. Not just Jason, but his big silly dog too.

Kate took in her silence. "You're not calling because you're upset about your job, are you? It's Jason, isn't it?"

Emma could barely say the words aloud. "I've been throwing myself at him." She waited for Kate's condemnation, especially since her best friend had warned her to take it slow.

"Good for you."

"Excuse me?"

Kate laughed. "It's about time you joined the rest of us girls and gave in to the dark side. Women tend to throw themselves at hot guys. We can't help ourselves."

"It's not a good thing, Kate!"

"Why the hell not? The sex is great, right?"

"Right."

"You're having fun, aren't you?"

"Of course I am, but you told me to take it slow."

"Hey, if the getting's good, I say go out and get it. Forget I ever mentioned slow. Slow is for wimps. And you are definitely not a wimp. Besides, it's not like he's exactly pushing you away, is he?"

Emma giggled. Jason had jumped her bones repeatedly, with little to no provocation. "He's definitely not saying no."

"I think you're doing both of you a big favor. He's too much of a macho, pride-ball to give in to what he wants—which is you—but then you came along and took the decision away from him."

"What if he thinks all we're doing is having meaningless fun together?" Emma said, giving voice to her biggest worry.

She knew Jason wanted her. That much was obvious. But for how long? "I don't know how much longer I can hide my true feelings from him."

"Which are?"

"I love him, Kate. You know that. We all know it."

Kate sighed. "I don't know what to say, honey. I hope he'll be man enough to love you back, but . . . "

Emma finished her sentence. "I shouldn't count on it, should I?"

Kate's silence said it all. And as Emma hung up and went inside to take a shower, she didn't know if she felt better or worse. Because there was definitely no denying that every time she and Jason made love, another protective layer melted away from her heart. In no time at all, her love for Jason wouldn't be buried way down deep anymore. It would be right there on the surface, in plain sight for the world to see.

Only this time, if he rejected her like she had rejected him, Emma didn't know where she'd run.

Because there'd be no place left to go.

⌐◦

Jason's meeting in the city was long and intense. His last cookbook had hit the *New York Times* hardcover bestseller list and everyone was working overtime to make sure it happened again. He tried to throw himself into his work with the same passion he always did, and yet for the first time he wasn't all there, wasn't completely in the game. He didn't think his editor or the marketing and sales teams noticed his distraction, but he did. And it bothered him a great deal.

His entire adult life, Jason's goals had been clear and direct. He would work hard, succeed, and be satisfied with what he had achieved. Everything had worked out precisely according to his plans.

Everything except Emma. And now she was throwing another wrench into his life. Because this morning, he'd woken up with her in his arms and actually been overwhelmed with happiness.

There was no point in pretending it was anything else.

With every passing hour in her company he remembered why she was his best friend in college and why he'd fallen in love with her. She was funny and sexy and intelligent. And so damn beautiful it made his breath catch just to look at her.

Was it possible that she'd changed? Was she really ready to turn her back on her fake, stuffy world to be with him? He felt twisted up inside and it wasn't a sensation he cared to hold on to. Forcefully, he caught himself, took hold of his thoughts and emotions. At Stanford, he'd been nothing but a green boy with stars in his eyes. He'd seen what he wanted to see, loved because he thought it was his right.

A decade later, Jason knew better. He knew that love didn't really matter. That sex was just an illusion.

Jason wasn't stupid enough to think that he'd ever be free of Emma. He'd always want her. Which was all the more reason why he had to stick to his plan. The time had come to find out exactly what she was doing in Napa. Why she'd come to find him. Tonight he'd question her motives and, based on her answers, he might very well have more ammo for getting payback.

thirteen

Emma paced nervously in front of the winery. Jason had sounded so serious when he'd called her as he was leaving his meeting in San Francisco. Her brain immediately went to a host of worst-case scenarios.

What if he was going to tell her that he was done having fun with her, that she wasn't exciting enough for him? Sexy enough?

Or, what if he hadn't actually been meeting with his publisher today? What if he had a lover stashed away in San Francisco and after crawling exhausted out of her bed he realized he couldn't get it up with scrawny, pathetic Emma one more time?

Even though she knew how ridiculous it was to expect Jason to want to be with her again after all this time, after her past unfaithfulness, she'd still hoped. She'd still dreamed.

But she had a sinking feeling that tonight could be the end of it all.

"Emma," Jason called out, a picnic basket swinging from one hand.

She couldn't help but reach for him, kiss him with all of her pent-up desire. "I missed you today," she admitted, figuring there was no point in holding her cards close to her chest anymore. Not if he was going to discard her anyway.

His eyes darkened and her pulse quickened with desire. "I missed you too."

His words meant so much more to her than he would ever know. She held them close to her heart and prayed that he meant it. She followed him up the gravel pathway around the banks of a small lake that overlooked the grounds and the mountains beyond.

"I see you brought more food. If I didn't know better, I'd think you were trying to fatten me up some more. Like the big bad wolf."

He turned and gave her a very wolflike grin. "Everyone should enjoy food. It's one of the main pleasures in life."

Emma licked her lips at the word "pleasure" as it fell from his sensual lips. Jason certainly knew a thing or two about that subject. In only two days, she'd learned how much she'd been depriving herself all these years by not letting herself eat. Was being super skinny worth it? Really, what had it gotten her but hunger pangs? And a freezer full of unsatisfying Lean Cuisine microwave dinners.

"Besides," he said as he spread a thick, soft, red-and-white-checked blanket on the grass, "I like watching you eat."

Emma blushed furiously beneath his sensual gaze, remembering the way he'd licked the whipped cream from her cleavage in his living room the previous evening.

"Don't you mean you like eating off of me?"

He grinned again, taking her breath away with his all male beauty. She'd never find another man like this.

Jason was powerful, intelligent, and irrepressibly sensual.

"That's right," he said. "Thanks for reminding me. I think I've got some more whipped cream in the basket for dessert."

Emma shot him a seductive glance, hoping she could stall any serious conversations about her going back home and leaving him alone forever the same way she'd been doing it for the past several days. By distracting him with sex.

"Don't they say to eat dessert first?"

"Good idea," he said, but just as his lips were about to touch hers, he pulled away, his breathing ragged. "Emma, we need to talk."

Oh God, this was the end, just as she had feared. Even their shared passion wouldn't help her this time. Here she was the one who'd been wanting to revisit their past, and now that he was actually making them do it, she wanted no part of it.

"Okay," she said shakily, wishing she could run, but knowing she'd never be able to live with herself if she acted like a coward again. At twenty-one, she'd had the excuse of being young and naïve.

At thirty-two, she was all out of excuses. It was time to face the music.

"Why are you here?" Jason asked.

She stared at him. Was she brave enough to admit the truth? She wasn't sure she was, but he deserved nothing less from her, especially given how welcoming he'd been, when she had no where else to go.

"I wanted to see you."

He shook his head, a quick side-to-side motion that told her she'd have to do better than that.

"You've had ten years to come and see me."

She looked down at the blanket, at the lake, anywhere but at him. "I know. And I should have come earlier. But I couldn't." Finally meeting his eyes, she admitted, "I didn't think you'd want to see me."

But he didn't want to go there, they weren't talking about him, she could see that clearly stamped across his face. Right now, this was about her.

"You didn't know if I'd want to see you on Sunday either. That's not what this is about."

"Not entirely," she admitted.

"Steven was at the reunion with a young blonde. I'll bet that bothered you, didn't it?"

Her eyes opened wide with surprise. "You saw them?"

"They were hard to miss. Between his loud voice and her enormous, fake . . . "

Jason didn't finish his sentence but they both knew what he'd been about to say. Emma almost smiled then, but nothing about this conversation was funny. Not even her ex-husband's taste for extremely young silicone breasts.

"It didn't bother me," she lied.

Of course, he saw right through her. "Wanna try that answer again?"

His words should have been harsh, but there was an underlying softness that drove her to confess, "You're right. It did bother me. But not because I want him back."

"You don't?"

She shook her head vehemently and held her hand over her heart. "No. You have to believe me. It was a shock when he asked for a divorce, but I definitely don't regret it."

"Then what do you regret?"

The corner of her mouth quirked up. "That I never knew how young, blonde, and well-endowed he wanted his women to be, I guess. Including me."

Something changed in Jason's face. "Would you have changed for him?"

Emma thought about it for a moment. It was a good question. "No," she replied honestly. "I wouldn't have. I couldn't have. That's not who I am."

Because even though she'd been trying to act like a Playboy bunny with Jason, she knew how far from her essence that über-sexy caricature really was.

"So you didn't come up here to try and make him jealous?"

"No. No way."

"To prove something to him?"

To herself, maybe, but she couldn't say that. "I've got nothing to prove to him. I hope he's happy and now I can see that we weren't meant to be together. No matter what my parents thought."

"Ah, your parents."

Jason got that grim look that she remembered from the one family dinner she'd invited him to in college. She'd known he'd been uncomfortable, that he'd felt horribly out of his element, but she hadn't known how to fix things.

"I'm sure they're thrilled that you're in Napa with me, aren't they."

She took a deep breath. "They don't know."

One dark eyebrow went up, clearly mocking her. "Of course they don't."

"That's not fair. No one knows where I am. Only Kate."

"So you're running away. That's what these past few days have been?"

She didn't have anything to say to that, it was too close to the truth. A truth she didn't want to own up to. But even if she couldn't be honest about how she felt about herself, she could be honest about how she felt about Jason.

"Do you want to know why I came up here? Why I left my parents in the middle of Sunday brunch, praying that you'd be at your restaurant and that you wouldn't take one look at me and kick me back out onto the sidewalk?"

The set of his lips was hard, but his tone was soft. "Tell me why, Emma. I need to know."

Her voice on the verge of breaking, she said, "Because when you walked into our reunion and I saw you again I knew that I had to be with you. That I'd made the worst mistake of my life in college. And then in the lake . . . " She swallowed, but wouldn't let herself wimp out. Not this time. "When you touched me, I remembered. Everything. How you made me feel. How wonderful you were. It's never been like that for me, Jason. Like this. So incredible. Not with anyone. Only you."

She thought he was going to reach for her then, but he didn't and so she kept filling the space with words.

"I'm here because I want to be with you. To see if we can make this work, whatever it is we're doing. All I know is that when I'm with you, I feel whole." A bird chirped above them, but it didn't break the spell, nothing could. "I'm happy.

Please believe me. I may not have any other answers, but the one thing I know for sure is that I want to be with you. You're the only thing that makes sense."

A mix of expressions moved across Jason's face, through his eyes. Disbelief warred with hope, desire with pride. She could see it all and she didn't blame him. How could she? She was asking him to trust her. Now all she could do was pray that he would risk even half of what she was risking on him.

Because Emma already knew that this time, she was risking it all.

⌒

The smart thing to do would be to get up, head back to his restaurant, bury himself in work, and forget all about Emma. She was no good for him, she never had been, even if his heart—and his cock—wanted so badly to believe differently.

She'd answered his questions and yet, there was so much she hadn't said. But he was loath to press her, because if he did . . . shit, who was he kidding?

He wanted her to say all the right things so that he could convince himself it was all right to forgive her. That it was okay to lose himself in her body, her beauty, in the sheer pleasure of being with her.

He was doing it again. Giving up his power to her, letting her reel him into her web. Hadn't she just given him all the ammo he needed to destroy her? She'd said he made her feel whole. That by leaving her he could rip her heart to shreds.

Emma was as vulnerable as she'd ever been. She was an open wound, desperately trying to figure out what was going on in her life. Crushing her now would be easy. So easy.

But he just couldn't do it.

Couldn't. Do. It.

Stupid fuck that he was, everything in Jason refused to hurt Emma like that. And already he knew that tonight, and from here forward, he was going to do everything in his power to forget their past and give in to pleasure.

The pleasure of Emma's warm body and her sparkling company.

As he pulled a chilled bottle of Fumé Blanc from his basket along with two glasses, he gave credence to the part of his brain that told him he was giving up on his plan for payback way too soon.

Rather than make love to Emma, he should be fucking her raw. But no matter how he'd tried, he couldn't help but fall for her again.

Certain that he was headed for trouble, but unable to stop himself, he expertly popped the cork, then poured the wine and handed a glass to Emma.

Her hands were shaking slightly. Working to lighten her mood—better yet, to get her in the mood and out of her clothes—he said, "Don't worry, I won't bite. Unless you specifically ask me to, that is."

Emma laughed, but her hands were still trembling. He could see the relief in her eyes, feel it in the way her muscles relaxed as he intertwined his arm with hers, and said, "Here, let me."

She'd been scared that he was going to cut her loose tonight, but he hadn't, had he? Even if it was the smart thing to do.

The heaviness of his thoughts weighing on him, Jason was desperate to forget everything but the pleasure of Emma's touch. So when she opened her mouth to let him pour the dry white onto her tongue, he "accidentally" sloshed half the glass of wine on her chest.

"Uh-oh," he said, forcing a lightness he didn't yet feel.

She gasped as the bubbly liquid ran down the front of her dress, then giggled, saying, "Look what you've done. Now I'm going to have to take my clothes off."

Her lightness buoying him up just as he'd hoped it would, Jason reached for the straps of her tank dress. "My thoughts exactly."

He dragged the bodice down past her lace-covered breasts. Her nipples were sensitive from the combination of ice-cold liquid and his arousing touch and she moaned as his thumbs slid gently over her aching peaks.

He stared at her phenomenal breasts, plumping over the edge of her skimpy cream lace bra, even if he'd been either sucking or touching them twenty-four-seven for the past half week. You'd think he'd be over how hot she was by now, but he wasn't. Not even close. No wonder why he couldn't let her go.

"Your underwear should be illegal."

He bent his head down to lick the sticky liquid off her soft skin. He ran his tongue along the edge of the lace, which barely covered her puckering areolas, finally dipping his tongue in to taste her rosy nipples.

She arched into his tongue and her breasts popped completely out of her bra.

Reaching behind her back to undo the clasp, keeping his focus on her curves and his arousal, Jason murmured, "If I had known you were wearing this bra we would have skipped our little talk and gone straight to—"

She cut off his words with her mouth, tasting the wine on his lips, running her tongue from one tantalizing corner to the next, and he was glad she'd made him shut up before he said something, did something that would break the spell.

He ran his fingers down her rib cage to her stomach, finally caressing her skin along the seam of her sheer, wispy, matching cream panties. As he bent his head down to devour her breasts again, he slipped one finger into her wetness.

"Jason," she moaned as she shifted her legs slightly to give him better access to her body. He gently swirled her clit with his middle finger and she went limp in his arms.

When he pulled his hand away from between her legs to pull her dress all the way off, she tried to help him as much as she could, but her fingers were clumsy. He didn't think it was possible for him to be more turned on, but the evidence of her need almost sent him over the edge.

Seconds later, sitting naked before him in the moonlight, she ripped the buttons off his shirt. As he worked on his belt and zipper, she pressed fervent kisses to his chest, licking first one taut nipple and then the other.

"Your tongue is driving me insane."

He kicked his feet out of his pants then settled himself between her long, silken legs, kissing and licking all the way up the length of her legs, from her ankles to the damp flesh on the insides of her thighs, getting closer and closer to her cunt with his tongue and lips and teeth.

"I thought you weren't going to bite unless I asked you to," she said in a breathy voice.

He stopped his sensual onslaught and placed a kiss on her belly button. "I did promise, didn't I?" he said in heated undertones.

She nodded, which made her breasts shake erotically. "Good thing I didn't make any promises about sucking," he said as he drew one of her nipples into his mouth and sucked it eagerly. His hands started the slow progression up her thighs, taking his sweet time as he slid one of his fingers into her wet canal.

She pressed herself against his finger, crying out her pleasure. Sensing her growing urgency, he ran his tongue between the cleft of her breasts, dipping it into her belly button, heading for his ultimate destination with utter concentration.

Slipping one finger in and out of her in a slow, tantalizing rhythm, he bent his head between her thighs and nudged her legs even further apart. This was all he wanted. To be with Emma like this, to feel her wet and soft beneath him. He would give up everything for moments like this.

Pressing his whole mouth onto her swollen clit, he sucked it into his lips, brushing it repeatedly with his tongue. Her legs were wrapped around his torso and she was holding onto the back of his head with both hands. Licking and sucking at her core, Jason felt her muscles convulse around his finger, so he thrust his palm against her mound until every last spasm had rocked through her.

Barely able to contain his intense need, he pushed her back into the blanket and she opened her eyes, glassy and dazed with passion, giving him a lazy smile. "I love it when you lick me," she said, and he nearly exploded at her sexy words.

"I love to lick you too," he said, running his tongue over the light sheen of sweat between her breasts, so tantalizingly displayed in the moonlight.

"I'm giving you permission," she said as he suckled her, his shaft settling at the base of her slick passage.

He lifted his lips from her breasts just long enough to say, "Permission to do what?"

Looking into his eyes with a wicked gleam, she said, "To bite me."

Jason groaned and gently sank his teeth into the swell of her breasts, willing himself not to explode as he slid into her cunt and the hot, silky passage enveloped him in a flood of wetness. She threw her head back with an expression of ecstasy as he pumped harder and harder into her, as she took him all the way to her core. Lifting his hips until only the very tip of his shaft remained inside her wet heat, he tried to stave off his orgasm. But when she arched her back so that her nipples teased his lips, silently begging him to suck them, he couldn't take it any more. Tasting first one breast and then the other, he put his hands on her hips and drove into her.

Their pelvises rocked frantically and her breasts swelled between his lips as she neared her second powerful explosion. She milked him as she came, but even as he detonated within her Jason felt torn in two by his need for Emma. Just as he always had.

fourteen

The song of the birds woke her, and as usual, Jason wasn't in bed beside her. What she wouldn't give to wake up in his arms. Their lovemaking at the winery had made her feel closer to him than she had since they'd last been truly close in college. Still, she felt that leaving her to wake up in an empty bed was his way of holding something back.

When she looked back at the picture of their lovemaking these past days, their sexual encounters had been far more exhibitionist than intimate. She wanted more than that. So much more.

Her muscles slightly sore from the aerobics of their lovemaking, she slid from beneath the duvet and stretched her arms above her head. She heard the squeaking of a chair on concrete and tiptoed over to the French doors, peering out into the garden.

A beautiful sight awaited her. Jason was sprawled across a chaise lounge, manuscript pages for what must have been a new cookbook balanced on his knees, and she longed to brush away the thick, dark locks that nearly covered his eyes.

He seemed so private, so untouchable, and she contented herself with this chance to observe the man she loved. And to think things over.

Last night she'd had her chance to ask him some questions. Namely, "Why are *you* here with me?" just as he'd asked her. But she hadn't wanted to go there, to delve too deep for one simple reason.

His answer had the power to hurt her more deeply than anything else.

Emma had escaped into the excitement and passion of Jason's arms because her current life was crap. She'd had nothing that was truly worth holding on to. Not until now. But she was well aware that it was a far different story for Jason.

He'd already had the perfect life, job, house, the perfect everything before she'd waltzed back in. Frankly, she wasn't convinced that she wasn't just making things worse for him. She knew she was distracting him from his work. He was a very busy, in demand man, and the fact that he was willing to give so much of his precious time to her meant a great deal.

Her cell phone rang, knocking her out of her musings. She reached into her purse, on the top of his dresser, and flipped open the top to see who was calling.

Her parents. Again. She didn't want to answer it. Didn't

want to speak to them, but the way Jason had called her on her obvious avoidance of them, on the way she was hiding from their disapproval rankled. Because it was so damn true.

She was determined to try and face her demons, one a time. Especially if it meant gaining Jason's respect. Taking a deep breath she said, "Hello."

"Emma. Where are you?" Her mother didn't wait for an answer, not when accusations and guilt were so much more fun. "We've been trying to reach you for nearly a week. Do you have any idea how worried sick we've been about you?"

"Mother," Emma began, her brain whirring to come up with a way to explain the situation.

"That friend of yours, Katherine—"

"Kate."

"As I was saying, Emma, we finally called that girl and she refused to tell us where you were. Refused! Just wait until she's a mother and her daughter runs off in the middle of a meal without a word to her parents about where she is going."

Emma hated to hear her best friend be so mistreated. "She was only trying to protect me."

Jane sniffed. "At least she told us you hadn't been in a car crash. Your father nearly had a coronary over it all."

Emma sorely doubted that. Her father was in better shape than most thirty-year-olds. But it was better to humor her mother than to give in to the snort of disbelief gurgling around in her throat.

"Tell Daddy I'm sorry."

"You can tell him yourself tonight at dinner."

"No!"

She couldn't go back there. To her parents' house, to her house, to her life. Not yet.

"Don't raise your voice to me young lady."

Letting herself lash out at her mother for the first time in, well, ever, Emma said, "If you haven't noticed, I'm thirty-two, Mother. I'm not a little girl anymore who needs to tell you where I am every moment. I have my own life to live. And I'm living it!"

"I never thought I'd hear my own daughter speak to me like this. We raised you better than that."

Emma tried to fight back the guilt at telling her mother off, but it was no use. She couldn't change thirty-two years of behavior overnight. Even if she desperately wanted to.

"I'm in Napa. With Jason."

Silence met her declaration. "Jason? You don't know any Jason. Is he a new client?"

Emma hated to dash her mother's hopes that this was only about business, but for the first time she wanted to come clean, no matter the repercussions. And she knew there would be consequences.

But if she denied being with Jason now to her parents, wasn't it the same as turning her back on him in college?

"Jason Roberts. My friend from Stanford. He's a chef now. A world-famous, incredibly talented chef."

"I hope you're not breaking your diet, Emma."

Inwardly she fumed. How dare her mother tell her what she could and couldn't eat. She wasn't a toddler anymore.

"His food is divine," she declared.

"You cannot be serious."

"I am, Mother. And his food isn't the only thing that's wonderful."

She barely stopped herself from saying, *He's the best lover I've ever had, hands down.*

"I have to go now. Give my love to Daddy." She put her thumb on the end button. "I don't know when I'll be back."

Closing her cell, she turned off the ringer and shoved it in the back of the top dresser drawer.

"Nice performance," Jason said, leaning against the open French doors.

"I didn't know you were listening."

Raising an eyebrow, he said, "I'll make you breakfast."

She followed him through the garden and into the patio door that lead to the kitchen, wondering if she'd unwittingly passed another test.

"Think your parents are going to send out the cavalry?" Jason asked as he whipped eggs, butter, and fresh feta cheese for omelets. His words were light but he wasn't joking.

"No," she said, thinking, *I hope not.* "They're just over-protective," she said, sighing and wondering why she was defending them to Jason. She should have been apologizing to him for how they'd treated him all those years ago. Jason slid a full plate across the island and she admitted, "You know what I'm just starting to realize?"

"What's that?" he asked, a bite halfway to his lips.

She watched him chew, unable to turn off the part of her brain that wanted to leap across the granite and French him, all discussion of her parents instantly forgotten. Dipping her fork into the light and delicious looking omelet, she worked to get her mind around something other than orgasms.

"It's not all their fault."

Her companion didn't bother to mask his surprise. "How so?"

She took a bite and swallowed, closing her eyes with delight. "My God, you really do incredible things with food."

"Nice try."

She held up one hand in defense. "I'm not trying to change the subject, I swear."

"So then, back to mommy dearest?"

Emma tried to frown, but gave up with a giggle. "You really shouldn't call her that. She's not that bad."

"Emma," he growled.

"Sorry. What I was going to say before I got distracted by your godliness in the kitchen and your nasty nicknames for my mother is that all this time, *I'm* the one who has let them dictate my life to me. You're going to laugh, but this morning on the telephone was the first time I've ever really stood up to her. Ever."

Saying it out loud felt impossibly silly and immature. What kind of thirty-two-year-old woman took so long to grow a sliver of a backbone?

"What a wimp I am. Especially since I already feel guilty for hanging up on her."

Jason reached for her hand across the countertop. "You're here, aren't you?"

She nodded, unable to take her eyes from his strong hand across hers. It was the first time he'd reached for her, the first time she hadn't been the one to make the first move.

"Nothing wimpy about that."

It was the nicest, most encouraging thing anyone had ever said to her. And coming from Jason, she felt that it was almost absolution for her sins.

He couldn't believe she'd told her parents about him. He'd been so sure she'd make up some story rather than admit to slumming it with the poor boy they'd never had the time of day for. Stranger things had happened, certainly, than Emma standing up to her parents. Right now, though, he couldn't think of too many.

"Got any plans for today?" he asked, wishing for the first time that he didn't have to head into the restaurant.

He'd been torn all night long by his opposing goals. On the one hand, he desperately wanted to trust Emma, to be with her, to let himself love her. On the other, he'd never allowed a woman to come between him and his career, never planned on letting Emma get such a strong hold over him again, and all the sane voices in his head told him to watch out.

But in the end, he wanted to be with her more than he wanted to be without her, payback be damned. So he was shutting the voices of reason down. Pussy-whipped idiot that he was.

In an uncertain voice, she said, "Um, I was hoping I could help you out."

He raised an eyebrow in question. "With what exactly?"

His lavicious intent was clear and she laughed.

"At your restaurant." Before he could shoot down her idea, she added, "I could fold napkins or shine silverwear."

This time he laughed. "Nothing like putting your Stanford Economics degree to good use, is there?"

She snorted. "Putting my degree to good use is highly overrated, trust me."

It was the perfect opening, so he took it. "You haven't talked much about your job since you've been here."

Her face changed from bright and open to slammed shut. "That's because I haven't wanted to think about it."

"Don't tell me you got fired? Not Emma the perfect?"

Poking her fork in his direction like a deadly weapon, she said, "First of all, I'm not perfect. We both know that." She looked the fork in her hand as if seeing it for the first time and put it down. "And no I wasn't fired."

"Are you sure about that?"

"Unless I fired myself and forgot about it, yeah, I'm sure."

He whistled. "Of course you own the company. What was I thinking? You working for someone else? Laughable."

She bristled at that. "How so?"

"Let's put it this way," he said as he leaned across the table, "I'm not entirely sure that you won't have completely revolutionized the way my staff folds napkins and shines forks by the end of the day. They'll probably start calling you boss and saluting."

She grinned, all bright happiness again. "So I can come with you?"

"If you're sure you wouldn't rather be wine tasting and laying out by the pool?"

"I'm sure."

Emma'd never had a job like this before, one where she could let her mind wander and actually talk to the other employees. She'd either worked for her father's financial planning company or been building up her own mortgage brokering business. Serious, serious, serious. That had been her working life.

Oh, who was she kidding? Apart from laughing with Kate on the evenings when she could tear herself away from the office, her whole entire life had been serious. In and out of the office.

Until now.

Because when she was with Jason she laughed. Actually gave into belly laughs, probably snorted too for all she could control her happiness.

She didn't have to try so damn hard every second of the day to be perfect, to do everything just right. To make a good impression.

And she could even eat like a semi-normal person, without freaking out about every single bite going into her mouth.

Jason stuck his head out of the kitchen. "Hey, Julie, is Emma causing any trouble out there?"

Clearly comfortable with her gorgeous boss, Julie grinned and said, "No way. She's fantastic. Where'd you find her? I think she's even figured out a faster way to fold the napkins."

Jason's laughter rang out through the empty dining room. "It's amazing what you can pick up on street corners nowadays."

Emma loved being a part of Jason's team, even if it was just for the afternoon. It figured that he would surround himself with entertaining, relaxed employees, whereas both assistants in her office were so uptight she wasn't completely certain that they'd ever really smiled at each other.

The past three days had been amazing, but hanging out in Jason's restaurant, laughing with everyone, feeling like she was part of a laid-back team, was even better.

Eating breakfast with Jason in his kitchen was the most intimate thing they'd done yet. Sure, they'd explored each other's bodies in a dozen ways, but no matter how great the sex was, none of it had touched her nearly as deeply as Jason telling her she was brave for standing up to her parents. And now, doing a rote task in his restaurant made her feel closer to him then ever.

Maybe, just maybe, she thought to herself with a private smile, Jason was starting to let her into his life again. And this time, she wouldn't do anything to jeopardize their relationship.

"Emma," Julie called out from behind the wall that partly covered the front door, "someone's here to see you."

She looked up to see who it was and the spoons that she'd been polishing fell from her fingers onto the table. Jason had been right about her parents sending out the cavalry.

But it was worse than that. Rather than coming themselves, they'd sent her ex-husband, Steven.

fifteen

W hat are you doing here?"

For the first time, Emma didn't care about being polite. Even during their divorce proceedings, she'd been unfailingly gracious, whether or not Steven deserved it. But serving her with divorce papers was one thing.

Interrupting her idyll with Jason was another entirely.

Instead of answering her pointed question, Steven gave her the once-over. "Damn, honey. You look amazing."

Suddenly, all her pride in her new, carefree, pretty clothes evaporated. She wished she was wearing a huge dumpy sweater and corduroys. Anything to get her ex-husband, whom she definitely didn't want anymore, to stop looking at her like he wanted to eat her up. He was giving her the creeps.

"Answer my question," she said, forcefully enough that he took a step back in surprise. "What are you doing here?"

"Your parents were right," he said, with a pitying shake of his head. "You do need me to come bring you home."

For a moment, Emma thought smoke might rise up out of her ears. "Get out."

But instead of getting the hell out of the restaurant before Jason saw him like she so desperately wished he would, Steven acted as if she hadn't basically ordered him out of her life.

"Looks like Jason did pretty good for himself, doesn't it? Who would have thought he had it in him?"

Emma was this close to smacking the smug condescension off Steven's face. But since she knew violence was taking things too far, even for the "new" wild Emma, she decided she'd have to physically remove him from the premises instead.

"You didn't come here to see Jason," she said as she grabbed his arm and tried to push him back toward the door. "I'm sure you have a whole host of reasons that have nothing to do with whether you actually care for me or not. But you can say what you came to say on the sidewalk. People are working and we're disturbing them," she added, finally realizing just what a show she and her ex were putting on for Jason's staff. And here she'd been hoping to make some friends. Damn her ex and her parents for meddling.

She should have known better than to point out their audience. Steven loved spectators, especially when he thought he was doing something as selfless as saving his pathetic little ex-wife from her own bad decisions.

"Now look, honey," he began as he tried to put his arms around her.

She stopped trying to get him out the door and jumped back several feet. Being touched by Steven gave her the willies. The only man she ever wanted touching her again was Jason. How she'd lived with Steven for so long was suddenly beyond her and only served to highlight how numb she'd forced herself to be just to make it through the past decade.

"I'm not your honey."

He pouted and it wasn't his most masculine look. She would have giggled at how ridiculous he looked except right then he said, "Now come on, sweetheart—"

"My name is Emma."

The waitstaff were doing their best to go about their job of setting up the restaurant for lunch. While keeping their ears peeled for the juicy stuff, of course.

Steven rolled his eyes. "Okay, Emma, I know how hard you took the divorce and I'm sorry about that."

Between gritted teeth, she straightened her spine so that she was her full five foot six. "Don't you dare presume to know how I feel. About anything."

He held his hands up in mock surrender. "All I'm saying is that I've decided to take you back, to let you take care of me the way you used to. I know how you've missed having me around the house."

"You want to *take me back?*" She tried to stay calm, but it was no use. "I don't want to take care of you. And I certainly don't need you to take care of me. Since you seem to be at their beck and call, why don't you inform my parents that I don't need them to barge into my life anymore either."

But it was as if Steven wasn't listening to a word she was saying. Which, she knew from a decade of experience, he very likely wasn't.

"I know this is just your hurt feelings talking. Once you calm down and leave your little fantasy world you'll see that we're only trying to do what's best for you."

That was it, she was going to strangle him and the police were going to come and convict her of assault. There was no other way, not when Steven wouldn't listen to reason. But just then, Steven's eyes moved over her shoulder.

"Jason," he said, stretching his hand out and moving through the restaurant toward her lover as if they were long lost football buddies. "Long time no see."

Jason shook his hand, but his mouth remained a firm, tight line. Emma longed to explain that she had nothing to do with Steven's appearance, that she didn't want him here, but there was no chance.

"Very impressive place you've got here. Even if it is way out in the boonies. Maybe one day you'll be able to make the move into the city."

Jason's eyes were grim. "Maybe." He turned to Emma. "Is this your ride home?"

She shook her head, desperate for him to understand. "No. He was just leaving. Without me."

Steven gave Jason a man-to-man grin. "You know how the little woman is, she never knows quite what she wants."

"Good thing you know for her," Jason said, the irony thick as cream in his words.

Of course, Steven missed it completely. "I knew you'd understand. That's exactly why I'm here. To take Emma home. I think the events of the past few months have been too much for her. With the divorce and all." His mouth twisted into a look of derision. "Not to mention the fact that she's left all of her clients in the lurch this week. A very irresponsible move in this economic climate."

Jason moved toward Steven, clearly on the verge of physically throwing him out of his restaurant, but Emma slid between them, putting a hand on Steven's arm. "Everything is under control. Besides, my business is none of yours. Not anymore. Let's discuss this outside. Alone."

Responding as if she were nothing more than a petulant teenager who had never shouldered a responsibility in her life, Steven said, "Of course it's my business. And your father's. We've both been getting calls from customers we've referred to you."

The unspoken subtext of *Therefore, little girl, you owe me, and your father, and better do what we both say and come back to Palo Alto* hung heavy and fetid in the air.

She was furious with Steven for daring to corner her like this and with Jason for just standing there, silently judging her. But most of all, she was angry with herself for not having foreseen these events. Most people could take a spur-of-the-moment vacation from their business. But not her. Oh no, not with Mommy and Daddy tied into every single aspect of her life, including her client base.

And whose fault was that? Emma knew the answer. It was her fault entirely. For not having made the choice to become an independent adult years ago like normal people did.

All out of options, she let go of Steven, grabbed her purse off the counter, and swept out of the door before tears of frustration could start falling.

Jason crossed his arms and leaned against the wall, running his eyes up Steven's no-longer-fit frame. "That didn't go exactly as you planned, did it?"

Steven ran a hand over his heavily moussed hair. "She'll come around soon enough. Especially when she thinks about how much sense it makes to remarry me. She was heartbroken when I left her, you know."

Working not to register his disgust on his face, Jason merely raised an eyebrow in response.

"You can tell her I'll be in touch," Steven said, but just as he opened the front door, he turned and threw a parting shot at Jason. "Don't forget, *I'm* what she wants," he said. "She chose me before, she'll choose me again. I wouldn't make the mistake of forgetting what happened ten years ago in the quad, if I were you."

Jason wanted to leap out the door and slam Steven's head into the sidewalk. Hadn't he waited ten long years for the pleasure of beating Steven to a pulp? When Emma had put her hand on Steven's arm, asking to speak to him outside, just the two of them, his vision had gone from red to purple to black. How dare she touch that prick with the same fingers that had been loving him all week? But suddenly, he wasn't standing in his restaurant anymore. He was twenty-one again and his world was on the verge of busting to smithereens.

⁓

Stanford University Quad, Easter Sunday, Ten Years Ago

It was a perfect, warm April weekend in Northern California. Cloudless blue skies, students playing Frisbee out on the lawn and studying on beach chairs in bikinis. Having grown up in Rochester, New York, home to the endless April snowstorm, even after three years on the Stanford campus Jason continued to be stunned by the weather. Forget studying. He was going to surprise Emma—who'd been working hard on an Economics presentation all week—with a gourmet picnic lunch.

Jason woke up early to make sure he'd have the co-op kitchen to himself and dove into the new Julia Child cookbook he'd splurged on.

Emma didn't eat enough and he was always hoping that one day he'd find the perfect recipe she couldn't resist. He'd tried to talk to her about her eating patterns, wondered if she had an eating disorder, but she always adamantly refused to admit anything was wrong. He didn't know what else he could do other than continuing to cook awesome meals for her.

She was at church with her parents in the quad and he figured he'd grab her when the service let out at 11:30 A.M. He wasn't looking forward to seeing her parents again, especially not after the chilly reception they'd given him at her birthday party. They'd looked at him like he wasn't fit to be the dirt in the tracks of her tennis shoes, but he'd tried not to let it bother him.

He didn't care what her parents thought about him. Emma's opinion was the only one that mattered. And she loved him.

Last night they'd been walking through the quad and he'd pressed her up against one of the thick stone pillars and kissed her until she'd whispered her love against his lips. She'd seemed especially intense for the past couple of months and he'd chalked it up to working too hard. He never quite understood why she drove herself so hard, almost as if she expected constant perfection.

No one was perfect, but Jason figured the way she drove herself into the ground to achieve more and more all the time must have something to do with her parents. They withheld affection, dangled their approval over Emma's head like a big, juicy carrot she could never quite reach.

Their message was crystal-clear: Only if she was "good enough" would she get their love.

A fire lit in Jason's gut, the same way it always did when he thought about the way her parents treated her. Why couldn't they see what he did? She was funny and brilliant and, to him at least, so damn sexy he couldn't think straight whenever they touched.

He'd loved her from the minute he'd seen her and it hadn't taken long for her to confess she felt the same way.

Still, he had to admit that sometimes it bothered him how she insisted on hiding their relationship from her parents. They thought friendship was as far as things went. How wrong they were. If only she'd stand up to them, he knew she'd finally be free from all the pressure and stress of being their perfect little girl, but Jason didn't want to force this issue with her either.

In time, he figured Emma would come to this conclusion on her own. And he'd back her up every step up of the way until that day came.

A spinach and feta quiche still warm in his backpack, he made his way across campus, walking up the steps of the quad just as the bells struck 11:30. Heading into the shadows of an overhang, he waited for Emma to walk outside with her parents.

Emma's father walked out with his arm slung around the beefy, over-inflated shoulder of a campus football hero. Steven Cartwright. What the hell was that guy doing with Emma's father?

Jason and Emma had run into Steven at the local pub a couple of weeks ago and Jason had wanted to flatten the guy for the hungry way he looked at her. Evidently, they were in the same killer Economics of Third World Countries class. Emma hadn't wanted to stay long. Jason didn't blame her and they'd left without finishing their drinks.

Emma's mother walked out of the church next, her boring suit a perfect match to her boring hair, makeup, and pinched expression. Does she keep lemons in her pocket? *he wondered. Otherwise how else could she keep that sour expression intact?*

Finally, Emma emerged into the sunlight and Jason's heart unconstricted. She probably couldn't wait to get away from the dull super jock and her dreary folks.

He began to make his way around the side of the quad, planning on surprising Emma from behind the group. She could tell her parents they had to study for a big test or something. But just then the dynamic changed between Steven and Emma. Jason stopped dead in his tracks.

Emma's mother basically handed her daughter over to Steven, while her father pushed the jock in his daughter's direction as well. Emma and Steven met in the middle of her approving parents and before Jason could blink to clear his vision, Steven was bending down to kiss Emma, the same soft mouth he'd tasted himself only hours before.

Fuck! He'd kissed her! Some football player had kissed his girlfriend!

Jason dropped his backpack to the ground, intent on killing the blonde asshole, if that's what it came to.

But then, the unthinkable happened: Emma went up on her tippy-toes and kissed Steven back.

The ground dropped out from beneath Jason. His lungs weren't working right anymore and he couldn't think clearly. Instead of kissing that stupid football player, Emma might as well have ripped Jason's heart out and stomped on it.

What was happening? She was his. Mine, he thought.

The sunlight glinted off of something on her right hand and Jason watched as Steven held it up for her parents to admire. Emma's father slapped him on the back and for the first time in history, Emma's mother didn't look like a sourpuss.

Knife-sharp betrayal lodged itself in Jason's chest. But still, he refused to believe that Emma was a willing party to this. Her parents must have forced this guy on her. And even though she lived in fear of disappointing them, any minute now she'd pull the ring off, she'd tell the guy to get lost.

And everything would be okay.

Only everything wasn't okay. Because instead of telling Steven where to stick his kiss and his stupid ring, she was letting him hold her hand.

Worst of all, she was turning her face up to his, laughing at something he was saying.

Jason took off, straight toward them. In the back of his mind he knew it might be a better idea to cool off, to wait until Emma was alone so that he could hear her side of the story. But Jason wasn't interested in what was fair anymore. In doing the right thing. Fuck being the good guy. Blood drained out of his face, his whole body felt empty, devoid of his usual boundless energy.

"Emma," he called out.

She spun around and he knew. Guilt was pressed into her face, written all over her body.

She was betraying him. Leaving him.

For someone who didn't deserve her. And never would.

"Jason," she gasped, trying to pull her hand from Steven's grasp. But Steven held tightly to her and there she was, stuck between two men and her parents.

Jason would have felt sorry for her, except he couldn't go there. Not when everything he'd believed in had been ripped away.

"Looks like you're having a big happy family Easter, aren't you?"

His words themselves were innocuous enough, but not his tone. They burned his tongue, his lips as they fell.

"Can we talk about this later?"

She was pleading and a kinder man would have let her go, would have said, "Fuck it, she's made her choice."

But he wasn't interested in being kind. Or in making this easy for her. She was going to tell the truth, goddamn it, admit that she was a coward. And a liar.

He shrugged. "Seems like it would be better to clear the air now that we've got everyone here, don't you think?"

She shook her head, swiftly side to side, obviously expecting him to protect her from her parents one last time. Too bad she was assuming they were still on the same side, when she had clearly defected to the enemy camp.

The sick thing was, just like he'd always known but hadn't wanted to admit during the past three years, a guy like Steven was a perfect fit for her. They would have blonde, dull kids, who got straight As and went into the family business.

Fuck.

Forcing his lips up into some resemblance of a smile, Jason turned to her mother. "Jane, your daughter and I have been dating."

Jane gasped. "You? That's impossible. Emma, tell me it isn't true."

But Emma just stood there, one tear tracking down her cheek.

Any other time Jason would have brushed it away. Now, he barely watched it fall.

"Walter, looks like you've found a much better candidate for your daughter, haven't you? I assume he's going to work for you upon graduation, keep everything neat and tidy in the family?"

Steven let go of Emma's hand then, puffing out his chest and moving toward Jason. "You've got that right, buddy. You're history. Emma doesn't want anything to do with you anymore. She's with me now."

Bile rose up into Jason's throat and he had two choices: Be sick or beat the crap out of Steven.

He chose a swift right hook into Steven's bedrock jaw. It hurt like hell when his fist hit bone, but the pain was good, reminding him that he was still alive. That he'd move past today, forget all about Emma.

One day she'd barely be a memory.

Steven came at him, but Jason was quick from years of holding his own in the kind of neighborhoods that Emma's parents wouldn't be caught dead driving through.

Jane cried out to warn Steven just as Jason was about to lay another slam dunk on his pretty face.

"He's not worth it, Steven," Emma's mother screeched.

The words not worth it, not worth it, not worth it *slammed around Jason's brain, getting louder and louder, running into each other.*

"Don't say that," Emma cried. "They don't mean it," she said, moving toward him, but already Steven had turned his back on Jason.

"You're mother's right, baby. He's not worth it. Let's go. We've sullied Easter enough with this trash."

Jason watched Emma stand there, watched her assess her two choices: Turn her back on her family, the perfect Wonder Bread, picket-fence future she would have with Steven, or risk it all with a boy who didn't look to have much of a future outside of a kitchen.

Another tear followed the first down her pale cheekbones. She'd made her choice.

He turned to walk away, but he couldn't. Not yet.

"Tell me this is what you want and I'll leave you alone."

She licked her lips, the very mouth that he'd been loving just hours ago, and said the words that condemned their love straight to hell.

"This is what I want."

Jason relived the scene as if it had just happened, as if ten years hadn't passed since the moment Emma had walked out of his life on the arm of an utter asshole. Ten years later, Emma's ex had come back for her. For all he knew, she and Steven had been reconciling for some time now and the country boy chef was a convenient way for her to make her ex jealous. No wonder why she'd told her parents about him. He knew something was up with that, knew Emma could never stand up to her mother in a million years.

Yet again, Jason was the perfect foil to get Steven to go down on bended knee. Steven might not want her, but more than that he didn't want to lose his ex-wife to trailer trash. And Emma likely agreed with him. Just as she always had.

Why the fuck had he actually thought she could change? That she could make the right choice for once? Especially when he knew exactly the choice she was going to make.

The safe one. The same damn choice she'd made before: A life of leisure over real love.

Well, that was fine. He was perfectly happy to let her screw up her life again. Except for one small thing: There was no way he was going to make it easy for her.

Because now that the lesson had been hammered home yet again, now that he'd been proven to be a lovesick fool for the second time, he wasn't going to let anything get in the way of his plan for payback. He'd just about been stupid enough to chuck it all after one great day with Emma and a few superb screws.

But he didn't have time for this right now. He had a restaurant to run. He'd find her after lunch and set his plan for revenge back into motion.

And this time there'd be no turning back. No matter what.

sixteen

Heading out blindly for a place to hide from Steven—God forbid he actually came after her again—Emma realized she only had one option. Jason's house. If Steven had the nerve to follow her there, she'd sic Marvin on him. As far as she knew, the huge dog couldn't hurt a flea, then again, didn't animals have a sixth sense about protecting people they cared about? At the very least, she knew that Marvin liked her.

Even if she was more confused than ever about his gorgeous owner.

What had he meant by *Is this your ride home?* He hadn't even waited three seconds before jumping to the assumption that she was leaving with Steven. That she wanted to.

How could he possibly think the last four days meant so little to her?

Sadness washed through her, tasting of defeat. The truth was, she knew exactly why he thought she'd choose to leave with Steven. She'd done it before and no amount of apologies or justifications for her behavior could change the past.

She'd held her worries, her fears, her sadness inside herself for thirty-two years. But after five days with Jason, she couldn't do it anymore. She didn't want to. Maybe that had been her problem all along: If only she'd been willing to admit to someone else that her life wasn't perfect . . . maybe she could have at least started thinking of ways to make it better.

Grabbing her cell phone, she dialed Kate's office, forcing down the part of her that told her she was being too needy. She and Kate hadn't talked this frequently on the phone since the summer between freshman and sophomore year in college. Then again, Emma had never really wanted to admit what a mess her life really was. Not until now, when she could no longer avoid the god-awful truth.

Kate picked up and a loud sigh of relief shot from Emma's lungs. "Thank God you're in."

"Emma! Did you get my messages about your parents forcing me to spill where you were? I've been trying to get ahold of you all morning."

"I did. After I had a nice little chat with my mother."

"Oh no. Was it bad? What am I saying? Of course it was bad. What did you do?"

"I told her I was staying with Jason and then I hung up on her."

Kate was silent for a long moment. "You're kidding, right?"

"Nope."

"Damn, girl, way to live your own life!"

The word "finally" hung in the air, but for once, Kate was tactful enough not to say what she so obviously meant.

Emma would have smiled at her friend's exuberant response, but she was all out of joy right now. "It felt great for about two hours."

Kate knew Emma's parents all too well. "They didn't drive up there to haul your butt home, did they? That's too much, even for them. You're in your thirties, for God's sake. Don't they know you're not their little girl anymore?"

"No, they didn't do that."

"Thank God."

"They sent Steven instead."

"Oh shit. That's so much worse."

"It was like a bad soap opera, Kate. Steven barged into Jason's restaurant, insisted I leave with him, and before I could get him to leave, Jason came out and got in the middle of it."

"I don't get it. Why would Steven have come?"

Emma laughed, a mirthless sound. "Especially since we both know he doesn't really want me back."

"You know I didn't mean it like that. He's an idiot for not wanting to be with you, but you're too good for him anyway. Are your parents holding something over his head?"

Emma forced herself to think clearly. "I'll bet they are. He mentioned something about my clients calling him and my father getting wind of it. I'll bet they've offered him a nice sum of money if he takes me back." Her words sinking in, she nearly sobbed, "How could my own parents think I'm so worthless that they have to buy someone to be with me?"

"Oh honey, they don't. They're just confused about who the best man is. They think it's Steven. We both know it isn't."

But Emma wasn't sure she knew anything anymore. Steven didn't really want her but would take her for the money. Jason acted like he wanted her one minute, and the next he was sending her away in another man's car as if the last few days hadn't meant anything to him at all.

"I take it Steven showing up didn't help anything," Kate said, breaking Emma's pained silence.

She sank down on Jason's bed, losing her tenuous hold on keeping it together. "He couldn't have picked a worse time. Jason was just starting to get comfortable with me again. I thought he was letting himself care for me, Kate. He has to know I'd never go back with Steven in a million years, doesn't he?"

"Have you told him?"

"Not exactly, but—"

"I don't want this to come out the wrong way, honey, but you chose Steven once before. How could Jason be certain that you wouldn't do it again?"

Emma hated how Kate was throwing her own fears back at her, making her actually look them in the eye. "Because I'm different now. I've changed."

"Are you sure?"

Emma shot up off the bed, her insides raging because she knew Kate was right. Four stolen days in Napa had barely made a dent in her life.

She hadn't really changed anything, had she?

Emma sank down onto the carpet. "I thought I was being so tough turning my back on my business and my parents for a few days, but what if I wimp out? I don't know if I'm strong enough to leave everything behind."

"Why not? What have you got to lose?"

She had to think about that. "Everyone's respect, I guess."

"Respect versus true love. Hmm, sounds like a difficult choice."

"Do you really think it could be that easy, Kate?"

She wanted Kate to say, *True love is always easy,* but wasn't the least bit surprised to hear, "No. Probably not. It'll probably hurt like a bitch and be the hardest thing you've ever done."

"Great," Emma mumbled, "that was just what I needed to hear."

"Maybe I should take some time off work and join you for a few days. Would that help?"

Emma wanted nothing more than to hold on to her best friend like a lifeline. But what she said was, "I think I need to fix this mess all by myself."

When the lunch rush slowed down, Rocco held out two beers and pushed open the door to the back alley. "Your life has become a goddamned roller coaster," he said to Jason. "I can't take it. I need a drink." Rocco downed his beer in one long gulp, then tossed the empty bottle into the Dumpster. Jason passed his over. "I take it you spent the past couple of days with Blondie? Showing her the sights?"

Jason shook his head over his stupidity. He'd done more than show Emma the sights. He'd nearly given her his heart again.

"I don't know what I was thinking."

Rocco shrugged. "You were thinking that she's hot and you were having a good time. Nothing wrong with that."

"I wanted revenge, not a good time."

"I remember."

"And I'm still going to make sure I get it."

"How so?"

"Her ex-husband wants her back."

Rocco squinted in the afternoon sun. "Yeah, so I heard. Sounds like he's a real prick."

"He is."

Rocco put down his second empty bottle. "So you're going to convince her to leave him for you and then once she's cut her ties you'll cut her off?"

Jason nodded.

"Doesn't sound like a very nice thing to do, boss."

"Tell that to someone who gives a fuck."

⟨◦⟩

Jason wasn't surprised to find Emma perched on the edge of his front porch swing. She'd fled his restaurant, but he had seriously doubted that she'd up and leave Napa so fast. Especially when he could tell she was only just settling in.

Her face was as pale as he'd ever seen it and her eyes were huge and frightened. But no matter how fragile she seemed to be, he refused to give in to the urge to comfort her, to feel sorry for her. After all, hadn't it been feeling sorry for her all those years ago that had gotten him into this whole mess? And then he'd gone and done it again. Stupid fuck that he was.

Not again. Not ever again. It had taken him years to get over her. Hell, he still wasn't over her. Given the way he'd behaved this week, he'd done nothing but dig a deeper hole for himself.

He'd taken the long way home to give himself time to pack his anger away, to manufacture a relaxed and friendly persona. In order for his plan to work, he needed her to think he was on her side. Moseying up the gravel pathway to his porch, he enjoyed watching her squirm, not knowing what he was going to say, how he was going to react.

Sitting down next to her on the porch swing, he said, "That was some unexpected visitor, wasn't it?"

She started, clearly shocked by his easygoing manner. "I'm sorry about that, Jason. He shouldn't have come here. Shouldn't have barged into your restaurant like that."

Jason shook his head, forcing himself to say the words he knew she needed to hear to make her stay. "I'm the one who should apologize."

"No," she said, turning to him, shaking her head.

He put his hand over hers, feeling how cold she was even though it had to be at least ninety degrees outside.

"Let me finish," he insisted. "I shouldn't have jumped to conclusions and made that comment about you going home with him." Giving her a look as filled with love as he could pull off considering she was the last person he wanted to love, he said, "I should have known you wouldn't walk out on me like that." He couldn't resist a little dig. "Not again. After all these years."

Instead of falling into his arms, Emma was staring at him, looking more confused than anything. Oh shit. Had he gone too far?

"Are you sure?" she asked, in a tentative voice. "You seemed so angry when you came out of the kitchen and saw him."

"Knee-jerk reaction," he said with a shrug. "He's not exactly my favorite person in the world," he said, thinking, *And neither are you.*

Jason knew revenge was going to be worth it in the long run. Too bad it was such a pain in the ass in the here and now. Because there was only so much lovey-dovey acting he could do before he hit his limit.

Still, just because he was going to be smart from here on out and firmly shut his heart off to her forever, didn't mean he was going to say no to any further seductions she had in mind. Seduction, of course, was all part and parcel of his plan.

Besides, sleeping with her was the only perk he had left and like hell if he was giving it up.

Emma could hardly believe the way Jason was acting. Rather than kicking her out of his life after seeing her with Steven, rather than mistrusting her motives—which he had every right to do, she supposed—he was acting more the devoted lover than ever.

But why, she wondered, should she be surprised by his support? Who in their right mind would want to go back to a cold sham of a marriage with a guy like Steven? Jason had always been more perceptive than anyone else she'd ever known.

She was trying to put her swirling emotions and newly budding happiness into words, when he said the one thing she'd dreamt of for so long.

"Move in with me Emma. Stay with me. Permanently."

Oh God, she was going to cry now. But only because all

her dreams were coming true. She'd thought her world was falling apart when Steven walked into Cravings, but evidently this was only the beginning. She couldn't speak, could only put her hands on the hollows of Jason's cheeks and kiss him softly, lovingly.

As her lips touched his, she almost thought she felt him flinch, but then he was taking her lips so passionately, so completely that she knew she'd been mistaken.

"Are you sure about this?" she said against his lips and when he said, "I've never been more certain about anything," she gave back into his kiss and made a decision.

From this point forward she needed to put her own fears away and stop imagining worst case scenarios. Ignoring her fears about the bubble bursting, Emma decided that she really was going to try to live her life one day at a time. Jason was offering her a miracle. And she was going to seize it—and him—with both hands.

"You don't have to rush back to the restaurant, do you?"

"Not for a couple of hours."

Her expression grew wistful. "Take me to bed, Jason." For once she didn't want to have sex standing up or on the floor. She wanted to feel like they were a couple, a real couple.

Certain he knew what she was asking from him, she held her breath as she waited for him to respond. It wasn't until he picked her up and carried her into the bedroom that she finally felt secure.

Laying her gently on the bed, he stared down at her, his eyes intense. For a moment, she thought he was going to speak, going to say something important. Was it too much to imagine that he was going to say, "I love you"?

But the moment passed and instead of making a passionate declaration of love he claimed her mouth. Ignoring a flash of disappointment that came from deep within, she wrapped her arms around his waist and clung to him, desperate for his touch.

Every time they made love she felt out of control, but knowing he wanted her to live with him took their sensual relationship to a whole other level.

"I want you so badly," she said, thrilled when he slid his hands beneath her skirt. Taking her mouth again in a hot kiss he found her slick and aroused.

"You're always so ready for me. So wet."

With a moan she broke away from his mouth. "I need you inside of me." She reached for him, trying to unzip his jeans even as she pulled him on top of her.

Moments later their clothes were off and he was poised over her naked body, her legs spread wide for him. And then he slid into her pussy and she arched her hips, wrapping her arms around his strong back, pulling his lips to hers. When the explosion came it rocked her to the core.

All of her dreams were coming true. Now the most important thing she could do was not chicken out. And the only way to make sure she didn't do that was to confess the deepest feelings in her heart.

"I love you, Jason. I never stopped loving you."

seventeen

Jason lay completely still in the dark, forcing his breathing to be shallow and even. Emma's head lay in the crook of his shoulder, one of her arms wrapped around his chest.

His lungs felt like they were going to burst. He wasn't getting enough oxygen in. He wanted to sprint around the neighborhood until he was too tired to think, pound Jack Daniels shots until he was completely numb. Do anything, anything at all, to get to the place where he could stop hearing her words. Stop hearing her say, *I love you, Jason. I never stopped loving you.* He needed to pull free of the web she continued to weave around him, binding him to her.

Using every ounce of self-control he possessed, he waited

until he knew for certain that she was asleep. Making the minimum of movements, he extracted himself from her clutches and grabbed his jeans and T-shirt on his way out the bedroom door.

He left the house without a second glance. Even his yard, his vines, which had once been his sanctuary, weren't enough distance for him now. Emma followed him like a ghost through his house, onto his front porch. He headed out his front door in his bare feet, out down the road, in no particular direction.

Right now he didn't care where he went. He just needed space.

No, he needed to never see Emma again. He needed to have never sought her out at the reunion. Why couldn't he have let sleeping dogs lie?

But he already knew the answer to that. Knew that he was as addicted to Emma as he had been at eighteen. And if he were going to be perfectly honest with himself—there was no point in anything else at this point—he knew he would always be addicted to her.

No matter what she did.

No matter how traitorous, how weak she was.

No matter what she said.

Jason knew that she'd said "I love you" to firmly lock him up in her trap.

Maybe yesterday he would have let himself believe that she meant it, that she was being honest with him. But he couldn't see things that way anymore. Not after seeing her with Steven and realizing once and for all how much better suited she was to being with her ex-husband than she would ever be with him.

He'd always known that Emma and Steven were two peas in a pod. Both golden, both privileged, both held hostage by the same rules of social propriety that had dictated their lives up until now and would continue to do so for the next sixty years.

They would have two golden-haired children, send them to only the best private schools, speak in hushed tones from across a heavily polished dining table, a table where the food wouldn't be any good.

And why should their food taste good? Life, for people like Emma and Steven, wasn't about joy. It wasn't about happiness. It was about coming out on top. Looking their best at all times.

Winning, no matter the cost.

Jason knew exactly why Steven had come all the way to Napa to take Emma home. He could practically see the wheels spinning in Steven's head: Like hell if he was going to lose out in the woman game to some low-life chef who'd had some lucky breaks.

In a way he had to appreciate Steven's way of thinking. And if this was just a man to man battle, then fine, Jason would get down and dirty and fight for what he wanted. And he'd win. Hands down. Jason knew that Steven wouldn't stand a chance. Because if Jason truly wanted Emma, he would have taken her.

Only, this war wasn't between Steven and Jason. Emma was Jason's true opponent.

The more his thoughts churned, the deeper his conviction grew that he needed to see his plan through. Because even though he was tempted to kick her out of his house now, to stop playing this game, to say, "I don't believe you'll ever love me," not like he loved her, he needed to wind things up with Emma on his own terms.

He'd left on her terms back in college. He'd accepted that he wasn't good enough for her, for her parents, for anyone or any part of her world.

But now she needed to know that the tables had turned.

And she wasn't good enough for him.

All of which meant that he needed to head back home, get back into bed with her, and continue convincing her that the two of them were going to be together forever.

He turned around and headed back toward his house, his legs heavy as cement, his heart cemented as well.

Still, something deep in his gut hurt. But that, he supposed, was just the price he was going to have to pay.

In the end, getting retribution was something he was doing solely for himself. Emma, he was convinced, would come out of this all just fine. She'd find herself another rich pansy to marry. She'd move back into her white-picket, two-story suburban paradise, and she'd forget all about him.

Any guilt he might have felt about the lies he was going to continue to tell her in the name of payback disappeared as he pictured her living her happily ever after with a Steven clone.

His mouth twisted grimly. The truth was, Jason knew he was the one who was going to pay the biggest price in the end. Because she would be living her new perfect life, while he would have to pick up the pieces and learn to get along without her.

Again.

Anger fueled him. Yes, he was going forward with his plans, but he was sane enough to know that he couldn't let things stretch on with Emma for much longer. Quite frankly, he couldn't take it.

The sooner she was gone, the better.

He'd have to work fast.

First things first, he needed to take everything away from her that she could easily go back to. Her home, her possessions. And especially her parents' love and respect.

~~~

"Let's go, sleepyhead."

Emma wrapped her hands around the hot cup of coffee Jason handed her. "Go?"

She didn't want to go anywhere ever again. She wanted to stay in bed all day. She was so tired. Utterly worn out from her confrontation with Steven. Drained from the fear she'd felt as she'd waited for Jason to come back to his house. Shattered and then put back together again at the wonderful realization that he not only wasn't going to kick her out of his life, but that he wanted her to stay with him permanently.

And then her confession of love last night, knowing he'd been fast asleep and hadn't heard her, but still wondering when he was ever going to say it back to her. If he was ever going to really love her the way she loved him.

No, she told herself, as she turned her attention to blowing the steam off the hot coffee, away from the odd confusion of her thoughts, of course he loved her. Why else would he ask her to move in? Tell her not to leave him? Say that he was sorry she had to deal with Steven, that he hadn't said the right thing at the right time because he'd been too surprised by her ex's appearance in his restaurant?

Jason smiled at her, a smile that spoke of his understanding of her exhaustion. And yet, something in his eyes said he knew what would make her feel better, give her energy to face her life again.

"To your house. To get your things."

It was as the roof had been ripped off of his ranch house and sun was streaming over the bed, straight onto her. She wiggled into a more upright position.

"You want to go with me? Don't you have to work today?" she asked, incredibly pleased that he not only wanted her to move in with him, but that he was going to take another day off of work to do it.

He waved his hand in the air. "Rocco's got things covered. And besides, you're so much more important than my job. Don't you know that?"

No, she didn't know that. And she wasn't even sure that she believed him. But she wasn't going to ruin everything, mess up this perfect moment, by saying that.

"Thanks," she said softly, but before she could get out of bed and give him a kiss, he was heading for the door.

"By the time you're showered and dressed, breakfast will be waiting."

He winked at her and then was gone. Emma put the coffee cup down on the bedside table and closed her eyes. Everything was perfect, all she'd ever wanted was coming to fruition. So then why did she feel so muddled? So unsure?

The easiest explanation was the one she grabbed hold of. All of her uncertainty, all of her fear about moving forward in this new life with Jason, must have come from her upbringing. From the way her parents had coddled her and then planned every last second of her future.

Moving in with Jason was the first time she had ever done something entirely on her own. Something that wasn't in her parents' plan or her ex-husband's plan.

That had to be the reason she was so frightened, why she wasn't jumping out of bed to embrace the day, to head to Palo Alto with Jason and pack up her things. Certainly he hadn't given her any cause to doubt his motives.

But questions jiggled away inside her nonetheless. As she kicked the sheets off her legs and headed for the shower, she wondered if he had really been asleep when she'd professed her love. Or had he just been pretending? And if so, why would he do that?

Not that she was going to ask him any of the above, of course. She didn't want to rock the boat. Not now that they were both finally on it.

A knock sounded on the bathroom door. "Five minutes to hot waffles."

Jason's cheerful voice worked like magic and her doubts vanished. The man she loved wanted to be with her. She couldn't possibly ask for more.

Jason whistled as they stood on Emma's doorstep two hours later. "Big house."

She bit her lip. "Too big. I guess I always thought I'd have kids to fill it, but . . . " She waited for Jason to reassure her, to tell her that they'd have plenty of kids together, but he didn't.

Shaking off her unreasonable disappointment, she unlocked the door. "It's nothing like your house," she started to explain, wanting him to be prepared for the beige-and-white world that she'd inhabited for so long, so different from his colorful, interesting home.

"I didn't think it would be," was all he said, and she couldn't decide if she was imagining the hard edge to his voice. But then he turned and smiled at her and she knew that she was doing just that.

Why did that little voice inside insist on being such a killjoy, she wondered helplessly? Any other woman would have been over the moon about moving in with Jason. No second thoughts, no wondering if it was the right step. No worrying if he really loved her as much as she loved him. No tormenting herself over whether they could really make things work, if they'd actually managed to resolve their past or if they were simply going to pretend nothing bad had ever happened?

Not having been inside her house in nearly a week, Emma was shocked by the sight before her. How had she never noticed how utterly lifeless it was? There wasn't a shred of personality on the walls, in the bookshelves, or in the furnishings.

"A decorator help you with this?" he asked. His words didn't hold any judgment, merely curiosity. Still, she felt frozen by his question, didn't know how to respond, how to admit that she hadn't even been in control of this one little aspect of her life, until he grinned and added, "Because I'm thinking you should ask for your money back, if that's the case."

She giggled then, glad that he'd broken the ice on this very strange trip to her house, the house she'd shared with Steven.

"She might have been color-blind," she managed to joke and was thrilled to see his eyes light up in appreciation.

"No shit. What, did she think the color police were going to come in here and arrest you if she used anything other than beige, gray, and white?"

Emma nodded, her giggles turning into full-on laughter. "My mother loved it," she finally managed.

Jason shook his head. "Of course she did. And that's why I'm about to institute a new rule."

Emma raised her eyebrow. She was impressed—and somewhat disappointed, to tell the total truth—that he hadn't taken a potshot at her mother again, especially when she'd given him the perfect opening.

"We're not taking one single thing out of here that *you* don't love."

She shook her head. "Then we can pretty much get back in the car right now."

He frowned. "You're kidding, right? You don't own anything that's really you? That you can't live without?"

Emma had to think about that. "No, wait. I do. It's in the garage."

Five years ago she and Kate had been to lunch in San Francisco when they'd walked past a gallery whose paintings had absolutely called out to Emma. Bright showy flowers, thick acrylic paint, chunky enough to dip your finger into. She hadn't bought one then, but she couldn't get the images out of her head. A week later, after a gala lunch, she'd gone back to the gallery, pulled out her business checkbook, and with shaky hands had paid for the painting.

But she'd never had the guts to actually put it up. Steven would have hated it. The saddest thing, Emma now realized as she pulled the large canvas out from behind boxes of old tax records, was that she hadn't bothered to hang it up even when Steven moved out last year.

"That's a Sam Marshall, isn't it?"

She looked up in surprise from the painting that evoked such a mixture of memories. "Yes, it is. You recognize his work?"

Jason nodded. "He's good friend of mine, actually. Lives and works just up the road. That was some of his earlier work, I believe. You've had it stashed in the garage all this time?"

Emma grimaced. "It never seemed to fit in with the rest of the house."

"No kidding."

She didn't bother taking offense to his blunt statement. Not when it was so true. Frankly, she didn't want to be in her house anymore. Not with Jason.

"I can come back and pack by myself another day."

But she could see the determination in his eyes. "Nope. I want to help you pack up everything you need today, even if we need to rent a U-Haul truck to drive it all back up to my house. That way you can put your house on the market right away."

She spun around, nearly dropping the painting. Jason reached out and grabbed it before the heavy gold frame clattered to the floor.

"Sell my house?" She barely left off the words, *Are you crazy?*

Jason's eyebrows furrowed in confusion. "I thought that's what we'd agreed on."

"We did. I mean, I'm going to move in with you, but I hadn't though about—"

"What do you need the house for? You're not planning on coming back here, so . . ."

A warning bell went off in the back of her mind. It wasn't like Jason to be so pushy. But as he waited silently, letting the implications of his unsaid words sink in, she realized that if she didn't sell her house, it would be akin to telling him she didn't have faith in their relationship. That she wanted a back up plan just in case things went wrong.

But nothing was going to go wrong this time, she was sure of it. Or almost sure of it, anyway.

Angry with herself for not having the guts, the faith, and certainly not anywhere near the kind of self-esteem she needed to be certain of Jason's love for her, Emma forced a smile.

"Of course, you're right. I guess things have been moving so fast that I haven't been thinking of all the details."

"You work with lots of real estate agents in your line of work, don't you?"

She nodded. "Yes, I do."

"Why don't you call one now, get the ball rolling? I'll bet a place like this gets snapped up pretty fast in Palo Alto."

Numbly, she pulled out her cell phone. He was right, of course he was. No time like the present to close out the rest of her past, a past she wanted nothing to do with anymore.

eighteen

J ason almost felt bad about what he was making Emma
do. Almost, but not quite. Because even though he was
taking away her potential refuge, this house was bad for her.

It reeked of submission and sadness and he couldn't stand
the idea of Emma going back to this house after he dumped
her ass. Yes, he wanted to hurt her, just like she'd hurt him.
But then, when enough time had passed, he actually found
himself hoping that she'd find the guts to create a good life
for herself.

One that she really wanted to live. Not one that some decorator hired by her status-obsessed mother had put together
for her.

The painting he'd just loaded into his car spoke volumes

about the real Emma. Too bad he'd never be able to trust that girl. Too much had come between them, too many lies, too much pride.

When he walked back inside the house she was throwing clothes into a huge beige heap in the middle of her enormous walk-in closet.

"Nice packing technique."

"I'm not packing."

He raised an eyebrow and surveyed the growing heap. "Then what, exactly, are you doing?"

A smile played on her lips as she emptied an entire wing of the closet onto the floor. "I'm giving everything away to charity."

"That's too bad," he said, grinning. "Some poor unsuspecting lady might accidentally buy these clothes. And wear them." He faked a shiver of fright.

Hands on her hips, she said, "What's your brilliant suggestion?"

"We could burn them."

She looked disbelieving for a moment and then laughed. "It's not a bad idea, but unfortunately there's plenty of wear in most of this stuff."

Jason picked up a truly boring khaki dress that he was certain would have washed Emma's pale features away entirely. "Calvin Klein. And it's still got the tags on."

Her face crumbled. "Isn't that horrible? I was so depressed with my life that I shopped to fill the void." She didn't seem to expect any reply. "Which obviously didn't work because I was just buying more of the same awful stuff."

Jason hated that he felt sorry for her and realized he had two choices. Either say something he was going to regret

later, like "Don't feel bad, everyone makes mistakes." Or
pick up an armful of clothes and take them out to the car.

He chose option two. "I'll load the car up and do a drop-
off at the donation center on University Avenue."

Any excuse to get out of this prison Emma had called
home. Steven's uptight, smug vibes fairly radiated off the
walls.

Shit, while he was at it, once he dropped the clothes off,
maybe he'd stop by a bar for a quick drink. He needed something to make it through the rest of the day.

Jason hadn't spent a lot of time near the Stanford campus
since he'd graduated. He'd been perfectly happy to carve out
a new life in the wine country, which seemed so far removed
from this suburbia, even though it was only ninety minutes
away.

Looking around at the soccer moms in their huge, unnec-
essary SUVs and the stressed-out college students downing
espresso shots while pretending to study at sidewalk cafés, he
wasn't terribly surprised to find he didn't miss it.

He liked his life in Napa, his work as a chef, the respect
he received from his colleagues and fellow locals alike. Trust
Emma to come back into his life to make him question everything he'd been comfortable with for so long.

It wasn't that something was missing in his life. Well, that
wasn't exactly true, he acknowledged, as he passed heaps of
Emma's unworn clothes over to the Goodwill volunteer. He'd
almost gotten married a couple of times, both women the
polar opposites of Emma. Lush brunettes, as free with their
bodies and appetites as they were with their emotions. He'd

thought they were women he could be happy with, spend the rest of his life with, have kids, the whole nine yards. But both women had called things off not long after the engagement, calling him emotionally unavailable. Saying he didn't know what he wanted. Accusing him of always prioritizing his work over them.

They were right about that last complaint. He always had been more comfortable spending long hours in his kitchen rather than going home early for a cozy drink by the fire.

Emma was the only woman he'd ever cut out on work for. Rocco had commented on it this morning, saying, "Never seen you take two days off in one week, boss. You feeling all right?"

Jason had insisted, "Never been better. Just have some important things to take care of."

He could practically feel Rocco's disapproval reverberating through the phone. "You gotta do what you gotta do, boss."

"Damn right I do," Jason said, slamming his cell phone shut, wondering exactly where Rocco got off acting so high and mighty about treating women right when Rocco was as big a player as they came.

Granted, he'd never acted out of a premeditated plan for revenge.

Jason was getting back in his car when he heard a familiar voice calling out his name. "Jason! Wait up."

"Kate," he said, reaching out to give Emma's best friend a hug. "How's it going?"

He'd always liked Kate, never blamed her in any way for what Emma had done. In fact, back in college, he'd wished he could have fallen for a girl like Kate. Someone easy and uncomplicated. A girl without a steel rod up her ass.

"I'm great. The question is, how are you? And what are you doing here in Palo Alto?"

"Doing good, thanks. Just dropping some things off for Emma."

Her eyebrows furrowed. "Why?"

Giving her one of his most reassuring smiles, the kind he employed on TV to relax everyone and let them know that he was a good guy they could trust, he said, "She's moving in with me."

Kate's mouth fell open. "Are you kidding me?"

He couldn't resist saying, "Surprised?"

Her open face grew uncharacteristically serious. "Whose idea was this?"

"Mine."

"Don't you think it's a little soon to be moving in together?"

"Not really."

She stared at him. "You love her that much, huh?"

He swallowed and forced out, "I do."

"Uh-huh." He could tell she didn't believe him, and he was trying to figure out a way out of the conversation when her pager and cell phone both beeped.

"Crap. I'm late for a meeting. Two, actually. Tell Emma I'll call her tonight."

As he watched Kate run off in impossibly high heels, Jason began to feel like Emma's social director. Steven and Kate could pass their messages on to Emma themselves.

⌒

Emma kept busy while Jason was gone, but after an hour had passed she started to worry. What if he'd changed his mind about everything and decided to head back to Napa without her? She hated how insecure she felt, but she couldn't help it.

It was only during those moments when she was in Jason's arms, when he was kissing her and making her feel like the only woman he'd ever want, that she felt truly safe. But all the befores and afters kept her on shaky ground.

Even now. When there was absolutely no reason for her to be worried anymore.

Well, except for the small matter of his not having said "I love you" yet. Looking at things in that light, putting her house up for sale and moving to Napa seemed extremely premature.

If she were brave, if she had any faith in herself at all—or in their relationship, for that matter—she'd say that very thing to him.

She heard his footsteps coming down the hall and relief washed over her. He'd come back. In the back of her mind she foresaw a hundred nights of waiting at home for him. Was she going to live the rest of her life worried about whether he was truly committed to her?

He smiled as he plopped down on her bed, but something seemed different about him, something seemed to have changed in his eyes and the lines of his face in the past hour.

"Is everything okay?" she asked, barely brave enough to turn her fears into that very general question. Granted, it wasn't *Are you sure about us?* Or, *Do you think we should take this slower?*

"I haven't driven around Palo Alto in years."

She cocked her head to the side. Now that wasn't the reply she expected at all. Especially since Palo Alto was all she knew. She'd grown up here. Gone to school here. Married and bought a house here.

"Does it feel strange to be back?"

He shrugged, then said, "It does, actually." Piercing her with his gaze he said, "Lots of memories I hadn't expected."

Emma wanted to comfort him. But the only way she knew how to do that was with her body. And she knew that having sex with Jason in the bed that she and Steven had shared—or anywhere else in her house, for that matter—would be horribly wrong.

They needed to get back on level ground, go back to Napa. He'd sacrificed another day at his restaurant and made the drive to support her in clearing out her things, in saying good-bye to her old life. She'd be forever thankful, she realized with sudden clarity.

This really was good-bye. To a home that never really was.

Besides, he wasn't the only one who wanted to leave this mausoleum. A couple of hours in this house was more than enough to convince her that selling was the right thing to do.

"I'm all done here. Let's go back to Napa. Right now."

He gestured to the two suitcases by the door. "That's it? That's all you're taking?"

She took a deep breath and scanned her bedroom once more. "I never realized how little everything in this house meant to me until today."

"I'm sorry," he said, but she didn't want him to apologize for making her see things straight.

"Don't be. How many people get a chance to start fresh? This is my second chance." She turned to him and ran her hand over his beautifully square jaw. "Thanks to you." Going up on her tippy-toes, she gently kissed his lips. "Ready to get out of here?"

"Hell yes."

He lifted her into his arms, carrying her out of the house and into his car. She felt like a blushing bride, even though she'd just been taken away from an old home, rather than brought into a new one. A minute later he threw her luggage in the trunk and backed out of her driveway so fast he left tire tracks on the beige pavers.

It seemed a fitting good-bye.

nineteen

Marvin's tail wagged excitedly as they walked up Jason's front steps and plopped her bags on his porch. "He must know you're staying."

Emma smiled. "Go to your restaurant. I know you've got work to do."

Jason seemed confused by her non sequitor for a moment. And then he smiled. "You sure?"

She nodded. "I've got some things to take care of as well. Mind if I use your home office?"

"Sure." She followed him inside and he flipped on his computer. "It's always online, so you're good for the Internet. Got some important business to take care of?"

She licked her lips, wondering if telling him the plan she'd

come up with in the car on the drive back to the wine country was going to freak him out.

"It's a big secret, huh?"

She grinned, finally deciding that since he was the one to
suggest she sell her house, informing him of her next set of
plans shouldn't be enough to make him run.

A voice in her head wondered, *What exactly, then, will be
enough to make him run?* but she forced it away, chalking it up to
nerves over the huge steps she was taking to change her life.

"No, not really. I just figured that since I'm selling my
house, I might as well move the bulk of my business to Napa
as well."

Something froze in his face and she stopped breathing.
Oh God, he thought she was coming on too strong. Maybe
he'd expected her to live in Napa but commute to Palo Alto
or do her work over the phone. After all, they'd never really
talked about her day to day, so he might have assumed she
could take care of things long-distance.

But then, he looked unexpectedly pleased and proud of
her for doing such a bold, brave thing. "Great idea," he said.
"You're right, it really doesn't make sense to have your main
office in Palo Alto anymore."

"I know it's a big step . . . " she began, uncertain of what
she was actually trying to say.

"The perfect step," he murmured, pulling her against the
hard planes of his body. "Exactly what I want you to do."

Emma wondered at his choice of words. *Exactly what he
wanted her to do.* She knew it was unreasonable to feel this
way, when he was being nothing but supportive, but she
wished he had said something more like, *"I just want you to do
what's right for you. Whatever will make you happy."*

But then he tilted her face up to his and kissed her slow and soft, making all of her unfounded doubts flee. "You're making me so happy."

She loved making him happy, making him feel good. Somehow, someway, she'd figure out a way to get over her stupid insecurities and accept the truth of Jason's affection. Without always waiting for the other shoe to drop.

"Looks like we've both got work to do. I'll see you tonight," he said, closing his office door softly behind him as he left.

Marvin sat at Emma's feet, staring at her expectantly. She almost felt as if he were saying, *Okay then, get on it with it.*

She grinned, and feeling braver than she'd ever been, opened her cell phone, logged into her e-mail, and began the process of changing her life for the better.

⌒

Jason felt like a complete shit. No matter how he tried to frame his actions, he was being an asshole. *But she deserves it,* he told himself, only to have that same self answer, *So she dumped you ten years ago. Get over it already!*

But that was just the thing. He wasn't over it. He wasn't over her. He never would be, and that made him angry. Angry enough that he'd just convinced her to sell her house and, now, restructure her business as well.

But now that the reality of leaving her with nothing to fall back on slammed into his gut, he didn't know if he could let her go through with it.

Rocco looked up when he walked in. "Wasn't expecting to see you here, boss."

Jason threw on an apron and washed his hands, glad to be back in the familiar smells and sounds of his kitchen. It was a place where he didn't have to think if he didn't want to, where he could get by with just his hands and his instincts.

He didn't feel like explaining himself to Rocco, so he simply said, "The trip went faster than I thought it would."

Rocco grunted. "Everything still going according to your master plan?"

Jason focused on slicing a pile of mushrooms. Really, none of this was Rocco's business. He should have never discussed his personal life with him in the first place.

"Having second thoughts, boss?"

Jason nearly sliced into his forefinger then. "Just shut up and get to work before I shove this cleaver up your ass," he growled, feeling like a prick for more reasons than one.

That same familiar voice from earlier in the day rang out with a loud tap-tap-tap on the kitchen door. "Anyone home?"

Kate's red curls bounced across her breasts as she let herself into Jason's private domain without asking permission. Rocco moved faster than Jason had ever seen a six-four, 280-pound ball of muscles move outside of a basketball court.

"I hope you're looking for me," his sous chef said, looking for all the world like he'd just been struck by a lightning bolt. Of true love. Jason wanted to puke.

Kate looked Rocco up and down saucily, her gaze resting on his thick right bicep. She ran one long, blood-red finger tip over a tattoo of a naked, voluptuous woman. Jason was about to drag her by her hair out to the parking lot to ask what the hell she was doing in his restaurant when she finally said, "I wasn't, but I'm certainly willing to reconsider."

"Kate," Jason interrupted in a hard tone.

She turned to him and put her smile away. Evidently, only Rocco deserved kindness today. Jason had an ugly, uncomfortable sense that she could see right through him. He didn't like it. Not one bit.

"Long time no see," she said in an equally hard tone.

Respect for the way Emma's best friend took care of her warred with his sense that all of his plans were about to be thwarted. "Let's talk privately," he said, not interested in having another big public scene in his restaurant.

For ten years, his employees had thought he was a nice guy who cooked great food. But now that dozens of skeletons were leaping out of the closet, he was sure they had to be wondering what else he'd been hiding all along.

Kate followed him out to the deserted back alley, the space he was starting to think of as his second office. He ran a hand over the light stubble coating his jaw. In so many ways Emma had been a ray of light—there was no point in denying that—but at the same time, he could feel himself getting burned, and one layer at a time his old skin was peeling away.

Leaving what behind, he wasn't sure.

"Nice alley," Kate said, covering her eyes against the bright late afternoon sun.

Not interested in drawing this out any longer than he had to, Jason cut right through the small talk. "I doubt you came here to talk about the view."

She turned to him, looking sad. "I wish I had. I've always liked you, Jason."

"The feeling is mutual."

"Okay then, since we're friends, why don't you tell me what's going on."

He stared at her, a muscle working in his jaw. "With what?"

Her hand fisted in frustration. "Don't play the dumb guy card with me. You know exactly what I'm talking about. What are you doing with Emma?"

He thought fast. "Rekindling the old flame."

"Uh-huh. So let me get this straight. You haven't been in touch with her for ten years and all of a sudden you want to be her boyfriend again? Just like that?"

"Why not?" he said, in lieu of anything better to say, because he certainly couldn't think of a story Kate would buy.

"One day you woke up and decided to let bygones be bygones?"

It was perfectly clear to Jason that Kate was one hell of a prosecutor. Not only did she see right through him, but she had a way of phrasing things that made him feel like a complete jackass.

"You've got it."

Kate's fierce expression changed so quickly, Jason was completely thrown off his defensive stance. "I know you still love her, Jason."

She let her words sink in, let him sit with them, stew in them, gave them time to run through his head again and again. It was the cruelest thing she could have done, a brilliant tactic on her part. Because he knew she was right. And that even if he stuck with his plans for payback, Emma wasn't the only one who was going to hurt.

He was going to lose everything too.

Only, he couldn't see another way.

Finally she spoke again. "Now that you're back together again, Emma won't let herself believe in anything but the fairy tale finally coming true. But you already know that, don't you?" Jason tried to keep his expression neutral. "And that's great if you really are her knight in shining armor, but as someone who's been there for her day in and day out for the past ten years—the same ten years that you were AWOL—I want you to know that she deserves that fairy tale. Every damn bit of it. The guy on the white horse. The red rose. The kiss on the lips. The perfect ending in the sunset. She deserves it more than any person I've ever known."

Kate stopped and Jason hoped, prayed, she was done reaming him in the heart. But she wasn't. Not quite.

"So if you are planning on letting her down—easy, not so easy, I don't know how you're going to do it—all I'm asking is that you do it soon."

The muscle in his jaw started twitching again, just as she added, "I'm not saying you don't have a right to be pissed at her, because you do. What she did to you in college was rotten. Just be honest with her, Jason. She deserves to know the truth about how you feel. Because if you don't tell her, I will."

With that, she brushed past him, back into the kitchen, calling out to Rocco, "I'll be at Jason's when you're ready to pick me up for our date tonight."

Jason's doorbell rang and Emma glanced up from the laptop keyboard where she was firing off e-mails to her office managers. Obviously Jason wouldn't bother ringing his own doorbell. Oh no, Steven hadn't come back, had he? Or worse, had her parents decided it was time to drag her back home?

Please God, not today, she prayed. She couldn't deal with one more thing today. Wasn't putting her house on the market and moving the main branch of her business to Napa enough for one day?

In no rush to find out who was waiting for her behind Jason's wooden red door, the doorbell had rung again by the time she opened it.

Her best friend grabbed her in a bear hug and she breathed out in relief. "Kate, I'm so glad it's you."

"Steven wouldn't have the guts to bother you two days in a row."

"I thought maybe you were my parents."

Kate shivered. "Let's cross our fingers that they'll wait patiently at home for you to come to your senses, okay?"

They both plopped down on an oversized sofa chair in Jason's living room. "I love his house. It's so colorful."

Emma nodded. "Me too. In some ways, I guess this was the kind of house I've always wanted to live in."

"So, how are you feeling?"

Emma bit her lip. "Alive for the first time in years."

"But?"

"Scared."

Kate nodded. "That makes sense. I mean, with you moving up here so quickly."

Emma frowned. "How did you know I'm moving in with Jason?"

"He didn't tell you that I saw him in Palo Alto outside of the Goodwill this afternoon?"

Emma shook her head. "No, he didn't."

Kate tried to brush it off, but somethings didn't ring true as she said, "Hmmm. It probably doesn't mean anything. We barely saw each other for thirty seconds. I was late to a meeting downtown."

All of Emma's fears rushed back, especially in the wake of the huge changes she was making. Why wouldn't he have mentioned seeing Kate? "What if it does mean something? I mean, I put my house on the market today and—"

"You what?"

"Not only that but I'm going to hire a manager for my Palo Alto office and open a new mortgage company here in Napa." Emma voiced her biggest fear. "But what if something goes wrong with us? What if we don't work out? I won't have much of anything to go back to, will I?"

Kate pushed her lips together so hard they nearly turned white beneath her bold red lipstick. "No, I don't suppose you would."

Trying hard to look on the positive side, Emma said, "But you know, when we were in my house today I realized that I don't need it anymore. I never liked it. I didn't even pick it out. My father did, with Steven."

"You never told me that."

Emma nodded. "It was a done deal by the time we drove over to it. My big birthday surprise."

"They bought you a house for your birthday? How about giving you a necklace or bracelet like normal people?"

"I always felt like I should be so appreciative. It was so big."

"And beige," Kate said on a giggle.

"I saw it through new eyes today. And I hated it. Every square inch. Every sofa. Every painting. Everything in my closet. All I took with me were two suitcases."

Kate's eyes grew considering. "Then it sounds like no matter what happens with Jason, you're doing the right thing in selling your house." She paused, then asked, "Do you like being out here in the wine country?"

Emma smiled and sank back into the cushions. "I love it. It feels like home. Even though I've barely been here a week, I already feel a hundred times more comfortable than I ever did in Palo Alto."

Kate squeezed Emma tightly. "I'm happy for you. Happy that you're making changes you've needed to make for quite a while."

Emma keenly heard what Kate didn't say. *I'm happy you're with Jason again, that things are working out so well for the two of you.* But she didn't want to fight with her best friend, she didn't want to have to defend her love for Jason and her new, big life changes, so she merely said, "Not that it isn't great to see you, but . . . "

Kate smacked Emma on the shoulder. "Don't worry. I'm not here to interrupt your sex-fest with the hunky chef." Emma's cheeks burned red, but she didn't deny that that was exactly what had been going on day and night. "I've got a date with a fella from Jason's kitchen. Big strapping lad with tattoos."

"Rocco?" Emma couldn't have been more surprised if Kate had just said she was a lesbian. "He's nothing like the zillionaires you usually go out with."

Kate smiled a secret smile. "I know. He's so much bigger. Hunkier. I just want to take a bite out of him."

Emma tilted her head to the side. "How'd you meet?"

Kate waved away her question. "Long boring story, you don't want to hear it. Now tell me everything that's been going on for the past week while I change into something lower cut and higher heeled."

Emma followed Kate through Jason's house, amazed at how effortless her best friend's confidence was. Emma would have given anything to be like Kate. But after this week, she knew that no matter how hard she tried to be a self-assured sex goddess, no matter how good Jason thought her moves were in bed, she was still the same Emma on the inside.

It was a hard realization, and yet, one that helped her see things in a true light. She was always going to love Jason. And she was always going to worry about not being good enough to keep him around. So really, if those were the two constants in her world, she might as well give in to them and let herself love him for as long as he let her.

twenty

Rocco picked Kate up a couple hours later. Watching brand-new sparks crackle between them, Emma wished she could hit the rewind button. If only she and Jason could start over again. From the first day they met. Their first kiss. If she knew what she knew now—which admittedly, didn't feel like a whole lot, although she was gaining smarts every day—she would never have chosen Steven. She would never have turned her back on a love that was so true, so powerful, for something plastic and fake and horribly overrated.

Tonight she would talk to Jason, really talk to him about her fears, her concerns. She had to. Sure, it had only been one day, twenty-four hours since he'd asked her to move in, and yet she couldn't go on wondering why, constantly asking herself if things could possibly work between them in the long term with so much unresolved history.

Her house and mortgage company were just details. Her reservations and unanswered questions went so much deeper than that.

Why had he come to the reunion? Why had he asked her to join him by the lake? In the lake. Why hadn't he turned her away when she showed up in Napa on Monday? Why had he asked her to move in with him by Wednesday night?

She'd sensed so much hardness in him this week even as he'd loved her better than she'd ever been loved before. She could no longer turn away from it, no longer deny his anger because it was the easy way out.

Unable to sit alone in his house any longer, she decided to go have dinner. At Cravings. She didn't want to bother him while he was working, and she wouldn't, but at the end of the night she wanted to make sure they talked. Until then, being in his restaurant was as close as being with him.

An hour later, during which she tried on all of her new outfits only to find each and every one of them lacking, she was seated in a nice, corner table of his restaurant where she could watch the action. Julie, the waitress she'd helped out the day before, winked at her and Emma felt that maybe, just maybe, this was a sign that everything would be okay. That everything would work out.

Everything on Jason's menu looked amazing and so incredibly decadent. Falling into her usual pattern of searching for the lowest-calorie item on the menu, she stopped and took a deep breath.

She didn't need to do this to herself anymore, did she? Jason said he'd think she was beautiful if she had lush curves, hadn't he?

Somewhere in the back of her brain, a voice asked, *"So now you're going to gain weight to make him happy? Isn't that the same thing as losing weight to please your mother?"*

But no, Emma refused to think that the two things could have anything at all to do with one another. Of course she wasn't eating fattening foods just because Jason wanted her to. What a ridiculous idea.

Fortunately, an instant later, she found she didn't need to worry about making any decisions about the menu when Julie came by her table with a big glass of champagne. "On the house, courtesy of the boss."

A glow started all the way down at Emma's toes. "Isn't that sweet?"

Julie raised an eyebrow. "Just between us girls, I've never seen him like this." Emma grinned but then Julie added, "Almost as if he's not here half the time."

Maybe that was romantic, but to Emma, something about it sounded not quite right. Jason had always been the most fully present person she knew. She didn't like to think of him being out to lunch while on the job.

"Oh. Okay."

Julie didn't seem to notice anything amiss, so Emma said, "I have no idea what to order. It all looks so good." And so fattening.

"No problem. How about I put together a meal for you of Jason's best?"

A customer across the room waved Julie over and Emma nodded quickly. "Go ahead and take care of your real customers. I'm just going to sit here and enjoy being pampered."

Two hours later, Emma had tasted heaven. Each bite was better than the next. She felt sated and sleepy, envisioning a night of slow, passionate lovemaking. Her irrational fears would be there in the morning at which point they could have their long overdue discussion.

Relaxing into the comfortable chair, Emma let a new-found, champagne-fueled sense of peace take her over, feeling certain that nothing could ruin her night.

⌒

Kate openly admired Rocco's enormous muscles over the glass of Pinot he'd poured her in the middle of a vineyard.

"Isn't someone going to come out here with a shotgun and nail us for trespassing soon?"

"If the owner was going to nail you," he replied with a lusty grin, "he wouldn't use a shotgun."

"So you're already thinking of nailing me, huh?" she said, sending his blood racing, and then added, "I take it you're the landowner in question?"

"You'd better not use too many lawyer phrases with me," he said, grinning even wider. "I'm just a lowly sous-chef. Although, I have to admit hearing you say things like 'landowner in question' is a huge turn on."

Knowing exactly what she was doing to him with her generous curves, her luscious red mouth, and her dirty, brilliant mind, she gestured lazily to the vines that surrounded them. "So you're a low-ranking kitchen worker who just so happens to own a huge vineyard?"

Pleased that she was impressed, he merely said, "Call it a lucky real estate move back when land was cheap a few years back."

She raised an eyebrow, but merely drank her wine. "I'll make a deal with you." His gaze was still on the vines, but he knew she could see how hard his cock was against the zipper of his jeans, that he was on the verge of pressing her back into the blanket and kissing that sassy, clever smirk off her face. "You tell me what you know about Jason and Emma and I'll make sure you get lucky again."

Rocco wasn't stupid. He knew that Kate had two reasons for going out with him. One, because she wanted him to fuck her brains out. Which he would gladly do. And two, because she wanted to save her best friend, Emma, from heartache. All afternoon, he'd struggled with his conscience where Jason was concerned.

On the one hand, they went back a long way, and Rocco hated the thought of giving up one of his most valued friendships because he squealed to Emma's girlfriend.

But what Rocco couldn't get away from—male bonding aside—was that Jason was doing the wrong thing. A bad thing. Something that could ruin not only his life, but Emma's as well. He saw the way they looked at each other, like they'd never seen anything so beautiful, so important, so perfect. Why couldn't Jason just admit how he really felt and get over the past?

Someone had to pull Jason's head out of his ass. And as Rocco took another long admiring glance at Kate's lush red curls, her long fingers—fingers that could do a hell of a lot of damage to his cock and hopefully would—he knew that if anyone had the panache to force Jason to own up to his stupid revenge plan, it was this woman. Not, of course, that he was going to give her any information for free.

"I don't know," he said, rolling over onto his back. "What's in it for me?"

Kate put her glass down on the wild grass and licked her lips. "Oh, so you're going to play it like that, are you?"

Rocco shifted slightly to give his throbbing erection more room in his pants. "Ever heard of buying off a defendant?"

She dropped her gaze to this bulging zipper. "I'm not going to buy you off, honey. I'm going to blow you."

"Sweet Jesus."

She ran her nails down his chest, stopping at the button on his pants. "You'll be yelling out a whole lot more than that by the time I'm done with you, but only if you give me what I want." She popped the button open on his jeans and gently held his zipper between her thumb and forefinger. "Start talking."

"Have mercy on me, lawyer girl," he begged.

Obviously no stranger to being in the driver's seat—both in bed and the courtroom—she shook her head. "You want me to let your cock out of prison, tell me something I want to hear."

Intense desire imprinted itself on Rocco's bad boy features. "I can't believe you're making me sell out my buddy," he said, acting like he hadn't already made this decision without her help.

"I'm getting bored, tattoo boy."

"Shit, you drive a hard bargain," he said, shifting again, pushing his pelvis up into her hand. Just as her fingers were slipping off the metal zipper, he said, "She screwed him over a bunch of years ago."

Kate's lips turned up just the slightest bit, letting Rocco know she was pleased that he'd finally decided to talk. She pulled his zipper down all the way and his fly burst open, hardly able to contain his massive erection.

"Don't tell me things I already know," she said, mistress to her slave. "One more slip and your cock will never know how good it feels to slide between my lips."

Rocco's words merged with his groan. "He wants pay-back. For what she did."

Her movements deft, she pulled his thick penis out from the waistband of his black boxer shorts. "Very nice work, Rocco," she praised, her fist closing around his throbbing cock. "Very nice, indeed." And then she murmured, "Payback, huh?"

He nodded, hoping she was going to be wrapping up the interrogation soon. He was this close to yanking her ankles over his shoulders and plunging into her, foreplay be damned. "Yeah, that's what he says. But they've been going at it like bunny rabbits for the past week."

"I guessed that," she said, bending her head so that her hair brushed across his about-to-blow cock.

He was impressed that he could still speak. "He's fucked in the head. Been trying to tell him that too."

Her breath a whisper against the soft skin stretched over his cock, she said, "Why would he take her back like this after all these years?"

"Because he loves her. He really does."

She shifted her head to look him in the eye and he knew that his reward had come. Opening her lips, she fluttered her tongue against his head and then sucked his shaft fully into her mouth, milking him with her throat.

Hot damn, he thought as he threaded his hands through her hair and pulled her closer, he was going to have to figure out a way to convince Kate to make regular wine country pit stops. Either that, or he was going to have to become a sub-urban boy toy. Which, frankly, didn't sound all that bad when Kate's plump red lips were sucking and pulling at his cock. And then as she drained him dry he lost sight of everything except the woman he was going to pleasure all night long.

"Emma Jane Cartwright!"

Jane Holden's crisp voice easily cut through the din of sound in Cravings. Her parents had come for her after all. Emma alternated between instinctively straightening her spine under her mother's disapproving glare and wanting to slink down beneath the tablecloth in embarrassment.

Julie was one step ahead of the production, quickly adding another chair to Emma's corner table and seating Jane and Walter as if nothing was the least bit strange about their abrupt, rather unpleasant entrance.

"You have sixty seconds to explain yourself, young lady," Jane bit out.

Emma blinked. How could she possibly explain something to her mother that she herself didn't understand? And really, what did her mother think was going to happen when the sixty seconds were up? That she'd run off chastised and crying?

Nonetheless, three decades of being her mother's daughter surfaced and she nearly said, "I'm sorry." But she could only get as far as "I'm" because something in her wouldn't let her apologize.

Not when she had nothing to apologize for.

Surprising herself, Emma said, "I've already told you."

"You've told us nothing, just a load of nonsense."

Julie returned with three fresh glasses of champagne and Jane picked hers up as if it had the cooties. Rudely shoving it back at Julie she said, "We have nothing to celebrate here."

Emma already had hers at her lips and even as Jane said, "Don't you dare drink that, young lady," Emma pounded her glass in one long gulp.

"Here, take this one too," Julie said, deftly replacing the empty glass in Emma's hand with Jane's untouched reject, muttering, "I have a feeling you're going to need it," in sympathy.

"Impertinent girl. I'll be sure to speak to the owner about her cheek," Jane huffed.

It was sick, Emma knew it was, but she smiled at the thought of her mother telling Jason to fire one of his friendly waitresses. Talk about a scene.

"Since you don't seem to be able to think clearly, your father and I are going to do it for you."

Emma merely sipped from her third glass of champagne. Funny, the last time she drank this much this fast had been last Saturday night. At the reunion. The alcohol had made her bold that night. She knew it was a cop-out, wished she was strong enough to stand up for herself without the benefit of a buzz, but since she wasn't, she desperately hoped it would do the same for her tonight.

"As soon as Mrs. Ellison told us that a FOR SALE sign went up on your house, we knew you needed our help. Immediately."

Jane's "we love you and know what's best for you" wasn't going to work. Not this time. If they really loved her they'd want her to be happy. Not get back together with an ex-husband she should have never married in the first place.

"Mmm-hmm," she said, taking another fortifying gulp of the bubbly drink.

"It was that boy who convinced you to do it, wasn't it?"

"Boy?" She wanted to hear her mother say his name, acknowledge his existence as a real person. And yes, even though Jason had indeed proposed the sale of her house,

Emma would never admit this fact to her parents. Never.

"That . . . . Jason Roberts." Jane nudged Walter. "Your father never did like him, did you? Tell her."

Her father shook his head, but Emma could tell that as usual, he was doing his damndest to stay out of it. Too bad. Because this time, Emma needed him to take a side. To have an opinion.

"Really, Daddy? What didn't you like about him?" she asked pointedly.

Jane spoke quickly. "He had no manners. No culture."

"I didn't ask you for your opinion, Mother. I already know how you feel about Jason. I asked Daddy."

Jane pinched her lips together and glared at Walter as if she were daring him to say the wrong thing.

Patiently, Emma waited for her father to respond. "Well," he finally said, "we thought you could do so much better."

Emma cocked her head to the side, thinking, *You actually thought that Steven was better for me?* But what came out of her mouth was, "Are you saying that you never had anything against him personally?"

"I never liked him, with his overly familiar behavior," Jane said and with one quick glare, Emma made it perfectly clear she was waiting for her father to respond. Besides, she wondered furiously, what was wrong with Jason coming across to strangers as friendly? Open? Approachable? It was better than all those society friends of her mother's who acted like they had regular pole insertions up their you-know-whats.

Surprisingly, her fierce look was working wonders on her mother. It might have very well been the first time Emma had ever seen Jane back down to let her father get a word in.

"No," her father finally admitted. "I had nothing against the boy."

Emma let this shocking news sink in.

"Enough useless chitchat," Jane fumed. "We informed the Realtor you were mistaken in putting your home on the market."

Emma got angry, then. Really, truly angry.

"How dare you?" Out of habit, she took a drag from her glass of champagne. Suddenly disgusted with herself for needing alcohol to make her brave, she pushed it away.

"Perhaps you haven't noticed, maybe I haven't given you any reason *to* notice, but I'm not a little girl anymore."

"No matter how old you are, we still know what's best for you," Jane insisted.

"No you don't." Each word fell from Emma's lips like a bullet. "And I'm not sure you ever have."

Jane's gasp was loud enough to cause diners at the surrounding tables to turn their heads. "How can you say such a thing? We've only ever had your best interests at heart."

Emma had never used foul language in her parent's presence. But there was a time and a place for everything.

"Bullshit."

Jane's hand slapped across Emma's cheek in the blink of an eye. "How dare you speak to your father and myself like that! Like some low-class tramp. That's what being here, with that boy, has done to you." Pushing her chair back, she wrapped her bony fingers tightly around Emma's wrist. "Get up right now, young lady. We are leaving."

Her mother had never slapped her before, but then Emma had never given her cause to do such a thing. Especially given that she'd spent the past thirty years playing the role of "perfect daughter" with such precision.

But Emma was surprised to find that she was stronger than her mother. By far. Maybe it was due to all that delicious food she'd been eating, which had given her a couple of extra pounds of strength.

Or maybe it was the knowledge that Jason wanted her. No one had ever truly really wanted her. Not like he did. The real her, not someone he was trying to mold into his own picture of perfection.

Jason's low voice held thunder and lightning as he stared at Jane with a look of utter hatred. And contempt. "Apologize to your daughter. Immediately. And then get out of my restaurant."

Emma hadn't heard Jason come out of the kitchen until he'd leapt to her defense. She was thrilled that he cared so much about her, but tonight, she needed to finally fight her own battles.

Calmly getting up from her chair, she stood before Jason, taking both of his hands in hers. "I know you want to help me, but please, let me do this on my own."

His jaw was tight as he stared at the raw skin on her face.

"You're hurt," he said, and the pain in his voice only served to solidify her feelings.

"I'm fine," she whispered. It wasn't true, but, "I will be fine," which she said next, was. "Please, Jason."

After a long, tense moment, he gave the barest of nods. "I'm not leaving you alone with them."

"Good. I don't want you to."

Busy gaping at their interchange, Jane found her voice again. "How dare you corrupt my daughter, you reprobate. You weren't good enough for her in college and you're certainly not good enough for her now."

Fire shot into Jason's eyes then and his hands bunched into fists. Emma moved between them. "This is between me and you, Mother. Leave Jason out of it."

"He's trying to ruin your life."

"No, Mother, he's trying to help me live it. And don't you dare ever so much as suggest that he's not good enough for me—or anyone else—again." Jane opened her mouth, but Emma put her hand up. "You've had your say. Now I'm going to have mine."

Jane grabbed her purse and was about to walk past Emma, when Walter forced her to remain where she was standing.

It wasn't an apology for her mother's behavior, certainly, but it was something. "I know you only want what's best for me. What parent wouldn't? And I don't blame you for that. But has it ever occurred to you that what you think is best and what I actually need are two different things?"

"You don't know what you need."

Emma thought about that. "Maybe not. But I'm trying to figure it out. And I need to do it my way."

Something that might have been admiration flashed in her father's eyes. Wanting them to understand, still needing at least a little of their approval, she said, "I will always appreciate what you've done for me. All you've given me. And I don't want you to think that just because I'm selling the house and moving my business to Napa that I don't—"

Jane's face turned puce. "Moving your business to Napa. My God, you really have lost your mind." She stalked out of the restaurant, leaving the distinct scent of Chanel No. 5 in her wake.

Walter looked extremely uncomfortable, but he remained where he was. "She's sorry for what she did," he said in a quiet voice and Emma nodded, knowing it was her father's way of apologizing. For everything.

He cleared his throat. "I don't know if I approve of what you're doing." He looked at Jason and it was clear that he wasn't just speaking about her house and business. He was talking about whom she loved as well. "But you're right, Emma. It's your life." Letting out a long breath, he said, "I'll talk to your mother, see if I can bring her around."

"Thank you, Daddy." Ignoring Jason's scowl, she leaned over and gave her father a kiss. "I love you."

Walter nodded and walked away.

It wasn't a perfect ending to their confrontation, but she felt like a sliver of an olive branch was laid out for the future.

And as Jason pulled her into his arms in the middle of the restaurant, Emma felt freer and more secure than she ever had before.

twenty-one

"We should leave," Jason said, reaching for Emma's wrap without waiting for a reply.

But rather than falling to pieces and crying all the way to his house, Emma's eyes were bright and dry. "I'm not in any rush to leave. I want to stay to help your crew clean up. It's the least I can do to repay them for being so nice to me."

What the hell? She'd just been through the ringer with her parents—doing a damn good job of telling them where to stick it, no less—and she didn't want to run and hide? Jason studied Emma carefully. Was she trying to hide her true feelings under a cloak of bravado for his benefit?

"You don't need to pretend to be strong for me, Emma. I want to take you home. You need me to be there for you."

It was the craziest thing. He wasn't feeding Emma a pack of lies about how much he cared because he was trying to get payback. He meant every word.

Not because he wanted to trap her into trusting him.

Not because he had some kind of ulterior motive.

But because he truly wanted to take away her pain.

He cared about her. Loved her. Honestly loved her, inside and out. Past and present.

He'd wanted to kill her mother for slapping Emma, for hurting her. And in that moment, when he'd been about to commit murder in front of dozens of strangers, he'd made a powerful realization: In trying to get payback for the way Emma had betrayed him so many years ago, he wasn't any better than her parents.

Everyone thought they had their reasons to control Emma, everyone thought they were justified in causing her pain.

Including him.

But they were all wrong.

Kate was the only one who really knew the score. Just as she'd said, Emma deserved to be happy. Truly deserved it.

Jason wanted to give that happiness to her. To start, he'd worship her with his body, make her cry out in pleasure to erase her tears.

Somehow, someday, he'd make things up to her.

Because even if she never found out about how he'd planned to hurt her, he knew. And he hated himself for it.

"Get back into the kitchen," she said with a soft smile on her lips. "I'll help Julie bus the tables and when you're done we can go home."

The word "home" sounded like "heaven" to Jason. "Are you absolutely certain?"

She nodded. "There have been enough scenes in your restaurant for one week. I want you to take care of your final customers. Go finish the job you do so well."

Bending down, he began to kiss her possessively, just as he had all week. But he no longer wanted to take her by force. He didn't want to own her anymore. Softly, so softly, he ended the kiss and she pushed him back toward the kitchen.

"Don't worry, I won't go anywhere. I promise."

Emma knew exactly why Jason had been acting so protective, why he wanted to bundle her up and carry her back to his house like a knight in shining armor. And she too was surprised that she didn't want to scream in frustration, didn't want to cry over the way her mother had behaved.

It was the very opposite, in fact.

She'd never felt this sense of freedom before. It was scary to be living her own life, to be in charge of making her own decisions. But my God, she felt like she could finally breathe.

A small smile playing on her lips, she cleared her table. Julie rushed over. "You don't need to help me with this, honey. Especially not after what you've just been through. Sit down and I'll bring you another drink."

But Emma merely laughed and waved Julie away. "I want to help. Thanks for everything."

Julie frowned. "Can I at least get you some ice for your cheek?"

Emma bit her lip. She'd almost forgotten about the slap. "That's probably a good idea."

Julie grabbed the dirty plates from her. "Go on, grab a seat at the bar. This place is almost cleared out, thank God. What a night."

"You said it," Emma murmured as she followed Julie to the deserted bar. Moments later, the ice was cool against her heated skin. "Thanks for the ice."

Julie laid a hand over hers. "Don't mention it. If you ever need to talk . . . "

Emma simply nodded and smiled as Julie left her to her thoughts. It was the oddest sensation, being able to pinpoint the exact moment that her world had turned around.

She was a beautiful butterfly exploding from its cocoon. From here on out, she was going to embrace life. No more looking out for pitfalls, no more watching every step, every word out of her mouth so carefully.

She was going to leap and know that when she fell, it would be straight into Jason's arms.

⚓

Jason watched his pastry chef plate the final desert and unwrap his apron, throwing it into the laundry hamper. Initially he'd wanted to head back to his house for Emma's sake. But as he counted down the minutes until he could shut down the kitchen for the night, he realized the real reason he wanted to be alone with her was for himself.

The only way he could shed his sins, the only chance he had to be absolved of his dishonorable plans, was to start making things up her right that very instant.

"You guys got things covered?"

His crew nodded and he let himself return to the dining area. To Emma.

She was sitting at the bar looking more beautiful than ever before. There was a new radiance about her. Something he couldn't put his finger on, but undeniable nonetheless.

As if she could feel his presence in the deserted dining room, she spun around on the bar stool, the very stool he'd so roughly taken her on earlier in the week. He'd wanted to teach her a lesson about who was in charge, he'd wanted to push her as far as she would go, but now . . . now all he wanted was to love her.

"Fancy meeting you here," she said, smiling up at him.

A faint red patch stood out on her otherwise perfectly creamy skin and he saw red all over again. "Are you all right? I never should have gone back to work."

Knowing what had set him off again, she covered her cheek with her hand. "I'm fine. It doesn't hurt anymore." Moving toward him, she took his hands. "What needed to happen happened. I honestly think that my relationship with my parents might finally be on the right track."

He opened his mouth to protest, to call her mother a bitch, but she stopped him with a finger to his lips. "I know you want to protect me, and I love that you were willing to stand back when I needed you to. Thank you for letting me fight my own battle." She shook her head. "I honestly don't know how things are going to turn out with my parents. With my mother, anyway. But I've got to believe things are going to be better from here on out. And I do."

Going up on her tippy-toes, her lips a breath away from his, she whispered, "Now take me home." Walking hand-in-hand through the warm darkness, she said, "I know why you love living here so much. It's beautiful and filled with amazing, caring people."

"It's your home now too," he replied, his voice thick with emotion.

And when she said, "I know," he couldn't resist the urge to swing her into his arms.

"Jason," she protested on a giggle. "You can't carry me all the way to your house."

"Just watch me," he said, knowing he would carry the weight of the world on his back if it would make her happy.

She tilted her head up and as he kissed her he could have sworn it was the very first time he'd ever tasted her lips.

"Hurry," she whispered into his neck and he fairly sprinted the last hundred yards to his front porch. The look Marvin gave him from one barely opened eye seemed to be saying, "Finally, you fool, you came to your senses. Whatever you do, don't mess things up this time."

He kicked his front door open, then shut, carrying Emma through his living room, his kitchen, down the long hallway to his bedroom.

Gently he laid her on the bed. She sat up, reaching for his shirt, and he put both hands on either side of her face and kissed her with every ounce of emotion he'd stored up since that day freshman year when he saw her for the first time.

"Let me make love to you tonight, Emma. Let me give you pleasure. All I want is to make you happy."

Delight flew across her features and he knew then that she hadn't expected so much from him. He'd been taking advantage of her need, of her desire, and although their love-making had been extraordinary on so many levels, it had lacked the most important thing of all: Love.

He wanted everything about this night to be perfect. For it to be their first real night together. He wished candles were lit, that soft music was playing. "I know I must smell like a kitchen. I can take a quick shower."

Emma simply smiled and nuzzled her face into the place where his neck and jaw came together. "You smell exactly like you."

So many of the women Jason had been with during the past decade had insisted that he shower before coming to bed. They said he smelled like a deep fryer, or some nights, worse. But Emma, his Emma, wasn't like any of them.

Jason had always known she was special, unique, but he'd stupidly let the weight of his own baggage over their breakup grow heavier and heavier with every passing year. Until he'd convinced himself that he'd been wrong all along about her innate goodness. Until he believed that there was nothing extraordinary about Emma at all, only what he'd concocted in his imagination.

How misguided, how stupid he'd been. Only by the grace of some higher force had he been given yet another chance at redemption.

Wanting to hold her, to kiss her for hours, he swung Emma up on top of him, her light weight only serving to ignite his already overheated desire. She laughed then, a happy sound full of affection, and he knew that he was going to spend the rest of his life trying to make her laugh. Keeping her happy.

"You're so beautiful, Emma," he said reverently.

Through her smile, she said, "No one has ever said that to me before. Only you."

"Everyone else is blind."

He took her lips again, brushing against her mouth so lightly that he couldn't tell where her breath ended and his began. Every last nerve, every cell in his body leapt into awareness. The curve of her breast against his chest. The insistent beating of her heart through her ribcage. The gentle swell of her hips into his hard, rigid muscles.

She tasted like his favorite part of summer, when the cherries fell from the trees. Her lips were plump and red and sweeter than any berry had ever been. She moved against him, making an impatient sound, and he knew he could take her then, slide all the way into her wet, slick warmth. But tonight wasn't about getting off, about a quick rush of pleasure.

It was about worshipping the woman he loved.

Smoothing one hand down the curve of her back, unable to resist her hips, her ass, he nibbled on her lower lip, his tongue finding the small, sweet crevasse in the very middle.

"Don't tease me, Jason," she begged.

He smiled, running his fingers through her soft hair, enjoying the silky feel of it wrapping around his knuckles, the sensitive center of his palm.

"I'm not teasing you," he said, "I'm loving you."

Her blue eyes stilled on his and he thought she understood him then, knew that tonight was his way of apologizing for being so rough, so punishing, that he was sorry for everything he hadn't had the strength to be.

Emma had never seen this side of Jason before. Back in college, when they'd kissed and fooled around, they'd still been kids. This week, when they'd had sex there had always been an edge of danger to it. Almost as if he were continually pushing her to see how far she'd go.

Tonight he was neither a young man exploring her body nor a bitter ex-boyfriend trying to teach her a lesson.

Instead, he was the lover she had always dreamt of. And she sensed that he was trying to say with his body what he could not say in words.

And then he was kissing her again and her thoughts floated away in a tangle of so many sensations: the heat of his skin as he caressed her through her clothes, the solid strength in his thighs as she straddled him, the way his tongue slipped and slid against hers, turning her insides to molten lava.

She never wanted to forget this kiss, the way Jason's touch was reverent and yet dangerous at the same time. She could feel his restraint in the faint trembling of his muscles as she ran her hands over the hard planes of his chest, around to his tight rear.

They were both still fully clothed, but instead of wishing she was wearing nothing but sexy lingerie, Emma savored this sensation of making out with Jason with only the barest skin-to-skin contact.

It made every touch so much hotter. Every nerve in her body focused in on his lips on hers, his tongue as it teased the corners of her mouth, his teeth as they gently bit down on the sensitive tip of her earlobe.

She felt as if they were coming together for the first time, only this time, there was nothing that could ever come between them.

Emma had lost Jason once. She refused to lose him again.

He moved one hand slowly up her ribs, finally finding the underside of her breasts. Through her dress, his touch was like a whisper of wind blowing across her. And yet, she'd never been so attuned to his body. To her own.

"Jason," she breathed, his name a prayer on her lips, and

then he was rolling them over and his hot, heavy weight was pushing her down into the mattress. Instinctively, she pressed her hips into his, wanting him against her, inside her, touching her.

Loving her.

"I wanted to take this slow, but I can't resist you, Emma." He pulled one strap of her dress down over her shoulder, exposing one aroused breast to the dim moonlight streaming into his bedroom.

"I don't want you to resist me," she said, hearing the pleading tone in her voice, knowing that it was okay to plead, it was okay to beg. Because he felt exactly the same way.

His tongue came down over her flesh then and she reached for him, pulling his mouth down onto her, silently urging him to suck harder. But she already knew that he would lave her nipples slowly. That while he was tempting her mercilessly with his teeth and tongue and lips, he would slide the other strap off her shoulder and cover her other breast with the callused heat of his palm. That he would squeeze and stroke her skin as if he were touching her for the first time.

She knew this because tonight was the first time they had ever truly made love. She opened her eyes then and looked at him, his dark head at her breasts, and something in her bloomed into life.

He must have felt her gaze upon him, because he looked up then and smiled at her. He was so beautiful she could hardly believe that he wanted her like this. That he'd chosen her out of all the women he could have had.

As if he sensed her innermost thoughts, he moved the pad of his thumb across her lower lip and she trembled at his touch.

"You're all I've ever wanted, Emma."

His words were soft and yet she felt them in the deepest recesses of her heart. And knew them to be true.

His hands were on her breasts again and the bad girl that she had finally gotten to know this week lifted her hips in a clear invitation, and he took it, cupping her bottom with both hands, pulling her wet heat against the erection nearly breaking the zipper of his pants.

"Touch me, Jason," she begged, but he didn't reach under her skirt. She'd known he wouldn't, that she would have gone off like a rocket at the slightest touch. He was seducing her, thoroughly, inside and out. And he was bound and determined to take his time.

He reached around the back of her dress for the zipper. "I want to see you naked."

She shivered at his words, at the light play of his fingertips on her spine as he pulled her zipper down, releasing her from the outfit's silky confines.

And then her dress was gone and he was staring down at her clad only in her panties. She shook beneath the heat of his gaze. She thought maybe he'd break and touch her then, slip a finger beneath the sheer, thin lace. A muscle was jumping in his jaw, the one that said he was this close to pressing his lips into her, tasting her, making her scream with pleasure.

"I used to dream about you lying on my bed like this. Your breasts bare, wearing only panties."

Her breath quickened as he began the slow process of taking off the last barrier between her body and his hands, his mouth, his cock. His fingers danced over her belly, past her hipbones, down her thighs, tickled her calves; his mouth followed, memorizing the lines of her body, the sensitive dips and valleys.

He kissed and touched her everywhere but the one place crying out for him. Her thighs separated as he slid her panties off and a flood of moisture escaped. She'd never been this wet, this ready, this enraptured by Jason's touch, his kisses. By the man himself.

With trembling hands, she reached for his clothes, pulling his shirt off over his head, glad there were no buttons, knowing she would have ripped through them, clumsy in her passion. He helped her with his pants, throwing them into a heap along with his boxers.

Gloriously naked before her, Emma reached out for him. All week she'd been intent on showing him her tricks, on making him admit the force of his desire for her. She'd tasted him, swirled his head with her tongue, taken him deep into her throat, all the while hoping, at least in those moments when she was giving him pleasure, that she was in control of something.

She didn't want to be in control tonight. She didn't need to be. She gently stroked his hot, hard, silky flesh with the very tips of her fingers, closing her eyes so that she could feel every inch of him.

He kneeled over her, perfectly still, and she could feel him shaking beneath the force of his need. They had all the time in the world, but still, it was time.

Moving her hands from his shaft, she pulled Jason down on top of her, opening her thighs to welcome him, wrapping her legs around his waist.

He stared at her then and without ever pulling his eyes from her, he slid into her, and she'd moved to take him deeper, deeper, until she could no longer keep her eyes from closing, her head and neck from thrusting back in the pillows. His mouth found her breasts again, his finger her clitoris, and together they drove together, riding each other in a flood of emotion and lust and deep, true love.

Her muscles clenched against him and he grew harder and bigger with each thrust until the moment when she felt that he would pull out, when he would think of safety over everything else, but this time there was no going back. Only the sure knowledge that she'd finally made it to heaven.

twenty-two

E mma woke with a smile on her lips. Jason wasn't in the garden, he wasn't in the kitchen making breakfast, he hadn't left her a note saying he'd call her later. He was right here with her. At long last, everything was absolutely perfect.

"Good morning sunshine."

She opened her eyes and giggled. "Hi."

Gently, he kissed her and her body stirred with awareness, an immediate responsiveness to Jason that she knew would never fade.

"There's something I want to ask you," he said and butterflies fluttered in her belly. Deep in her heart she knew what his question would be. And her answer.

After last night, everything was crystal-clear. They were going to be together forever. She'd heard wedding bells before, but they'd never been a symphony playing just for her.

The loud clicking of high-heeled shoes sounded outside the bedroom door just then, badly interfering with the wedding march in Emma's head. Could Kate have any worse timing?

"Emma? Are you in there?"

"Go away," Jason said and Emma giggled again, feeling exactly the same way about her best friend's near interruption.

She was just about to snuggle back into his chest, preparing herself for his oh-so-important question, when the unlocked doorknob turned.

Kate poked her head in. "Hey you guys. Sorry to disturb but I need to talk to you for just a second, Emma."

Emma shot her friend a look that said, *Not now! Jason and I are having a really, really important moment.* But Kate just wasn't getting it.

Damn her.

"Can't it wait?" she pleaded, wondering what could possibly be so important that Kate was dragging her out of Jason's bed.

Kate shook her head. "Nope. It can't. I desperately need to talk to you. I'll wait for you out back."

Kate walked through the bedroom, out the French doors, and into Jason's backyard. Emma turned to him, unable to believe the stunt her friend was pulling.

"Oh God, I'm so sorry about Kate. She dropped by last night, but she never came back, so I figured she had a hotel room. I know this is terrible timing, but if something's happened to her I need to find out what it is and help. I promise to try and make it quick, okay?"

Something flashed in Jason's eyes that looked like dread. He picked up her hand and Emma worried at his sudden change in demeanor. Sure, Kate had barged in at a really inopportune moment, but that didn't mean everything was ruined.

"Promise to remember one thing while you're gone, okay?" His words held an oddly serious tone, almost somber.

"Of course," she said, giving his hands a squeeze, smiling encouragingly.

"I love you."

She gasped then, finally hearing those three words she'd so desperately longed for.

"I've always loved you, Emma. And no matter what, I always will."

"I love you too," she said, putting her hands on his face and kissing him to show him that he didn't have to ever be afraid to say he loved her. Not wanting to leave, but knowing the sooner she dealt with Kate, the sooner her friend would leave them alone, she smiled and said, "I'll be right back. And then we can continue where we left off."

Jason nodded but didn't meet her eyes and as she slid off the bed and wrapped his thick robe around her, she was struck by the oddest sense that everything had gone from absolutely perfect to not quite right in the blink of an eye.

Shit. Kate must have pulled the details of his payback plan out of Rocco. Jason wished he could blame his longtime friend for telling her, but the whole situation was his own damn fault, wasn't it? First coming up with his ridiculous plan and then having the nerve to brag to Rocco about it. He was sure Rocco had put up a fight—a small one, at least, in the name of friendship—but Jason now understood that there was no point in lying to women. It would only come back to bite you in the ass. Rocco had done what he had to do.

From the moment Jason had run into Kate in downtown Palo Alto he'd sensed disaster. Only then, he'd merely been concerned about the failure of his payback plan.

Now his whole life was at stake.

Why hadn't he told her himself? If only he'd been man enough to confess everything last night. She would have forgiven him. She would have understood that he'd only acted out of some stupid sense of wanting her to feel the way she'd made him feel back in college.

She would have loved him anyway, he was sure of it, if he'd only owned up to being a complete idiot.

What if hearing about his plans for revenge from her best friend turned her against him? Jason got out of bed and threw on a pair of jeans. He couldn't let Kate tell Emma what he'd done, he had to tell her himself.

Because without Emma, he now understood, he had nothing.

~

"If you hadn't noticed, Jason and I were sort of busy in there. Couldn't you wait to tell me all about your hot date with Rocco?"

Kate didn't grin at Emma's teasing recriminations. In fact, she looked about as nervous as Emma had ever seen her, which immediately made her worry that something bad actually had happened to Kate last night.

Emma rushed over to squeeze beside Kate on one of Jason's chaise loungers. "Are you okay? You didn't get into any trouble last night, did you? I was just teasing about you bothering me."

"No," Kate said, her eyes serious and more than a little sad, "I had a great time with Rocco last night. I need to talk to you about something else."

Emma's mind raced with possibilities. Did this have to do with her parents? With Steven?

"I wish I didn't have to do this, I wish I didn't have to tell you anything. But I do, Emma. I have to."

Emma stopped breathing for a long moment. Finally, she said, "What is it?"

"It's Jason."

Her breath left her lungs in a rush and she smiled at Kate, wanting her to understand that things with Jason were perfect, better than perfect even. "I didn't get a chance to tell you because everything happened so fast, but after my parents came by his restaurant last night—"

"Your parents were here?"

Emma nodded. "It was difficult. But good. I stood up to them, Kate. And things are already different with my father. My mother's a different story, but, well . . . I guess that's something we're going to have take time to work out."

Kate opened her mouth to say something, but Emma wanted to finish. "Jason was wonderful. He let me fight my own battle, and then afterward everything was different between us. All that stuff I was so worried about, me chasing him, our lack of intimacy, it all disappeared.

"He loves me, Kate. He just told me, right before I came out here to see you. But I already knew. I knew last night. We're going to be okay. I know we've had our problems in the past but this time everything's going to work out. Trust me, it will."

Kate nodded and Emma felt good that they'd had this talk. She knew Kate had been worried about her, but she hadn't known that there was such urgency to it.

"I believe that Jason does love you, honey. But—"

Emma frowned. "But? There aren't any buts," she protested, even though she'd been living in a world of what ifs and whys ever since the moment Jason had approached her at the reunion.

"There's no nice way to say this . . . " Kate paused, visibly pained by what she was about to say and Emma almost hated her friend in that moment as she waited for Kate's proclamation, no matter how irrational, how unfair it might be. "He might love you, but I don't know if he's capable of loving you the right way. I think he might still be too damaged over the way you broke up in college."

"Stop it!" Emma screamed at Kate, pushing away from her on the chair, wanting to get away from her friend's awful words, all of which confirmed her biggest fears.

Right then, Jason stepped out of the sliding glass doors. Emma's heart clenched as she looked at him, bathed in the morning light, wearing only jeans. She'd never seen anyone as beautiful as him, and knew she never would.

"I'll let you tell her," Kate said to Jason and his lips were a tight line as he nodded. Emma didn't know what was going on and she wanted to run away, leap over the back fence and disappear if it meant that she could be oblivious and happy for one more precious moment.

Kate's eyes gleamed with unshed tears. "Don't leave anything out this time," she said to him before turning back to Emma. "I'll be waiting inside if you need me."

Emma's head was spinning. Please God, why couldn't everything work out for once?

Jason walked across the grass, onto the pavers. When he didn't sit down next to her, a little piece of her heart disintegrated.

"I don't know what Kate has already told you, but I'm the one who needs to come clean, Emma. I'm the one who needs to tell you the truth." He stopped talking, swallowing hard. "Everything is different now, but at the beginning of the week I invited you to stay with me to settle the score between us."

Emma's heart splintered, but didn't completely break. Mostly because she didn't want to believe what he was saying.

"No, you couldn't have," she said, but her voice sounded hollow, like it was coming out of a long, narrow tube.

He didn't agree or disagree and Emma unleashed her fury onto him. "Why would you say something like that? I'm finally happy. You just told me you love me." Her words grew shriller and shriller until they were piercing and raw coming from her throat.

"I do love you, Emma." He reached for her, but she flinched and he pulled back. All of the warmth left her body. She felt cold, so cold again. As frigid as the night she'd seen him again at the reunion. The night he'd . . .

Oh God, everything was so clear now. Too clear. The demanding sex, how quickly he'd suggested she give up her house and business in Palo Alto, the way he'd encouraged her to believe that she was more important to him than anything.

She'd thought everything was moving too fast, that he wasn't the sweet Jason she used to know, and she'd been right. But she hadn't wanted to trust her instincts.

Stupid girl. Just like she'd always been, evidently.

"I'm sorry, Emma, incredibly sorry that I've acted like such a fool. But I couldn't go through with it. I love you too much."

Emma simply stared at him. She noted the pleading in his eyes, his body language, but sympathy couldn't penetrate her disillusionment. Emma's voice was as ice cold as her broken heart. "What exactly was it that you couldn't go through with?"

Jason swallowed once, then twice. All of the muscles in his upper body jumped then tightened as he said, "I wanted payback."

"What else?"

"Nothing else."

"Don't lie to me, Jason."

"I was going to reel you in and spit you out after you got rid of your house and your business." Jason held her gaze and if she weren't so distrustful of everything he was, she would have been impressed with his strength in the face of dishonor. "Like I thought you did to me. But I was wrong. I know that now. Please forgive me. You've got to forgive me."

Emma hurt so bad that she no longer felt anything at all. Carefully she stood up. "Thanks for telling me everything, Jason."

"Emma, I—"

Whatever Jason had been about to say froze on his tongue as her frosty eyes met his.

"You win."

He tried to grab her hand, but she pulled it away. "How long were you planning this?" And then, she said, "No, I don't care. I'm just glad I was stupid enough to go along with your plan. I made things easy for you, didn't I? The girl with stars in her eyes who thought true love was actually going to conquer all."

"Don't talk like that, Emma."

"I'll talk however I want!" she screamed, losing her extremely tenuous hold on her emotions. "You bastard!"

But as quickly as the hurricane had surfaced it was replaced by another ice age. "We're even now, aren't we?" she taunted, knowing she was hurting him, but knowing he'd never hurt as badly as she did right now.

Silently, she dared him to disagree. But he didn't. And that almost made things worse.

"I was an idiot," he said. "I should have gotten over you marrying Steven years ago."

"You know what? I don't want to hear about what you should have done. All I know is what you did do. What you would have done if I had let you. My house, my business, my parents. You tried to take them all away from me."

"I'll make it up to you."

She went on as if she didn't hear him, unable and unwilling to store up any of her hurt, her bitterness. "I've been guilt-ridden over what I did to you for ten years. Ten goddamn years. And I'm sorry for the way I dumped you. I was a thoughtless, spoiled bitch. You should have been angry with me. A real man would have been angry. Why couldn't you have been honest about it? Told me what you actually thought of me? Instead of playing games with me. With my entire life."

Feeling as if she were seeing Jason for the first time, she said, "You know something else I just realized? What you've made me see? You and Steven are exactly the same. You both thought you could manipulate me, make me jump around like some wimpy little puppet. And you both succeeded. I hope you have fun slapping each other on the back over a beer sometime soon."

"Emma, I'm nothing like Steven."

"No," she said, shaking her head, "I'm not sure you're half the man he is. At least he asked me for a divorce, at least he had the common courtesy to actually end our relationship before he screwed me over. Whereas you were screwing me over the entire time, weren't you? Every time you touched me. Every single time we—"

No, she couldn't say it. She couldn't say "made love." Not now that she knew how far from the truth those words really were.

"But I love you. You love me."

Emma laughed, a completely humorless sound. "How could I love you, Jason? I don't even know who you really are."

twenty-three

Standing alone in his backyard, Jason felt her loss as keenly as he had ten years ago. He still remembered every word that had been spoken in the quad that Easter, the way he'd said, *"Tell me this is what you want and I'll leave you alone,"* the way she'd admitted, *"This is what I want."*

Courtesy of hindsight, and more than a little maturity, Jason was finally ready to admit that Emma hadn't actually told him the truth that Sunday afternoon.

She'd told him exactly what he'd wanted to hear, what everyone was pressuring her to say. But she hadn't ever, at any point, said what *she* really wanted.

But she'd been brave enough to sit in his restaurant

and admit that she'd always loved him. That she'd made the wrong choice because there was so much pressure from everyone to be with Steven.

Jason knew he could have fought for her. And that if he had, he probably would have won. Sure, it would have been painful. Ugly too.

But if he'd loved her enough, wouldn't he have done anything to be with her? Even forgiven her for needing some help, some backup, in dealing with her world? A world that he knew to be as ruthless in its own way as a low-rent back alley. Just because people had money didn't mean they were kind. More often than not, they grew accustomed to getting their own way. To pushing the weak around to suit their own needs.

He hadn't wanted to forgive her for the way she'd behaved that day. For the way she'd betrayed him. But hadn't he practically pushed her into Steven's arms?

Today, Jason saw everything in a different light. One where he was no longer the good guy, the one who'd been wronged.

In fact, as far as he could tell, he was the one who should have been groveling at Emma's feet. Because the one time she needed him to be there for her, to really *be* there, he'd bailed out like an insecure, immature fool.

And now that he'd finally been given a chance at redemption his twisted pride had taken him way off course.

Jason wasn't sure there was a way back into Emma's heart. All he could do was hope and pray that the third time was the charm.

It was all he had.

⟆

"Stop defending him. I don't want to hear it."

Kate flopped next to Emma on the bed. "I'm not defending him. I'm just trying to help you see both sides of the story."

Emma sighed. The thought of going back to her cold, empty house, of looking at the FOR SALE sign and remembering how stupid she'd been to fall for Jason's lies, hook, line, and sinker, had been more than she could bear. So she was currently holed up in Kate's house, giving her best friend free reign to pester her with some silly notion of true love.

"I know the way I dumped him for Steven was horrible, Kate. I've been living with that for ten years. I was a shallow, weak person."

"No way. I could never be friends with a loser like that."

Emma smiled despite herself.

"Look, why don't you give yourself some points for A, being a kid whose parents were in charge of her whole life and B, finally taking that life back in Napa this past week?" Emma opened her mouth, but Kate shoved a pillow into it. "And then, maybe you could give Jason some points for being hurt and wanting to feel like he was in charge, but then *not actually acting on it because he realized he was being an idiot and that he loved you*!"

Emma threw off the covers, said, "I'm going for a run," and locked herself in the bathroom.

She stared at her pale face, the bruises beneath her eyes, and knew that everything Kate was saying was true. But just because things were true didn't mean you could necessarily believe them.

Take her mother. She knew her mother loved her. But it didn't mean that her love was healthy or good for Emma in any way.

The same went for Jason. He'd meant it when he said he loved her. She understood that from a place deep within. But that didn't mean that he'd fulfilled his need for payback, for revenge. It didn't mean she believed he wouldn't continue to punish her again and again over the years for her stupidity, her youth, her bad decisions.

After changing and leaving the bathroom, Emma jogged down the front steps and down the sidewalk. Her stomach grumbled and she was glad for it. She hadn't eaten anything yesterday, almost as if she were punishing herself for daring to trust Jason, for daring to believe her life could be better, that she deserved more.

Her old patterns were reemerging: running on a empty stomach, feeling virtuous for not allowing herself to eat. The familiarity of returning to the way of life she'd always known comforted her, and she felt almost as if she were returning to herself. She was no longer in the fantasy world she'd been living in with Jason, a world where she didn't work 100 hours a week, where she ate anything and everything she wanted.

A world where love actually meant something.

She crossed University Avenue at the light on a crowded Sunday morning in downtown Palo Alto filled with babies in strollers and parents. And lovers.

The sight of a couple walking hand-in-hand, sipping from a frosted drink in a clear Starbucks cup nearly felled her in the middle of the street. Tripping, she barely kept from skinning her knees on the pavement.

Somehow she made it to the other side of the street. And

knew that she couldn't do this to herself anymore. Couldn't keep falling down and almost getting run over because of bad decisions.

All her life, she'd starved herself, thinking that if she was skinny enough then maybe she'd be happy. But really, hadn't she only been doing that to make her mother happy?

And now, now that she was falling back into the black hole, she realized there was another person she wasn't eating for: Jason. Hoping her frailty would punish him. Make it perfectly clear how much he'd hurt her.

Back in college, she'd known he'd been worried about her eating and exercise patterns. But he was too gentle to force her to admit that she had a problem. And then, in Napa, she ate to make him happy—every decadent bite of food a way to teach her mother and her ex-husband a lesson.

Had she ever made one single decision for herself?

Her stomach grumbled again and her legs shook from lack of energy. Today would mark her first official solo decision: She was going to stop hurting herself on purpose.

And she was never going to eat or starve for anyone else again.

Minutes later she was sitting at an outdoor table enjoying a sesame seed bagel with cream cheese. It wasn't decadent by any means, but neither was it a weight-conscious choice.

But it did taste damn good, mostly because she knew it was her very first baby step in the right direction. At long last.

⌒

"Sorry I screwed everything up for you, boss."

Jason continued chopping chives. He'd been chopping

and thinking all morning, trying to figure out his next step, the right move to get Emma back. She'd only been gone one day, but it felt more like a year.

"You're a bastard, that's for sure. I thought I could trust you," he said, and then, "But you did what you had to do. What anyone would have done who wasn't a complete prick like me."

"Are you feeling all right?"

"Emma was going to find out sooner or later."

"But she left you, man."

Jason nodded. He didn't exactly need Rocco to point that out. He could feel Emma's absence in every breath. He saw her all over town, in every room of his house, in his kitchen.

But she wasn't actually there. And it was his own damn fault.

"Yeah, she did." *And I want her back.*

He didn't need to say the words aloud for his friend to hear them. All along, Rocco had known the score. He'd tried to warn Jason about his stupidity, but he'd been too blinded by self-delusion and wounded pride to actually take notice and listen.

"You should know, Kate's been trying to get your lady to see reason."

Jason put down his knife. Was it possible that he actually had an ally? He'd thought himself lucky to have even Rocco in his corner after the way he'd been behaving.

"You're kidding, right?"

"Nope. She seems to think you're capable of being a stand-up guy."

"I can't believe it. I thought Kate would want to slice my balls off and feed them to a pack of wolves."

Rocco grinned. "That was her first idea, actually."

Jason picked the knife back up. There went his only ally. "Great. Glad to hear it."

"But mostly she thinks you guys belong together. Underneath her tough lawyer suit she's just a big, soft romantic."

Jason raised an eyebrow, trying not to be a selfish bastard who only thought of himself. Something in Rocco's voice seemed to say that his buddy was unleashing his own gushy, romantic side as well.

"I take it things went well on your date with her last night."

"You could say that. I'd call it spectacular, myself. She is one hot, smart babe."

Jason smiled at his friend's enthusiasm for a very unlikely candidate. Although, he had to admit, hot, smart babe was a good description for Kate.

"I'm heading down to Palo Alto in a couple of hours. Gotta admit I'm kind of looking forward to seeing what the world looks like in black-and-white Pleasantville."

"It's not actually that bad. There are a few slashes of color here and there."

Emma's blue eyes were the first thing that came to mind. And her lush red mouth. And those polished pink toenails in her sexy sandals.

"Then why haven't you been back for so long?"

Jason didn't reply. Why bother when they both already knew the answer? Obviously, he'd been scared shitless about seeing Emma again.

Because after all these years he couldn't stop loving her.

Rocco acted like he'd just had a spur-of-the-moment idea.

"Why don't you come with me? Sam and Judy can cover for us. We'll make it a road trip."

Jason almost laughed at his buddy's transparency. But the thing was he couldn't head back to Palo Alto. He wasn't ready to see Emma yet. He hadn't figured out a plan of action. If he was going to win her back he needed to act with finesse, make her see that she couldn't live without him. He'd been trying to choreograph a big romantic reconciliation scene for the past twenty-four hours but nothing he came up with was any good.

Roses were cliché.

Getting down on one knee and proposing to her was just plain stupid, especially since she couldn't stand the sight of him.

He'd even thought about trying to get her out to a baseball game, saying he was sorry on the huge screen above the stadium, echoing it with a Goodyear Blimp trailing a sign that said, "Please forgive me, Emma. I love you. I mean it." But since neither of them were baseball fans, it just plain didn't make any sense.

What was the point of a big gesture if it didn't reference their history together?

Rocco stepped in right then and saved Jason from himself. "I can see your overeducated Stanford brain going a million miles, boss. Maybe for once you should turn that thing off."

Rocco was right. Jason's plans sucked.

"Might not be a bad idea," Jason agreed, and then Rocco grinned and turned back to peeling a stack of green apples.

twenty-four

Emma showered and joined Kate in the kitchen for a cup of coffee. "You look a whole lot better all of a sudden," Kate remarked.

"Funny what a huge epiphany and a bagel will do for a girl," Emma said with a smile.

"Oh thank God, you ate. I was wondering if I was going to have to tie you down and force-feed you."

Emma groaned. "Not you too."

"Look, honey, you know I was worried about you not eating enough in college and you seemed so much better recently, but then this stuff with Jason happened. I thought that maybe it would set you off again."

"Does everyone think I'm so fragile that they can't tell me when I'm screwing up my life?"

Kate bit her lip. "Would you hate me if I said yes?"

"Of course I wouldn't hate you. It just feels like things would have been so much better all along if everyone had been honest with me." She took a sip of coffee. "Actually, being honest with myself might have been a good first step."

Kate raised an eyebrow. "I take it this has something to do with your epiphany?"

"Only everything."

"Care to share?"

Emma grinned. "What? And miss out on watching you try to pull it out of me for the next week?"

Kate stuck her tongue out and Emma laughed. "I don't know why I'm laughing. It's not funny. Not at all. Basically, I realized this morning that I've lived my entire life for other people."

"To try and win their approval, you mean?"

"Jeez, maybe I should have asked you what was wrong with my life. I could have saved myself a good decade or two of misery."

"A lot of people are looking for approval," Kate said, obviously trying to make Emma feel better. "Oprah and Dr. Phil have made millions off it."

"Thanks for trying to soften the blow. But it's more than that. I wanted to make everyone happy. Everyone but myself, that is."

"And now?"

"Well, at least I know I'm sick of doing that."

"It's a good start," Kate said, refilling their cups.

Emma nodded. "Something else is really bothering me. Something I need to deal with right away."

Kate guessed, "Jason?"

"Glad to know you're not psychic after all."

"Not Jason?" Emma almost laughed at the surprised look on her best friend's face.

"Eventually, you're right, I'm going to have to deal with him."

"Because you still love him, right?"

"Can we not go there quite this moment?"

Kate held up her hands. "Sorry. I got carried away. So what's your next step then, if not Jason?"

Emma put her cup down. "My mother."

Yet again, Jason found himself driving ninety miles south from Napa to Palo Alto. Three times in one week he'd been down these freeways, these bridges. Each time because of Emma.

To be perfectly honest, he wasn't at all certain this trip was a good idea. He doubted she was ready to see him; twenty-four hours was not nearly enough time for her to cool down.

He'd been a prick, an utter jerk in every way, and he still didn't know what he was going to say. What he was going to do. The only thing he knew was that he had to see her.

Even if she ran from him, he'd come back. Over and over, until he wore her down, until he made her see just how badly he needed her, that nothing was right without her in his life.

On the drive from Napa to Palo Alto last Saturday, on his way to the reunion, he'd had only one thing in mind: Getting even. Now, everything was reversed.

He needed Emma's forgiveness. And her love.

Some things never changed and Emma was one hundred percent certain that her parents would be sitting on their back porch, eating Saturday lunch.

Strangely, she wasn't particularly nervous about the upcoming confrontation. So much else had changed in one week. Last weekend at Sunday brunch, she'd been a completely different woman. Uncertain, off kilter, with no sense of who she was. Or what she wanted.

One week later, she was armed with so much more. A new perspective. A budding self-confidence. And the knowledge that before she could possibly have a better relationship with her parents, she needed to have a frank discussion about everything that had transpired during the past thirty-two years first.

She used her key without ringing the doorbell, wanting the element of surprise in her corner. Walking through her parents' house, the house she'd grown up in, she took in everything in a different light.

For the first time Emma could see how she'd done little more than mimic her mother's decorating style in her own house. Not that there was anything wrong with Jane's furnishings—they were perfectly nice, quite comfortable, even—but they were all wrong. At least for *Emma*. From here on out Emma was going to live in a house that bore her individual stamp with rooms that were bright, creative, and made her happy.

She honestly hoped this house made her mother happy. And that's when she realized: Maybe Jane had been a product of the same rigid upbringing. The same all-beige, drab, perfect world. Maybe it was all Jane knew.

Emma halted in the middle of the living room, thinking,

processing this new theory. She could see her parents through the French doors that led out to the professionally landscaped backyard, her mother's spine uncomfortably straight, her father looking less stern than she ever remembered seeing him.

She took a deep breath and turned the knob on the French doors. Her parents whirled around, her mother exclaiming, "You almost gave me a heart attack! Why didn't you ring the doorbell?" while her father simultaneously stood and said, "I'm glad you're here."

Emma went to her father and kissed him on the cheek. "Thanks, Daddy," she said, smiling into blue eyes so like her own.

"Have you eaten?" he asked and she knew he was trying to tell her she was welcome in their house, no matter how her mother reacted. She loved him for that, glad to have him on her side as she treaded into muddy waters with her mother.

"I'm not hungry, Daddy. I wanted to come and talk to both of you, that's why I'm here."

Jane's mouth was a firm, tight line. "Unless you have come to apologize, young lady, we have nothing to talk about."

Emma stared at her mother. It was like looking in a mirror. Apart from her father's eyes, she'd inherited everything else from Jane. The same height, the same bone structure, the same light hair.

And all of that was okay, just as long as she could put a stop to inheriting her mother's snobbery and fear of living life. If Emma ever had a daughter, she didn't want to ever make the mistake of trying to groom her to be a perfect little lady who lived in the shadows of real happiness her entire life. Jason sprang to mind—she'd always thought he'd be a great father—but she couldn't think about him now.

Rather than crying, storming off, or even automatically apologizing to get back into her mother's favor, she asked, "What do you want me to apologize for?"

By the way Jane's hands trembled on her wineglass Emma knew she'd caught her mother off guard. "You know exactly what you've done to make your father and me so upset."

Walter spoke directly to Emma. "I'm not upset with our daughter, Jane."

Two spots of color splatted onto Jane's cheeks. "Of course you are."

Instead of backing down from his formidable wife like he usually did, Walter shook his head. "No. I'm not. What I am upset about is that fact that you two can't seem to work things out."

Emma bit the inside of her lip. He had a point.

"Do you know why that is?" Jane spat at Walter. "It's because your child is willful and spoiled and won't listen to reason."

Sadness, rather than anger, bubbled up inside Emma. "Do you really feel that way about me, Mother?"

Jane opened her mouth, but then closed it. "I've never been disappointed in you before."

"Even when Steven and I got divorced?"

"That was a different circumstance entirely," Jane said in her usual crisp tones. Emma could tell that her mother had composed herself again as she began listing off her daughter's transgressions. "But this week when we found out that you went chasing off after some boy from college, that you left your business in tatters, that you turned Steven away when he was concerned about you, I could hardly believe you were my daughter. And then, when you treated your father and me so despicably . . . "

Emma held one hand up to stop her mother from saying anything more. She hoped she could keep track of everything she needed to get off her chest, rather than falling back into her regular pattern of kowtowing to her mother on absolutely everything.

"Jason came to the reunion on Saturday night."

Jane waved a bony hand in front of her face. "I don't want to hear all the sordid details."

"They're not sordid, Mother. I love him. I've always loved him. Marrying Steven was a huge mistake."

"How can you say that? He was perfect for you. Successful, charming—"

Emma cut Jane off. "I know that's what you thought, Mother. I married him because I wanted you to be proud of me. I wanted you to be happy. I wanted Steven to be happy. And I figured that I could somehow learn to be happy, since it was what everyone else wanted for me."

Walter didn't say anything, but he looked miserable. Guilty, even.

"It's hard for me to admit, but I'm angry with both of you. For what you've done. For the way you treated Jason." She softened her tone. "But Daddy," she said, reaching for his hands, "I know you were only doing what you thought was right for me. What father doesn't want his daughter to marry the best man? The one with all the right qualifications? I know Jason didn't look like he was the best man for me. He didn't have money or connections or even direction. But I loved him anyway."

Walter cleared his throat. "He certainly seems to have done very well for himself."

Emma smiled. "If that's your way of saying you approve,

thank you. Although" —her smile fell away— "there isn't anything to approve of right now. But that's not why I'm here. I mean, it is, but only a small part."

She turned back her mother, who quite surprisingly was sitting quietly and listening, albeit with a vice grip on her rapidly emptying glass of wine. "As for leaving my business in tatters for a week, you're right. I should have thought things through, made a plan. But at least I learned something important: I've made the mistake of not delegating. I could have hired good people and trained them to take care of the office in my absence. Maybe then I could have had a life. Gotten out and met people. Made more friends. Had some fun. But I wanted to think I was the only one good enough to do the job right."

Jane spoke up then, her voice a tad gravelly. "No one does as good a job as you can."

Emma felt a softening behind her breastbone. "Thank you, Mother. Thank you for always telling me I was smart. That I could do anything. It was a great gift. But I'm finally ready to learn to pass on some responsibility to others."

Walter cleared his throat again. "Very good thinking, Emma."

Emma beamed at her father. All this time she'd been vying for their praise, but she'd never been able to enjoy it. Simply because she hadn't learned how to be proud of herself as well.

"As for Steven coming to Napa." She giggled at the ghastly memory. She couldn't help it, even though it wasn't remotely funny. "We all know he doesn't want to get back together with me."

Jane tried to protest. "Of course he does. He loves you."

"He loved the way I picked up his dry cleaning and made him dinner and threw dinner parties for his clients. I was the perfect secretary. But never his perfect wife." Jane's face fell even further. "I don't mean to sound bitter about it, and honestly while there was a time that I was, I'm not anymore. I just want to be honest with you so that you don't get your hopes up thinking we'll get back together. We won't."

Her parents were silent, taking in everything she had come to say, so much more than she had said in total for thirty-two years.

"As for the night you came to Jason's restaurant in Napa . . . " She took a deep breath, then let it out, not sure exactly how to tell them that while they'd hurt her, in a way, she'd been glad. It had forced Jason to show his true colors.

And for her to reevaluate everything that she'd been hiding from for so long.

Jane's eyes were nervous, her hands wringing her napkin. "I'm sorry."

Her words were so soft Emma almost missed them.

"I know," Emma said. "And I'm sorry too for not being able to be the daughter you always wanted."

Jane looked up, two tears falling from her eyes to the tablecloth. "That's not true. I've held on too tightly. Your father told me to let go, to let you live your own life. But I couldn't." Her mother sniffled and Emma felt something deep down in her heart break. "I thought you were happy."

Emma reached for her mother and wrapped an arm around her frail shoulders. "I know you did. I thought I was too."

Only she could never be happy without Jason. She suddenly remembered what he'd said at the reunion: It was now or never.

And in that moment as she held her mother in her arms, Emma knew that she'd only ever had one choice: Now.

twenty-five

W hat do you mean she's not here?"

Kate seemed to be enjoying Jason's frustration, given her smirk. "Like I said, she left an hour ago. Besides, what makes you think she'd want to see you anyway?"

Jason tried to come across as tough, confident. Based on Kate's expression—like she had a mouthful of water she was trying not to spit out—he wasn't doing a great job.

He slumped down on one of Kate's couches feeling like the pathetic idiot he was. "No, I don't think she wants to see me. But I was hoping to change her mind."

Kate patted his knee. "Well, when you've done something as stupid as tricking her into thinking you loved her—"

"I do love her!"

"I know that, you loser, but a little advice: The whole revenge angle as a way to woo chicks really sucks."

Rocco pulled Kate onto his lap. "Hot damn, woman. I've been waiting for you all my life."

Kate said, "I know," kissed him, then turned back to Jason. "Anyway, as I was saying, given how badly you screwed up I'd say it's a damn lucky thing that she loves the crap out of you."

Jason shot up off the couch. "She told you that?"

Kate shrugged. "Maybe. Maybe not. The point is, you've got a truckload of groveling to do." She got off of Rocco's lap and poked one shiny red fingernail into Jason's chest. Hard. "Down on your knees, begging for forgiveness groveling. Understand?"

Jason nodded. "Trust me, that's the plan."

She smiled and snuggled back onto Rocco's lap. "Good. In that case I can tell you where she went." Jason was already halfway out the door when she said, "Her parents' house. She said she had some unfinished business to take care of."

As the door slammed behind Jason, Kate pressed her breasts into Rocco's hard chest. "He's not the only one who should be on his knees right now."

Rocco shifted to get off the couch, but Kate put a hand on his thigh.

"Not you, sweetheart, me."

⁘

Emma drove through the Stanford Campus seeing it not as it was today, but as it had been ten years ago.

Easter Sunday. A day she'd never been able to forget. For months afterward she'd been haunted by the look on Jason's face when he saw her with Steven. Holding his hand.

She shivered at the memory. It was not a recollection that got better with age. It hadn't faded and her actions hadn't magically morphed into being good or right.

She'd had plenty of chances to tell Jason what was going on before that horrible Easter Sunday, but she hadn't the nerve to take them. Steven had been pursuing her for a while. Her parents had met him at a faculty function and taken an immediate liking to him. What parent wouldn't? Star football player, high grade point average, career prospects coming out of his ears. Emma had been swept up into his arms, his world, his future.

She'd loved Jason so much, but at twenty-one she hadn't known just how much a love like theirs meant.

That it would be the one true thing she would ever know.

So she'd taken the easy route, made the easy choice, the one that meant everything would fall neatly into place.

In many ways, she mused as she got out of her car in the Stanford quad parking lot, choosing Steven had been a relief.

It was as if some unseen force punched her in the gut. She caught herself on the hood of her car before she crumpled in the empty parking lot. My God, had she hidden from the truth all this time? Had she truly picked Steven because she was afraid of a life with Jason?

Had she chosen a frigid world because Jason's world was wild and scary? Because she hadn't wanted to risk having nothing but love to rely on? No money, no connections, no beige furnishings?

Yes, she thought, as she watched students hop on their bikes and hurry off to their next classes, that was exactly what she'd done. She'd wanted to blame her parents for pushing her into Steven—and away from Jason—because that way she'd never have to blame the real person at fault.

Herself.

Yesterday, she'd been so angry at Jason for wanting to make her pay for her sins. But had he actually followed through on hurting her?

No.

Instinctively she knew it wasn't just because he'd been impressed by the way she'd stood up to her parents in his restaurant. Or because she'd been his sexual plaything for a week, or harnessed her inner Playboy Bunny, or bought a new wardrobe.

Jason hadn't hurt her because he *couldn't* hurt her.

She'd known this all along, hadn't she? No one else had ever made her feel so safe, so beautiful. So loved.

He wasn't the one who needed to apologize to her. It was the other way around: She needed to apologize to him.

She pushed away from her car and headed for the Stanford quad to face her demons, praying for guidance that this time she could finally get it right.

⌒

Jason stood on the Holdens' front porch and rang the doorbell, trying not to feel like a nervous kid. Jesus, did he really need to remind himself that he could buy and sell these people ten times over? That he was a celebrity? A huge, indisputable success?

Emma's mother opened the door. "Jason," she said, only marginally glaring at him. Hot damn, he almost felt welcome.

"Mrs. Holden."

She opened the door wider. "Call me Jane. Come on in."

His mouth fell open. Jane? Come on in? Had he landed in some sort of anti-reality?

"Thanks," he said, managing to pull himself together before she had her proof that he really was as mentally deficient as she'd judged him to be in college.

Emma's father stood in the kitchen staring out the window. When Jason walked in, he turned and held out his hand. "Hello, Jason. We are extremely sorry about the commotion we caused in your restaurant. Aren't we, Jane?"

Jason could hardly believe his ears. Had Walter actually apologized? And forced his wife to do the same?

Jason kept his face expressionless as Jane nodded. "We are."

"I appreciate that," he said, unable to resist saying, "although the person you should really be apologizing to is your daughter."

Both of her parents' faces turned pink and Jason decided he could leave it at that. For now.

Clearing his throat, trying to be polite even if he wasn't sure they deserved it, he said, "Is Emma here? I'd like to speak to her."

Jane shook her head. "I'm afraid she left ten minutes ago."

Jason's hopes sank to an all-time low. "Do you know where she went?" he asked, not bothering to mask his dejection.

"I'm sorry, we don't."

"Oh."

"We'll let her know you stopped by next time we see her."

Jason nodded, unable to speak. Jane and Walter followed him to the front door.

"We won't get in your way again."

Jason turned, shaken out of his funk. "Excuse me?"

Walter's complexion had gone ruddy. "We know she's in love with you. All we want is for her to be happy."

A million questions rushed through Jason's mind. Were they implying that he made her happy? How did they know she was in love with him? Was it because of what had happened in college? Or had she declared her love for him ten minutes ago in their kitchen?

Again, he couldn't speak. Only nod and get back in his car. He clicked open his cell phone and called hers. No answer, only her voice mail. He clicked his phone shut.

Jason was down to instincts and instincts alone. He needed to head back to the place where everything in his life had broken apart. Stanford University. The quad.

Because maybe that was the place where everything could be put back together again.

─⚭─

Emma stood in the center of the quad, oblivious to students whizzing around her on their bikes, professors carrying armloads of files and books back to their offices, freshmen girls giggling as they gossiped about which boys in their dorms they currently had crushes on.

Ten years receded and she was standing in this exact spot. Watching her world break into a million pieces.

Looks like you're having a big happy family Easter, aren't you?

The memory of his words hit her as squarely in the gut as they had a decade ago. She should have run to him, made him understand that she didn't want any part of the life she'd been groomed for. She should have said, "No, we're the opposite of a big happy family. You're my family, Jason. Just you."

But when she was twenty-one she hadn't said that, had she? All she'd wanted was for him to go away, she'd begged him to go away so that she could keep her safe, tidy life. God, what a little coward she was.

And when Jason had said, *"Walter, it looks like you've found a much better candidate for your daughter,"* she hadn't denied it, all she'd done was cry.

It was no wonder Jason had walked out of her life for ten long years. The question that had been tugging at her subconscious all week returned with a vengeance: Why had he come to the reunion? Had he been looking for her? And had he been simply looking for revenge? Or, possibly, a way to rekindle their love?

Emma desperately wanted to see him. To talk to him. Right now. She wanted to steel up that brand-spanking-new backbone of hers and ask him everything she'd been too afraid to ask. Lest he leave her.

"Tell me this is what you want and I'll leave you alone," he'd said. Ten years later, Emma desperately hoped for the chance to tell him the truth.

Because this time, she knew exactly what *she* wanted.

Jason Roberts. For life.

twenty-six

J ason took the steps two at a time. And then he saw her.
  He stopped cold, his heart taking off like a rocket inside
his chest. One beam of sunlight shone through the clouds,
lighting her hair up like a halo.

Jason grinned. Emma was definitely not a saint. Not even
close, judging by the things she'd done with him this week.

Everything was going to be all right. He didn't know why
he knew it, how he knew it, he just did. The pressure was still
on, but at the very least Jason knew his love for Emma wasn't
going anywhere, even if she justifiably stomped away at the
first sight of him.

He moved away from the steps, and as his long legs ate
up the distance between them she reached for her cell phone.

He grinned again, knowing exactly who she was calling even before his phone buzzed in his pocket.

Waiting until he was standing directly behind her, he flipped open his phone and said, "Hello, Emma. I was hoping you'd call."

She spun around so fast, her phone slipped out of her grasp and clattered on the cobblestones beneath their feet. Her face lit up and he wanted nothing more than to reach for her, to pull her against him, to soak up her warmth, her essence. But what was between them couldn't be resolved with a kiss.

"I'm glad you're here," she said, softly, and his smile matched hers.

"I've been looking for you," he said and she looked adorably confused.

"But no one knew where I was going."

"I knew. Where else could you go?"

She bit her lip. "I need to apologize to you, Jason, for so many things."

"No, I'm the one who needs to apologize." He hated himself for what he'd almost done to her. She needed to know that.

It was the strangest thing, but in this moment that should have been so tense, so awful, she actually giggled. "Okay then, should we do rock-paper-scissors to decide who goes first?"

He couldn't help it, he laughed too. And started counting. "One, two, three." He made a fist and she held two fingers straight and open. "Rock to your scissors."

"I guess that means round one goes to you, doesn't it?"

There wasn't anything hard in her words, but they were far too close to Jason's inner thoughts during a week in which he'd wanted nothing but to crush Emma's spirit. Instantly he sobered.

"We don't need to do this," he said, but she had sensed his abrupt mood change and she was already counting. "One, two, three."

This time her hand was flat like paper and his was a rock again. "You got that one. Looks like we're tied, huh?"

Emma looked into his eyes. "Let's just leave the score even, okay?" He nodded and she said, "I know you would never hurt me, Jason."

She couldn't let him off that easy. He wouldn't let her. "But I almost did."

"Okay, so you thought about it. You even told your friend about your plans. But when it came right down to it, you didn't follow through. I honestly don't believe you ever would have."

The words burned coming out of his throat. "Your house. Your business." He paused, not willing to let himself off this hook this time for anything. "Everything I made you do in bed."

"I didn't do anything with you that I haven't dreamt of doing for ten years. I had a wonderful week with you," she said fervently. "The best of my life. And I'm not going to let anything ruin that for me. As for my house, we both know I needed to sell it."

She had that look on her face, the one that said she should have been able to figure that out on her own. Jason hated to see her doubt herself. "You did what you had to do. At your own pace. There's nothing wrong with that."

"Bullshit!" she exclaimed, continuing to surprise the hell out of him. "There's so much wrong with what I've done, with how I've lived that I don't even know where to start."

Instinctively he wanted to protect her, even if she was doing a damn good job of fighting her own battles—even those within herself. "Don't, Emma. You don't have to go there. We don't have to go there."

"Don't you dare tell me that, Jason. You know damn well it's time for both of us to get everything off our chests. All of it. Because while you could have never followed through on hurting me, I clearly had no problem doing that to you. Ten years ago. Right where we're standing. I let the man I loved walk away. I let *you* walk away."

"Your parents—" he began, but she cut him off.

"Had something to do with it, but not everything. *I* was the one who couldn't cut it, Jason. I was afraid of being with you outside of the little bubble we'd created for ourselves."

"What do you mean? I'd never given you any reason to be afraid of me."

She shook her head. "Not in that way, not physically, of course not. I was afraid of everything you are, Jason. Everything that's made you who you are today."

He was trying to follow her, but nothing she said was making any sense. "I don't get it. You didn't leave me because your parents forced you to be with Steven?"

Her voice was pitched low as she admitted, "I wanted to be with Steven because he was safe. You were dangerous. Wild. I never knew what would happen with you from one minute to the next. I was afraid of a life that I couldn't predict down to the second."

"Steven gave you that." Jason's voice was flat. It wasn't a question, merely a statement that cut right through him.

"He did. I look back now and can't believe I ever thought I wanted a perfect, boring life. But I did want it.

And it was the worst decision I ever made. Because for so long I refused to allow myself to be happy. The food I ate, the house I lived in, the way I ran my business, and the man I married; it all tied into not liking myself very much. At all, really."

"And now?" It wasn't a question he wanted to ask, not now that he felt like he was breaking in two all over again, but he couldn't leave today without knowing the truth. About everything.

"Well, I'm pretty new at this happiness thing. But the one thing I know for sure is that you make me happy." She teased him, saying, "Even when you're plotting revenge against me you still make me happy."

Jason didn't know what to say. He should be groveling, like Kate said. Begging her for forgiveness. He wasn't good enough for her, he knew that, but he was going to try his damndest every single day for the rest of their lives to be a better man. For Emma, a woman who deserved nothing less than the very best.

"I can't stand to hear you joke about what I did, Emma. I was a bastard. An idiot. I'm going to spend the rest of my life making it up to you. If you'll let me."

Her eyes grew big then and he could almost feel her in his arms, but then she pulled into herself again and he could hardly breathe.

"Tell me why you came to the reunion last Saturday, Jason. I need to know." Reading his mind, she said, "And don't tell me it was because of your stupid payback plan. I deserve to know why you really came back, don't I?"

Emma had never wanted to touch Jason so badly. She wanted

to hold him, tell him she loved him, make plans for the future. But she knew none of that made sense until everything was out on the table.

He stared at her and she couldn't read his eyes. Was he confused? Angry? Did he think she was an idiot for not seeing the obvious? Finally, he spoke.

"Ten years ago, I screwed up."

She frowned. "*You* screwed up?"

He nodded. "Yeah, I fucked up big time. I always swore I'd be there for you and then the one time, the one goddamn time you really needed me, I bailed. Walked out of your life."

"How can you say that? I made you go. I pushed you away."

"I wanted you to do it, Emma. Don't you see? I never realized that I was as scared as you were. More, maybe. I'd never met anyone like you. And I'm not talking about your family money, your upbringing. I'm talking about the woman you are. The woman you always were. You made me feel things, big things I couldn't control. Do you know what it's like to go through life thinking you're bigger, badder than anything the world can throw at you, only to be blown completely off course by a little blonde girl with big blue eyes?"

Emma was reeling from his confession. Standing was impossible with her knees shaking so hard. She sat down hard on the stones. Jason moved closer, sat directly in front of her, and when he reached for her hand she gave herself over entirely to his warmth and her elemental need for all that he was.

"I screwed up at least as bad you did, Emma. Worse even,

because I didn't stay to fight for you. I just let you go. And then I blamed you for ten years for everything. Let you sit with that blame."

"You felt this way last Saturday?"

That muscle started working in his jaw and she reached out for it. He covered her hand with his and rubbed his cheek into her palm. Just being here with Jason like this was enough for her. She could sit in the quad with him forever and be happy.

"If I had I wouldn't have been such an idiot all week. I saw your name on the reunion list and I couldn't stay away from you. Not for another second. I told myself it was because I was finally going to get you out of my system, teach you a lesson, but now I know exactly why I fed myself such bullshit."

"Why?" she whispered.

"Because as long as I believed my own lies it meant I could be with you again. And being with you was all that mattered. It *is* all that matters. You know that, don't you?"

She felt her eyes grow wet. "I do. And I'm not ever going to forget."

He kissed her, then, and when his lips touched hers, she came fully, completely alive. Gently, she slipped her tongue between his lips, letting it dance with his in a way that was completely familiar and yet entirely new.

"I swore I wasn't going to ask you this today, but I have to."

Tears of joy streaming down her face, she stared into the eyes of the man she would always love. Whom she was certain would always love her. No matter what life threw at them.

"Emma, will you marry me?"

She couldn't stop smiling as she said "Yes" and kissed him. Six months later, when they returned to that very spot—Emma in her gown and Jason looking extremely hot in a tux—and she said "I do," the same exact smile lit her up from the inside out.